Sneaking Suspicions

Book One of The Tharon Trace Mysteries

Jan Hinds

ISBN: 10:1499295375
ISBN-13:978-1499295375

Sneaking Suspicions

Book One of The Tharon Trace Mysteries

By

Jan Hinds

Published by Jan Hinds

Copyright© 2014 by Jan Hinds

License Notes

DEDICATION

To my father, Frank, whose steadfast love anchored my life and who taught me to approach each new challenge with confidence as if I'd been doing it forever. I'm still working on that Dad.
I miss you.

And to my mother, Ellen Mary, my cheerleader and champion, who teaches me by her example that the best kind of person to be is a kind person.
I love you Mom.

TABLE OF CONTENTS

ACKNOWLEDGMENTS

I want to thank those who have encouraged and assisted me in completing this book.

A very special thank you goes to Katie Eden of Katie Eden Photography (katieedenphotography@gmail.com) for her excellent help in designing the cover. Just to show her determination to get the best shot, shortly after getting home from taking the cover photograph, the Sheriff's department showed up at her door investigating a report of suspicious activity with her car at the edge of the woods.

I give my heartfelt thanks to my editors, Linda Deam, Terri Reid, Geraldine Hofer, Janet Schafer, Amy Holt and Christy Hinds for your help and patience with my many drafts and revisions.

Most of all, my heart is filled with gratitude to my wonderful husband Roy, who, after making all my other dreams come true, is supporting my dreams as a writer.

Jan Hinds 2014

PROLOGUE

"Indiana? What possible reason would we have to send troops into Indiana?" General Adamson resisted the urge to mop the sweat from his brow. The orders made no sense. Why would the government invade any state, let alone Indiana? He'd heard of no threat against the state; unless President Hamron considered the state itself to be a threat. Few other states could boast the autonomy from the Federal government that Indiana consistently maintained, regardless of the disasters that plagued it.

Adamson had heard that widespread rumblings about secession were escalating and many believed Hamron's election to a second term had been rigged. "It's my understanding Indiana suffered heavily from the pandemic in 2051 and lost nearly half their population. Not much has changed in the past five years. Their economy is still quite weak, though it's making some signs of recovery. I don't see any threat coming from them."

Vice President Larkin grinned at the general's obvious discomfort. He rocked back in his plush desk chair and steepled his fingertips thoughtfully. His silky voice had a dangerous edge when he spoke. "As you well know, General, threats come in all forms. It can be as specific as a direct assault or as veiled as a simple question." He leaned forward, resting his forearms on the desk and looked Adamson in the eyes. "By the way, how are your lovely wife and those two strapping boys of yours? I understand the older one has twins. How old are they now? Three? And he has another one on the way? You and your wife must be so proud."

General Adamson's mouth went dry as he tried to swallow past the lump in his throat. He locked eyes with Larkin. There was nothing veiled in the threat to his family. He'd been keeping his own personal file on the accidents and the missing family members of officers under his command. Though the ranks were filled with honorable service men and women, he found himself surrounded increasingly by officers whose allegiance he questioned. Even men and women he'd served with most of his life turned cruel and intolerant. At least now he understood why. In a quiet, defeated voice he asked, "What do you want me to do?"

With a toothy grin bordering on a sneer, the Vice President's steel gray eyes gleamed with triumph. Nothing made Larkin happier than cutting off at the knees one of the few remaining military leaders yet to fall in lock step with the administration's agenda. "Assemble strike forces but tell the men they're on training maneuvers in the Midwest for the month of November. I believe four teams of five hundred each should be sufficient. As you said, there's not likely to be resistance. Station them in Michigan, Illinois and Ohio and have them primed to follow any order without question. Do I make myself clear?"

General Adamson rose to his trim six foot seven height and fought the contempt threatening his features. "Crystal clear, Mr. Vice President. Is there any specific threat they

2

need to be prepared for?"

Larkin's left eye twitched as he sat back and smiled up at the tall man he'd been itching to cut down to size, "Hostage rescue."

General Adamson paused at the door. "Is President Hamron on board with this action?"

Vice President Larkin's smile faded, "I assure you this mission is sanctioned at the highest levels, but you understand the delicate dance in politics these days. Plausible deniability is paramount."

With his lips in a tight line, General Adamson nodded once and left the office.

As he walked through the outer office into the corridor, he had to step aside for the First Lady's security detail. His heart ratcheted a notch or two when he saw the tall man with skin the color of dark caramel leading the entourage. He was at least two inches taller than Adamson and his amber eyes flickered in recognition when he saw the general. Verdine was his old college teammate and one of the few people he trusted completely.

The First Lady's petite frame was dwarfed next to most adults. Walking behind Verdine she might appear childlike, if not for her paper thin skin stretched taut by far too many face lifts. She inclined her head to him, "General Adamson, so good to see you. I trust all is well with you?"

"Quite well, Mrs. Hamron."

With a wave of dismissal, she entered the Vice President's outer office and walked straight through, entering the inner office unannounced.

Verdine took a guard position alone in the corridor.

Adamson brushed his bent index finger over his upper lip and tugged his ear, "Do you have the time, Agent Verdine?"

Verdine raised his wrist and lifted his sleeve with two

fingers, "I have nine forty-five, General."

Adamson dipped his chin, "Thank you." He walked down the hall with squared shoulders and a hopeful heart.

***

General Mitchell Adamson rode his bicycle on the trail that wound through the secluded Virginia countryside at two in the morning. Leaving all electronics at home, he cycled past the dark figure stretching his long legs in front of a bench near the well worn trail. As Adamson turned his bike onto a less traveled path, he glanced to the left and saw Verdine weaving noiselessly through the woods. He smiled at the graceful strides that would make an antelope jealous.

Panting hard, Adamson stopped his bike next to a limestone outcropping.

Verdine, barely winded, leaned against a tree deep in the woods near the rocks. He grinned, "Mitch, you're slowing down in your old age."

Adamson shook his friend's hand, "Thanks for meeting me. We won't be able to talk like this again. Larkin put the screws to me today. He threatened my family. The president wants me to set up a force to invade Indiana." He cast his eyes nervously over his shoulder. "Do you think the President wants to start a civil war?"

Verdine rubbed the dark stubble on his chin, "It's possible he doesn't know about this. You saw the two major players today. Those two have been intimately chummy for the past year."

The First Lady's papery skin and Larkin's premature balding pate flashed through Adamson's mind and induced an involuntary shudder. "I can't envision her choosing Larkin over her husband in the bedroom."

After a moment of quiet, Verdine's deep voice rumbled, "Never underestimate her. I've never met anyone more dangerous or devious in my life."

"What can I do? They're going to start a civil war and they want me to lead it. If I don't, they'll destroy my family."

Verdine paused before answering. "My friend, you're going to have to do the unthinkable, at least for a while. You're going to have to do what they want. It's our only hope of saving your family and the country."

CHAPTER 1

November 9, 2056

A chill wind blew across the schoolyard and seeped through Tharon Trace's thinly lined gray wool coat causing her to shiver. The coat had been sufficient the day before with temperatures near sixty. Clear blue skies had graced northeastern Indiana, casting a perfect backdrop for the vibrant maples bordering the schoolyard—but overnight the temperatures dipped below freezing and the leaves fell from the trees, leaving bare branches to scratch at the sky.

Tharon watched a purple ridge of clouds muscle across the rolling hills to the west of Sandy Creek, bathing the land and the town in shadows. She smiled wistfully at the younger children repeatedly shuffling the leaves together into huge colorful mounds and then squealing with delight as they jumped into and flattened them.

As if she were a mind reader, Veronica Miller scoffed in her ear. "Look at them getting so excited about a bunch of dumb leaves. Honestly, there are so many better things they could be doing."

Tharon sighed, knowing it was futile to argue with Veronica who simply couldn't fathom the pure joy of jumping into a pile of leaves. Shivering again, she knew it was less from the cold than the favor her new best friends expected of her. She never thought she'd long for second grade again, but sixth grade was rapidly becoming the pits.

Her other new best friend, Tracy Walker, was the younger sister of Kaid Walker. He and Helm Harris were in the seventh grade and, without rival, the most popular boys in middle school. They were also on Veronica and Tracy's radar since both girls reasoned the two boys were their tickets to popularity as well.

Tharon couldn't help but suspect ulterior motives for Veronica and Tracy wanting to be friends with her since she was about as far down the popularity totem pole as you could get in a rural Indiana school.

Tharon put off talking to Kaid as long as Veronica would let her, yet she felt compelled to launch one more complaint. "Do we have to tell the boys we like them? Can't we just say we like them without telling them we do?"

With a coaxing voice Veronica pleaded, "Just tell Kaid I like him. That's all you have to do. In fact, you don't even have to say anything. Just give him my note and wait for his answer." She thrust a folded piece of notebook paper into Tharon's gloved hand.

Veronica flicked her long straight blond hair over her shoulder. She folded her arms, raised an eyebrow and impatiently tapped her right foot on the cracked asphalt of the school yard. "We *all* promised, Tharon. Look, Tracy's talking to Eddie for you right now," she nodded her head in the direction of the bleachers where Tracy talked with one of the Edwards twins.

Tharon's nervous gaze traveled across the school yard to Tracy Walker who flicked her long straight black hair behind her shoulder in a perfect mimic of Veronica. But Tracy wasn't talking to Eddie: she huddled deep in conversation with his identical twin Everett. Tharon shook her head; Tracy never could tell the twins apart.

Everett glared at her from the bleachers with more contempt than usual. He was someone you didn't want to cross.

Tharon had learned that the hard way four years ago when she had accidentally worn her work boots on the bus. Everett kept taunting her, calling her a stinking pig and other insults that had her near tears. If she'd just kept her mouth shut that probably would have been the end of it, but no, she had to say *smeller's the feller* to him. The other kids laughed until Everett turned his glare on them.

It had been her eighth birthday and she remembered it vividly. At the end of recess, Everett pulled her behind the dumpster and threw her down in the sticky pungent filth that seeped from it. Then he straddled her and pummeled her chest with his fists.

Eddie pulled Everett off her when he saw how savagely his brother was beating her, but not before Everett landed a parting kick to her ribs and left her with a warning that if she told anyone, no one would believe her because it would be their word against hers, and if she told, he'd beat her again.

Eddie at least seemed sorry and didn't call her names, but he never tried to stop his brother from ridiculing her. And she had no doubt if it came down to her word against theirs, he'd side with his brother.

No one crossed Everett. Not even his brother. In that way he was like Veronica.

Right on cue, a huff spewed from Veronica's lips reminding Tharon that she'd agreed to talk to Kaid, who had hurt her more deeply than the Edwards twins.

Nothing stings worse than the betrayal of a friend—unless it's the betrayal from two friends. And it was the *nothing* that stung.

Kaid Walker and Helm Harris had been her best friends since she was seven until the past spring when suddenly they just stopped. Stopped playing with her, stopped sitting with her on the bus, stopped talking to her. The cold ache bore into her heart again. She had no idea what she had done that caused them to no longer like her.

Veronica and Tracy had filled the friendship void left by Kaid and Helm. At least the girls kept her too busy to brood about missing the boys. Veronica's forceful enthusiasm filled the summer with sleepovers, shopping, and theme parties such as polishing nails, karaoke, and makeovers. Veronica's latest scheme, to get boyfriends before Thanksgiving, edged Tharon way outside her comfort zone.

Given her history with the twins, common sense dictated the Edwards twins would be the last boys Tharon would choose to like. She chewed on her lip, trying to remember how that happened. She recalled a conversation in which Veronica and Tracy claimed Kaid and Helm as *theirs* and pestered Tharon to pick a boy. They shot down every safe suggestion she made as unsuitable. Finally Veronica said, "I think you should pick one of the Edwards twins. Which one do you like more?"

Of course she said she liked Eddie better. He at least hadn't beaten her. And somehow that innocuous declaration linked her to Eddie in the blasted boyfriend scheme. The only consolation she had was that she didn't want a boyfriend in the first place and was confident Eddie would never agree.

She shook her head wondering how she'd ever given Veronica the power to sweep her along in this silly plan.

The wind pressed a mass of rustling leaves across the ground like a hoard of fleeing rats tumbling over each other, and skittering towards Tharon. In many ways she identified with the leaves, tossed about on the whims of a greater force. Veronica was the wind. Tharon was a leaf rat.

Veronica's foot tap turned to a stomp and snapped at Tharon's attention. She looked at Veronica and couldn't mask the hurt in her voice, "I don't know why you want *me* to do it. Kaid's hardly said two words to me since last spring."

Veronica took a deep breath. When she spoke her tone was deceptively calm, the way the wind gets still right before a bad storm. "I'm sure he's just busy with sports now. He doesn't have time for his little neighbor and her little games."

Tharon averted her eyes at the stinging insult, mainly because it rang so true to her.

Veronica placed a fuzzy pink gloved hand on Tharon's shoulder, "Look, I don't think he hates you," she stood tall, flipped her hair behind her shoulders and smoothed her jacket. "It just means he's ready to go from a friend who's a little girl, like you, to a genuine girlfriend, like me."

Self-consciously fingering her long brown pigtail braids, Tharon looked down at her thrift store jeans and shoes and realized Veronica was right. Even though there were only a few months difference in their ages, Veronica was much more suited to be a girlfriend to any boy, especially someone like Kaid.

The realization left her with a pang of longing for the easy friendships she missed. It wasn't that she wanted Kaid as a boyfriend, she didn't want to have a boyfriend, but she ached for her old friendships with Kaid and Helm and all the fun they'd shared playing in the woods and on the farm.

Maybe she should stop trying to hang on to a childhood that no longer existed.

More as a moan of dread, than to dispute the point, she repeated, "I thought we were just picking boys to like. I didn't know we were going to tell them we liked them."

Veronica stomped her foot again and planted her hands on her hips. Her fitted pink down jacket hiked up, exposing the sequined pockets of her blue jeans. "We agreed to all get boyfriends before Thanksgiving. We can't be friends if we don't keep our promises to each other. Just give the note to Kaid now, while he's alone, and I'll go talk to Helm for Tracy. Honestly, it isn't that hard."

Tharon shoved her hands into her coat pockets and scuffed the soles of her shoes as she dragged herself across the schoolyard. She exhaled her own visible sigh into the cold air and trudged toward Kaid.

Kaid Walker's dark hair, blue eyes, dimples and friendly nature brought a smile to the lips of all the sixth and seventh grade girls—including Tharon. The Walker and Trace families were close friends, and she, Kaid and Tracy had practically grown up together. She'd always felt comfortable around Kaid—somewhere between friendship and siblings—not giddy and nervous like most of the girls. At least she did until he turned his back on their friendship. Now she didn't know what to feel.

The closer she got to Kaid, the more apprehension filled her heart. Would he snub her and treat her like a little kid? Even though the next day she was turning twelve—there was a big difference between her twelve and his thirteen.

Sure, they couldn't stay kids forever, roaming the woods on imaginary quests, climbing trees and playing till dusk every night. She just never dreamed the transition away from that happy childhood would be so abrupt. She thought, whatever else changed, that they'd always be friends.

She never thought she wouldn't be good enough for his friendship. Her nervousness mounted and she felt like a hive of bees were swarming inside her chest, trying to sting their way out.

Kaid hopped from one foot to the other trying to warm up as he waited his turn at flag football. Visible white puffs of breath burst from his mouth and accented his cheers for his team. His jet black hair poked out from under his tweed newsboy cap. Even from a distance she could see his dimples.

She envied those playing and wished she could play too, but Veronica had decreed that flag football wasn't a proper activity for popular girls. Tharon frowned. Before Veronica opened her eyes, she'd lived in blissful ignorance of the value of popularity. She felt another tug at her heart as she longed again for the time spent hunting with her father, or long days exploring the woods with Kaid and Helm.

She thought *what is wrong with this picture?* The faces of the girls on the field were filled with smiles and laughter, while her nervous apprehension for delivering notes and scheming about boys felt crippling.

Kaid turned as she neared him. "Hey, Tharon, want to play?" he nodded toward the field and his face broke into a dimpled grin.

His easy smile threw her off. She muttered, "Well, I'm not sure," then glanced back at Veronica whose frown turned into a radiant smile when Kaid followed Tharon's gaze. "I'm supposed to tell you that Veronica likes you." She fumbled in her pocket, and passed the note to Kaid.

He unfolded the note, glanced at it and stuffed it into his pocket. "Why are you supposed to tell me?"

She shrugged. "Veronica and Tracy said we have to

have boyfriends before Thanksgiving."

Kaid shook his head, "I knew Tracy was up to something. She's been way too nice to me lately."

Tharon plunged ahead before she lost her nerve. "Veronica picked you and Tracy picked Helm." *Why on earth did I ever agree to this?*

Kaid crossed his arms and gave her a crooked grin, "So who did you pick?"

Tharon shook her head, "I didn't want to do this but they said I had to like someone too so I picked Eddie Edwards." *Actually, Eddie was picked for me.* She kicked at a stone and it popped out of the dirt. Why did the plan seem wonderful when Veronica talked about it but when she explained it, the scheme sounded lame?

Out on the field Helm snatched the football from the air and sprinted for the goal. His strong legs pumped hard as he pounded the sod and stretched the gap between him and the pursuing team. He crossed the end zone and danced a victory jig.

Kaid jabbed the air with his fist and shouted, "Way to go, Helm!" He turned back to Tharon, "So do you like Eddie?"

She smiled at Helm's dance and shrugged her shoulders. "Not really," she admitted.

He raised an eyebrow at her, "So why are you saying you like him?"

She shrugged her shoulders again and held up her palms, "Because Veronica and Tracy said I had to pick someone and they took the two best boys." She blushed as soon as the words escaped from her mouth. She watched Helm jog easily to the sidelines. His blue knit hat popped off and his thick light brown hair danced in the wind.

Kaid moved in front of her to block her field of view. His mouth stretched into a wide grin and Tharon was sure he'd sprouted an extra dimple. "So you think Helm and I are the best boys?"

She laughed nervously, her face still burning. "Well, if I had my own choice it wouldn't be Eddie Edwards."

Kaid's face turned thoughtful. He shoved his hands in his jacket pockets and kicked at the loose stone which Tharon had lodged free. "Who says you don't have your own choice?"

He had her completely confused. "Veronica and Tracy already chose you and Helm."

Kaid met her eyes and his dimples were replaced by a serious expression, "Just because they chose us doesn't mean we have to choose them." The dimples returned and he playfully asked, "So which one of us would you choose?"

Her breath caught in her throat. How could she answer that? From the corner of her eye she saw Veronica approach Helm and her heart lurched. No. If she chose and was rejected, there was no coming back from that—either for the one she chose or the one she didn't. If she just had their friendship back, that would be enough. She tried to sound casual, "I think I choose not to choose anyone."

He held her gaze a moment longer, an unspoken challenge for her to pick one of them, and then he laughed.

She laughed too and felt her nervousness dissolve, melding back into their old familiar friendship.

He said, "You can tell the girls that we choose not to choose either. Come on, you can be on my team. We're receiving." He fastened a yellow Velcro flag around her waist.

Tharon hesitated, "I really shouldn't." She could almost feel the mental daggers Veronica shot at her back.

He took her by the shoulders and forced her to look into

his eyes, "Seriously? Can't you decide anything for yourself? You never used to be so wishy-washy. Don't let my sister and Veronica control you. Do you want to play?"

How could he act like he could pick up their friendship as if nothing had happened and how dare he accuse her of being wishy-washy? Her expression hovered between anger and happiness and she wasn't sure which won.

She shoved against his chest, "Yes I want to play. But I'm giving you fair warning, my hesitation had nothing to do with your sister and Veronica." She knew that wasn't entirely true and felt a little guilty for saying it. She forced herself to not look at Veronica and jogged onto the field.

While she waited for the kick off, she chanced a look at the sidelines where Veronica talked to Helm. She wondered if he would agree to be Tracy's boyfriend. She wasn't sure she wanted to know. The thought of him liking Tracy stabbed at her heart in an unsettling way that surprised her. She didn't realize she was staring at Helm until he winked at her. Her heart fluttered. She smiled and felt their old familiar connection even from all the way across the field. Was that just her imagination?

Tharon focused on the game and only ran the wrong way once. Playing pushed the dread at facing Veronica out of her mind and for the first time in a long time she simply enjoyed herself. When the bell rang she purposely avoided catching up to Veronica and Tracy.

Kaid punched her shoulder lightly, "Did you have fun?"

Still trying to catch her breath, she smiled, "Yes. That was great."

Kaid's dimples danced as he teased her, "I see why you were reluctant to play. You aren't very good at football at all."

She playfully backhanded his arm.

Helm swept in between them and slung a protective arm

over her shoulder, "Leave her alone, Kaid or she'll start ignoring us again."

The icy ache lodged again in her chest as she breathlessly whispered, "It wasn't ever me who walked away from our friendship." She shrugged off Helm's arm and ran back into the school.

With a measure of finesse she successfully avoided Veronica and Tracy the rest of the school day but as they lined up to get on the bus she knew she had to relay Kaid's message.

Tracy bubbled as she huddled close to her friends. "Oh, my goodness, I thought I was talking to Eddie, but it was Everett. He got mad because he wasn't included and he likes Veronica." She gave Veronica a sly look then turned to Tharon, "I talked to Eddie in art class and he agreed to be your boyfriend," she beamed at Tharon. "Isn't that exciting?"

In spite of her shock, Tharon managed a less than enthusiastic, "Great."

Veronica chimed in next. "Well, I talked to Helm and he said that you were like a sister to him, Tracy." She gave Tracy the briefest of sympathetic pouts. "He said he likes someone else but he wouldn't tell me who it is. I'm so sorry."

Tharon's face flushed as she wondered who Helm liked. Her stomach twisted into knots and her heart sank. Helm liked someone. Why did that fill her with such sadness?

Veronica ignored Tracy's crestfallen, *Oh* and turned to Tharon. "So what did Kaid say? Tell me everything. You and he were talking and laughing a lot. Does he like me?"

Tharon's mouth felt dry. She focused her attention on the frayed threads on the toe of her shoe. "Well, it isn't that he doesn't like you. He just doesn't want to pick a girlfriend."

Veronica's mouth dropped open. She glared at Tharon, "Exactly *what* did he say?"

Tharon tried to swallow the lump in her throat. In a voice barely above a whisper, she said, "He said he chooses not to choose."

Veronica frowned at her. "And just what did you say to him? Just what were you talking and laughing about? What did you say about me? Are you trying to keep him for yourself?"

"I didn't say anything about you. Listen, I don't want to have a boyfriend if you two don't have one. I didn't want to do this anyway. I'll just tell Eddie that I'm choosing not to choose either."

Lightning flashed in Veronica's eyes. "Do you think I can't get a boyfriend if I want one? I imagine I'll have a lot better success without you stabbing me in the back."

Tharon sputtered, "I didn't say you couldn't get boyfriends. And I didn't stab you in the back."

Veronica spoke low but her words were laced with venom, "If you didn't stab me in the back, then why don't you want Eddie now? You were just covering all your bases to make sure you had a boyfriend and we didn't. Did you poison Helm against Tracy too?"

Tharon shook her head, "No, that's ridiculous! I never picked Eddie. You picked him for me. And I only agreed to Eddie because you and Tracy had already picked Kaid and Helm."

Veronica stabbed her index finger at Tharon and sneered, "So you admit you wanted Kaid and Helm for yourself. How many boyfriends do you need?"

Tharon balled her hands into fists at her side. Tears seeped at the edges of her eyes. "I'll tell Eddie it was a mistake and I'm sorry. I never wanted anything to do with this stupid, childish, boyfriend scheme in the first place!" *Oh crap! I just called Veronica's plan stupid.*

Veronica's face turned hard as stone. She folded her arms and tilted her head, "No, *I'll* tell him for you."

Veronica and Tracy shouldered past Tharon to pull the Edwards twins aside and talked with them in low tones. At length the four of them turned to grace her with looks of withering hatred, except for Eddie who simply looked sad.

Tharon climbed numbly up the bus steps and walked down the aisle in stunned silence, searching for a place to sit. She glanced at her friends bunched up on a seat with Sarah Felger. Veronica sneered at Tharon with hatred still blazing in her eyes. Tracy looked from Veronica to Tharon with confusion and sadness. Sarah opened her mouth to say something to Tharon but after one glance at Veronica next to her, she closed her mouth and gave Tharon an apologetic shrug.

Tharon found an empty seat and scrunched up next to the window alone. She turned her head to the frosted glass and blinked back the tears threatening to betray the pain in her heart. What was wrong with her that she couldn't keep friends?

She felt someone sit down next to her. She knew it was Helm even before she looked at him. His comforting presence overwhelmed her. She brushed at her moist eyes with the back of her hand and turned to her new seatmate.

Helm's hazel eyes smiled at her. "Hi."

Warmth coursed through her, "Why are you sitting with me?"

Helm spoke low, so only she could hear him, "Because you're upset and I'm your friend."

She searched his face. His boyish softness was giving way to stronger angles, but his eyes still smiled before the rest of his features caught up with them. The only word that came to her as her heart warmed to his familiar companionship was a quiet, "Thanks."

Her lips curved into a contented smile as she sank against Helm's arm. She looked up and saw Tracy standing in the aisle glaring at her.

Oh crap.

CHAPTER 2

The school bus stopped to let Eddie and Everett off at their father's sprawling farm. The sign at the edge of the road heralded the proud beacon of 'Royce Edwards Corporate Farms: A Subsidiary of CalVin Industries,' in bright green lettering. The sign towered twice the height of the bus and remained lit up all night long.

A smooth black asphalt lane snaked a half mile to the three story red brick farmhouse sitting on the highest hill for miles around. Two massive, bright red barns loomed behind the house and three low, long, white buildings fanned out from the circular drive to the right of the barns.

Tharon heard the twins moving up the aisle from the back of the bus. She dreaded facing Eddie. She never wanted to hurt anyone, no matter how badly they may have treated her.

Everett stopped by her seat. His curly red hair poked out from the edges of his stocking cap and his green eyes glared at her. The all too familiar anger lines pinched between his eyebrows. "Kind of childish to hold a grudge since second grade, isn't it?"

Tharon's face burned. It had been more than a year since Everett had referred to the beating he gave her exactly four years ago. She'd never told anyone. Why hadn't she? It wasn't fear or intimidation—not anymore— at least, not since her father had trained her to defend herself. Why did she never tell anyone? She wasn't embarrassed. Was she trying to protect them? No. Not them. It was to protect Eddie. He'd been immediately sorry and she'd frankly forgiven him.

Everett, however, was another matter. He never passed up an opportunity to mutter a cutting remark or call her a name. But rarely did he say anything when someone else could hear him. He lacked the courage to show his open hostility to her in front of anyone.

Tharon glared back with grit and steel in her eyes. She raised an eyebrow and her lips curled in a tight smile that challenged him to reveal the secret threat, "What happened in the second grade?"

Everett flinched and glanced at Helm.

Helm looked from Tharon to Everett, "What's your problem Edwards?"

Everett grunted and continued up the aisle.

Eddie paused and looked at her with a sad expression. She wondered how identical eyes could look so completely different. Where Everett was all hard lines and hatred, Eddie showed a gentle kindness. The hurt in his eyes pierced her heart.

She said, "I'm sorry, Eddie, I'm just not ready to have a boyfriend."

Eddie's gaze traveled from her to Helm, "It sure looks like you're ready."

A pang of guilt coursed through her as she watched Eddie lumber to the front of the bus and trudge to their long driveway. He shoved his hands in his jacket pockets while he waited for Everett to get the mail. Her eyes met his one last time and his sadness twisted the knot in her chest.

She didn't want to have a boyfriend but she realized it wasn't all Veronica pushing Eddie on her. She did like Eddie, not in a *boyfriend* way, nor the *brother-friend* way she liked Kaid, nor even in the *I-like-myself-better-when-I'm-around-you* way that linked her to Helm. She wanted to be friends with Eddie—to get past the past. Had she destroyed that chance forever?

The bus turned onto Little Sandy Creek Road. As they neared Helm's bus stop, he nudged her with his arm and whispered, "Are you going to be okay?"

Tharon leaned against his arm, "If I survive the ride home."

He frowned, "This is my fault, isn't it?"

She gave him a crooked grin, "Yes, if you and Kaid hadn't been such jerks and ditched me, none of this would have happened."

He tilted her chin up to look at him and whispered, "I know. It's not what you think, though. Call me if you need me."

It was on the tip of her tongue to say something corny like, *I'll always need you,* or, *consider yourself called,* but even thinking it made her want to gag.

Tracy and Kaid's stop was another half mile down the road. Kaid gave Tharon a playful punch on the shoulder when he passed her but Tracy looked back at her and burst into tears. "I hate you! I never want to speak to you again. Stay away from me."

Tears swelled in Tharon's eyes and the lump in her throat grew to the size of a softball. She couldn't have spoken even if she could think of something to say. She never wanted to hurt anyone, how is it she'd managed to hurt almost all her friends?

Kaid tried to sooth his sister, "Tharon didn't do

anything. Don't be mad at her."

Tracy's tears evaporated into fury, "Didn't do anything? She poisoned Helm against me and she poisoned you against Veronica."

Kaid's anger rose as he rose to Tharon's defense, "She did no such thing. She never said an unkind word to us about either of you. Tharon, Helm and I have been friends for a long time. The best times I've had in my life have been with them. I wish I'd never agreed to stop hanging out with her."

Tharon's heart thundered in her ears as his comment sunk in. She found her voice, "Who did you agree with?"

Kaid blinked, and looked at her. It took a long moment before he said, "I promised not to tell."

Veronica Miller stood and rounded on her. She spoke quiet enough that her father, Chuck, the bus driver and her fourteen year old brother Cody, couldn't hear, but loud enough for Tharon to feel the contempt laced in her words, "It was your mother! Did you really think that all of a sudden Tracy and I couldn't resist your sparkling personality? You're such a slob, such a loser and half the time you smell as bad as those pigs you raise."

She climbed onto the seat and gripped the seatback as she hissed at Tharon, "Your mom begged our moms to make us be friends with you to get you to change. I guess she doesn't like you any more than we do."

Chuck Miller looked in the mirror above his head to see what was taking so long. "Kaid, Tracy, you need to get off now, I've got to get home and milk the cows."

Tharon looked at Kaid. Sadness clouded his features and she knew that Veronica spoke the truth. He backed towards the door and mouthed *I'm so sorry.*

Tharon clutched her backpack to her, she could barely breathe. The mile to her family's farm seemed to take an eternity. When Chuck stopped the bus in front of the drive, as usual, Veronica and Cody were the only other students left on the bus.

She hurried to the exit. Cody looked up from his chemistry book and smiled. He started to repeat their customary playful banter, "Hey, Dork, have a nice—" he saw the tears streaming down Tharon's face, "Hey, what's wrong?"

She shook her head and wordlessly ran off the bus, being careful to hide her face from Chuck.

Chuck called after her in his cheery voice, "Have a nice evening. I'll see you in the morning bright and early."

She ran past her tri-color English Shepherd, who sensed something was wrong. He whined and tried to nuzzle her hand as she ran. "Not now Shep."

Bounding up the steps, she burst into the house and threw her backpack onto the bench in the foyer, "Mom! Where are you?"

Lista Trace emerged from the kitchen wiping her hands on a dish towel. Her blond hair was gathered up in a perfect French twist; her porcelain skin flushed crimson on her cheeks; a smudge of flour dusted her chin. The gathered floral apron ballooned out over her growing baby belly. With warm brown eyes she looked at her daughter reprovingly, "That's not a friendly greeting. Can we try that with better manners?"

Tharon jutted out her chin, "Is it true? Did you tell Kaid and Helm that you didn't want them to spend time with me anymore? Did you beg Tracy and Veronica's mothers to make them be friends with me?"

Her mother paled, "Yes, but let me explain—"

"Explain what? That you didn't like the person I was? That I wasn't the perfect girly daughter you wanted so you picked Tracy and Veronica to mold me because that's what you want in a daughter? How could you?" Her voice caught in her throat, "Do you know how many nights I cried myself to sleep because I missed Helm and Kaid?"

Lista twisted the dish towel in her hands, "I just wanted you to broaden your circle of friends—to let you experience the feminine side of life to see if you'd like it."

For once Tharon didn't try to hide her anger and hurt, "How could you not trust me to find my own way to the person I want to be? Why didn't you trust me to choose my own friends? Tracy and Veronica even had me convinced I shouldn't go hunting with Dad anymore. Was that your idea too?"

Her mother took a step toward her but stopped when Tharon flinched. Lista said, "Ever since you were little you've spent every minute you could playing in the woods with those boys or hunting with your father. I wanted us to have something in common."

Tharon backed to the door, "You should have left me alone." She grabbed her winter coat off the hook by the door and shouted at her mother. "Veronica and Tracy hate me. I don't think they ever wanted to be friends with me. Don't ever try to pick my friends for me again. Ever!"

She slammed the screen door open and rushed down the steps without stopping to shut the front door. Tears streamed from her eyes, blurring her vision, but she didn't need to see clearly. She could find the way to the woods blindfolded if she had to.

As she navigated the narrow strip of sod between garden beds in the field on the south side of the house, her shoes slid on the rotting remnants of pumpkin vines. She crashed onto one knee as Shep nosed under her arm to stop her from falling. Her arms wrapped around him and she buried her tear stained face in his fur. "At least you've always loved me."

On the other side of the gardens the old growth timber towered ahead of her, its stark branches waving her onward in the wind. After brushing off her knee, she resumed her path to the woods.

Her mother called from the front porch, "Tharon, come back! I'm sorry!"

Tharon tugged her winter coat on over her wool coat and saw her father, Tom, as he climbed onto the tractor to pull the manure spreader from the cow yard. She could tell that he'd been making trips all day; a trail of manure meandered around the barn and up the grassy lane to the fields beyond the orchard.

She stood and looked at the farm: her mother on the porch, her father's strong back as the tractor faded from view, Maisy Baker's cottage beyond the house with the plume of smoke rising from the chimney.

Of course she'd be back. Of course she'd forgive her mother. Of course she'd survive. But at that moment she just wanted to be alone and cry. The only other place in the world that she felt at home was in the woods. She turned her back on the farm and stepped beyond the tree line, never imagining the peril in her chosen path.

CHAPTER 3

Helm sat in his bedroom whittling over the wastebasket. The dog figurine he'd been working on for over a year was nearly done. He'd started it before Tharon's mother asked him not to see or talk to her. He kept working on it because it helped him still feel linked to her.

He smiled as he put the finishing touches on the figure—an exact replica of Shep—he finished it in time for her birthday the next day. It had saddened him to watch Tracy and Veronica monopolize her time and try to turn her into a clone of their personalities. He wondered if she'd really been happy or was she just pretending to be? All he knew for certain was that for the first time since May, she seemed like his Tharon again.

His Tharon. When had he started thinking of her as if she belonged to him? No. He didn't feel like she belonged to him. He felt like he belonged to her. He shook his head, if Kaid ever had any idea he thought things like that, he'd never hear the end of it.

Helm remembered how miserable he'd been all summer and fall. It was a good thing he'd kept busy with baseball and football otherwise he'd have gone crazy. His heart ached that she hadn't seemed bothered that he wasn't around. He missed her. Had she missed him too?

In that one unguarded moment when he caught her staring at him from the football field, their connection flowed back into place, like a current drawing them together. He hadn't imagined it either. He saw it in her eyes on the bus. Nothing on heaven or earth would take her from him again. Not if he could help it.

Angela Harris knocked on her son's open door. Her short brown hair curled in an unruly mass to frame her oval face, which was creased with concern, "Lista Trace just called. Tharon was upset when she got home and ran off into the woods. Her mother wanted to know if you know where she's going."

Helm closed his pocket knife and shoved it in his jeans pocket. "She's probably gone to the climbing tree. I'll go find her."

Angela's hazel eyes opened wide, "It's freezing out. I'll just call her mother, I'm sure her parents will find her."

Helm fumed, "No! I'll dress warm and take my bike. She needs me. I never should have agreed to stay away from her. I haven't been much of a friend this year but I'm going to make up for it." He looked at his mother with defiance in his eyes. "No one is ever going to keep me from being her friend again."

Angela blinked at her son's anger. Helm almost never raised his voice, "I've got some hot cocoa on the stove. I'll put it in a thermos for you. She's probably cold out in the woods."

Helm put on a hooded sweatshirt and dressed as warm as he could while still keeping his clothes loose enough to climb the tree.

By the time he got his coat on, Angela was fussing with the cap to the thermos as she hustled from the kitchen. "I'm sorry you and Tharon are upset." In her own defense she added, "I was trying to be a friend to Lista at the time."

Helm dumped the contents of his back pack on the floor and shoved the thermos inside. He opened the door and stopped long enough to say, "I know you all meant well. But none of you give Tharon enough credit. She didn't need to change for me. I like her fine the way she is." He hesitated a moment, sorry he'd snapped at his mother. He kissed his mother on the cheek, "I'll call you from the Trace's when I get her home."

He pedaled down the gravel road as fast as he could. The cold bit into his face and he ducked his chin as far into his collar as he could.

Kaid must have gotten the same message because Helm caught up to him by the time they passed Maisy Baker's cottage. Maisy rushed towards Tharon's house, her black hair whipping out of the frayed ponytail streaming behind her. "Find her, boys! Bring her home!"

"We will," they shouted in unison.

Helm and Kaid were neck and neck. They exchanged a worried look as they crossed the concrete bridge over Little Sandy Creek. During most of the year the stream was low enough to cross on stepping stones they'd placed across its path.

They'd never seen the water that high so late in the year before. The muddy water flowed angrily under the concrete bridge before it curved and cut through the woods parallel to the road. The tree covered hillside on the other side of the stream sloped up gradually near the farm but grew steeper farther into the woods.

Helm hoped the current wasn't higher than the footbridge Tharon's father had helped them build three years ago to provide them a safe place to cross the stream after storms. He sighed in relief when they came to the bridge and found it above the current. He gripped the

29

brakes and dragged his foot to steady himself as the rear wheel skidded to the side on the gravel.

Kaid mirrored his stop. They carried their bikes across the bridge and leaned them against a tree on the other side.

Helm tried to look through the trees to the oak at the top of the hill but the trees at the base were too dense to see the crowns near the top of the ridge. He ran up the gradual slope to the clearing of what they called their climbing tree with Kaid close on his heels.

Shep barked before Helm saw the tree and his tension eased. If Shep was there, Tharon was safe.

Shep raced down the slope to meet them and urged them to follow him back to the oak which towered in a clearing filled with a tangled patch of black raspberry canes. The tree's large branches angled out almost perpendicular to the main trunk like arms beckoning to cradle them; dead branch stubs stuck out from the trunk providing one-sided rungs up to the larger branches, whose tips still gripped dried cinnamon colored leaves. Tharon sat in the middle of the crown with her back to the trunk.

Helm called up to her, "Are you all right?"

She leaned forward and grabbed the massive branch while bracing her feet against the main trunk and locked eyes with him.

When he saw her sorrow it cut him to the quick. He jumped for the lowest branch stub and swung his weight from branch to branch until he was even with her.

She choked, "How could you agree to not be friends with me? How could you not tell me? Am I that bad of a friend?"

"No. I made a terrible mistake," he glanced up at Kaid who climbed up and perched on the other side of her. "*We* made a mistake. Our moms made us promise to leave you alone so you could make friends with the girls. I didn't like it. I never liked it. I told my parents if I ever saw you unhappy, or if you wanted to still be friends, the deal was off," he struggled to not look away. "But you didn't seem to miss us."

With her eyes focused on the limb holding her she said, "I thought you outgrew me. That's what Veronica and Tracy kept telling me—that I was just a little girl and now that you're in the seventh grade, you were ready for someone better than me."

Kaid snorted, "And they thought it would be them? Don't ever listen to those two, they're wacked. As if we'd like them more than you. They don't hold a candle to you."

Tharon leaned back against the trunk and tilted her head at Kaid in disbelief. "Oh, please, are you kidding? They are both so much prettier than me, and they know how to dress nice and style their hair. I'm just," she made a sweeping gesture from her head to her toes, "plain old me."

Helm straddled the thick branch she was on to face her and steadied his balance with one hand on a branch above them. He said, "I don't know what mirror you're looking at, but there's nothing plain about the girl in front of me. You're smart and funny. You work hard. You've got a great imagination and you're very pretty." He took hold of her hand and squeezed it, "Have I ever lied to you?"

She held Helm's hand and looked him in the eyes. "No. But neither of you said a word to me? You just dumped me? Didn't you like the person I was either?"

Kaid shrugged his shoulders, "You know my mom. What else could I do? Besides, you never called to ask us to come over anymore."

She looked up at Kaid in disbelief, "But I did. For weeks I called you but your mom always said you were too busy."

A flash of anger lit in his eyes, "My mom never told me."

She turned her attention to Helm, "What about you?"

His face turned crimson, "You never called me, or I'd have come."

She gripped his hand tighter. "I wish I would have called you. I've missed you both so much." She looked from Helm to Kaid, "Let's make a pact here and now; no one will ever break up our friendship again."

Kaid's dimples punctuated his smile, "It's a deal."

Helm's hazel eyes looked deeply into hers and his heart pounded in his chest. "Agreed."

A burst of wind rushed through the crown and the branches danced in celebration.

Helm let go of her hand to grip the branch, "Are you about ready to go down? It's freezing up here."

She swung her foot up and pulled herself to stand on the branch, "Honestly, even as cold as it is, this is the happiest I've been in a long time. We probably won't be able to climb again until spring. Are you up for going a little higher before we go back down?"

Kaid and Helm looked at each other and shrugged. Kaid said, "I guess we owe you at least that much."

***

As she climbed she paused to look at the Miller's now empty cornfield and beyond it to their house and barn. It hadn't been bad, having friends who were girls. She felt a stab of regret and wondered if Veronica meant what she said about never wanting to be friends with her. She hoped not.

She wished she could say she didn't care what Veronica and Tracy thought, but that wasn't true. She did care. The thought that all these months they'd been pretending to be her friends gave her a new icy ache that gnawed at her chest with a chill colder than the wind that whipped through the trees.

The breeze tossed strands of her brown hair as they escaped her braids and twisted about her face. Her cheeks stung and she was glad her pride and anger hadn't stopped her from grabbing a warmer coat before she stormed out of the house. She suffered a pang of guilt for the way she'd treated her mother. They rarely had cross words between them and she knew her mother had good intentions, even if she was wrong.

Shep sat beneath the tree watching her. Occasionally he circled the tree, whining and barking nervously; or stood on his back feet, pressing his front paws against the tree trunk and yowling at her as if chiding her to come back down.

The knot in her stomach unclenched and she relaxed into the climb. All her senses fell into the automatic rhythm of climbing; her cold ungloved hands gripped the rough fissures of the bark, testing each handhold and foothold for soundness; she hefted herself higher and higher, unified with the tree and the sky and her friends.

Helm followed her in a counterclockwise movement until the branches became thinner and bent slightly beneath their weight. The wind picked up and swayed the crown, rocking them back and forth in a circular bouncing motion.

All three clung to the tree trunk. Kaid's arms ringed the tree and Tharon around the shoulders; Helm's encircled the trunk and her waist.

Tharon wrapped her arms around the trunk and one of Kaid's arms. Though she was frightened, she felt exhilarated and free as she swayed, one with the tree. There was nowhere else she'd rather be and no one else she'd rather be with. She hugged the trunk in gratitude.

"This is so much fun!" she squealed with delight.

Kaid glanced down, then squeezed his eyes shut, "Can we go down now?"

Helm clenched his teeth and said, "I think I've got my fill of tree climbing until spring. Maybe fall."

Tharon looked down at Helm. Her face beamed at him and he couldn't help but return her radiant smile. She took in all the view she could before they climbed down. To the north she saw her home; the house, barn, chicken coop, pigpen, and even the scarred outline of the workshop cut into the hillside behind the barn. A thin plume of black smoke floated up from the chimney of Maisy's cottage before the wind caught it and swept it away. Farther down the road she saw the rooflines of the Walker farm. "Kaid, I can see your house."

Kaid opened his eyes to gaze down the road. "Hey, yeah, I see it too. This is kinda cool."

A white van drove toward them and stopped directly below them in the middle of the road. From their vantage point they could see down the steep hillside to the gravel road.

Two men got out of the front of the van. The man who emerged from the passenger side was big and burley. It was hard to tell if he even had a neck. The driver was shorter and thinner and wore a purple baseball cap over his dark stringy hair. They opened the back of the van and pulled a third man out. His hands and feet were bound and they dropped him onto the gravel road. He wore no coat, just dark blue work pants and a matching shirt.

They were too far away to hear what the men were saying.

Helm's fingers dug into Tharon's waist. Kaid held her tight and they watched in silence.

She glanced down at Shep who growled low; the fur

stood straight up on his back from his head to his tail. She prayed he wouldn't bark but knew the odds of that happening were slim to none.

The back door behind the driver slid open and a fourth man stepped out. He wore a black cowboy hat with a white band. His leather jacket had fringe hanging from the shoulders and matching tan cowboy boots stuck out from under his jeans. He smoked a thin cigar, drew a long drag from it, blew smoke through his nose and mouth, and tossed the stub into the swift current of the swollen stream.

The burly man forced the bound man to kneel in front of the cowboy. The cowboy said something to the kneeling man who shook his head and screamed, "No! It wasn't me! I swear it wasn't me!"

The cowboy pulled a gun from underneath his jacket and shot the kneeling man in the head.

Tharon drew in a breath to scream but Kaid covered her mouth with his hand. He whispered, "Don't scream. They'll see us."

Shep ran down the steep hill barking at the men.

The cowboy kicked the body and sent it rolling down the short bank into the creek. He looked up when he saw the dog barreling down the hill toward him. He raised his gun and shot at Shep.

Tharon gasped and Kaid and Helm both gripped her tighter.

Shep staggered and swerved to run along the stream. His bark faded as he passed the footbridge and headed for home.

The cowboy shot again and this time Shep's barking stopped, no whimpering, only silence and the wind. They couldn't see through the trees to his body but all three stared in the direction of the ridge, praying Shep would circle back to them. He never did.

Tharon strangled a sob, "Oh, Shep."

They'd been so intent in watching for Shep that they didn't see the men get back in the van. They only heard the engine start and saw it continue south toward the Miller farm.

Although it was hard, they waited in the tree until the van disappeared from sight; then silently they worked their way down the tree. Helm dropped from the lowest limb and caught Tharon as she let go of the branch. She buried her face in his chest; his jacket absorbed the tears streaming from her eyes. He wrapped his arms around her and held her until Kaid landed behind them.

They scanned the road and woods and stood still, listening, but heard only the wind rustling through the trees and the rush of the stream below them.

Kaid tilted his head to the quiet, "I think they're gone. Let's take the ridge path to Tharon's house and get some help."

Tharon snapped her head away from Helm and broke from his grip. She turned to Kaid, "You go get help. I'm going to Shep."

"I'm not leaving her alone," Helm said. "She's right, you go get help." He followed Tharon down the slope.

Kaid hesitated only a moment. "I'm not leaving her either." He looked at the road nervously as he side-stepped rapidly down the more gradual slope the boys had climbed earlier as he tried to catch up with his friends.

Shep lay in an unmoving heap. Tharon was ten yards from him when the big man and the cowboy stepped from behind the large trees clustered at the base of the hill. The cowboy aimed his gun square at her chest. Her breath caught in her throat but through her tears she managed to choke out, "You killed that man and you shot my dog." Anger blazed in her eyes and burned in her chest.

The cowboy's sneering grin creased his sandpaper cheeks. Curly, blond hair covered his collar and he spit tobacco juice from the side of his mouth, "You can thank your dog and those bikes for us catching you. If that dog hadn't come running at us we'd have never looked up and seen ya. When we seen them bikes we knew where you'd come down. Now that we know you saw everything—" he raised the barrel to target her head. "We can't let you brats run home to tattle on us, now can we?"

"No!" Helm shouted and jumped between Tharon and the cowboy.

The big man put his thick hand on the gun barrel and forced it to point at the ground. "Burt, we ain't killin' no kids. I draws the line there."

Burt sneered and spit on the ground, "Right, moron, and just what do you suggest we do with them?"

"You got the brains so you figure somethin' else out. Somethin' that don't include shootin' kids." The big man balled his massive fists.

Burt sighed and scratched the back of his neck, "I suppose I can figure something out. Damn it, Carl, someday you're going to give me a stroke." He pulled his phone from his pocket and hit the screen. "Marty, we got 'em. Get back here."

Kaid saw Burt lower the gun as he spoke on the phone. He glanced to the right and gambled they might be able to get away if they dodged through the trees. He grabbed hold of Helm's and Tharon's sleeves and pulled them backwards and toward Tharon's house.

Burt jerked the gun to aim at Kaid. "Carl, if they run I'm shooting them. You okay with that?"

Carl nodded his head and held his meaty finger up in front of the three trembling friends. "Don't run. I'll take care of you, but don't run. Okay?"

Their eyes were wide with fear. They bobbed their heads as one. The boys each held one of Tharon's hands and huddled together with her in between them.

The van whipped around the curve and skidded to a stop near the footbridge. Marty, the man with the stringy hair and purple baseball cap, jumped down from the driver's seat but kept the motor running. He stood at the edge of the road and asked, "Why are they still alive?"

Burt sneered, "Carl has qualms about killing kids. Come on. Let's get them in the van," he pulled three long black zip ties out of his jacket pocket and handed them to Carl.

Carl fumbled with the zip ties, forming each into wide loops. He pulled Helm's hands behind his back and slipped the loop over them and tightened it; he did the same to Kaid. When he turned to Tharon he said, "I'm sorry about your dog, little girl. Just do what Burt says and I'll make sure you don't get hurt."

Tharon's mouth went dry. Her heart was beating so fast she thought it would explode. She closed her eyes and remembered the self-defense and survival training her father had drilled into her since she was little. Suddenly she wished she'd paid closer attention. She crossed her wrists behind her back with the sides of her wrists touching as Carl cinched the plastic strap around them.

Carl herded the children to the footbridge while Burt brought up the rear with his gun poised to discourage them from running away.

The foot bridge creaked under Carl's weight. He led Tharon across first and left her with Marty whose long skeleton-like fingers gripped her shoulder like a vice to hold her in place. He reeked of old sweat and motor oil and said, "Don't you get no notions of fussing. *I* got no qualms about killing brats. See?"

Tharon nodded her head. She decided of the three

captors, Marty was the most dangerous. Even if Carl tried to protect them and convinced Burt to keep them alive, she worried that Marty might kill them anyway. She looked him up and down, noting his Adam's apple bulging from his thin throat; his pale gray eyes, cold as steel, seemed about to pop out of their sockets; dark patches rimmed beneath his eyes.

Carl returned to get the boys. In the distance they heard the faint cries of Tom Trace calling Tharon's name.

Helm took a deep breath to yell for help, but before he made a sound, Carl clubbed him on the side of his head with his meaty palm. Helm's legs buckled and Carl caught him before he hit the ground.

Tharon drew a breath to scream as well but Marty gripped her tighter and pulled a ten inch knife from a sheath at his side. She shivered under his leering grin. Her chest twisted with the cold ache of dread and fear as she watched Carl scoop Helm over his shoulder and with an iron grip on Kaid's shoulder, forced him to cross the bridge.

When they were half way across, a loud crack sounded through the woods as a plank broke in two under Carl's weight. He wobbled precariously and Tharon feared he'd take Helm and Kaid into the stream with him.

She sighed when he regained his balance and they made it safely to the road. Her father's voice sounded nearer. He must be running fast. She strained to look for him through the trees. As much as she wanted him to find her, she had no doubt Burt would kill him on sight and Carl would do nothing to stop him.

Carl plopped Helm onto the floor in the back of the van and lifted Kaid up next to him.

Marty shoved Tharon toward the back of the van so hard that she tripped on her own feet and began to fall.

Carl, with surprising swiftness for his size, rushed to her and caught her before she splayed out face first in the gravel. The gentle way Carl cradled her in his arms unsettled her.

In a voice edged with anger that frightened her, he said, "Marty, I'm telling ya, ya got no need to hurt no kids. You hurt any of these kids and I'm gonna hurt you. I'm gonna hurt you dead."

Marty's upper lip curled in hatred but he glanced at Burt and said nothing.

Tharon looked into Carl's sad blue eyes as he gently sat her on the floor of the van next to Helm's unconscious body. "You hurt Helm," she said softly.

"I'm sorry. He shouldn't of tried to yell." He patted her head gently. "Don't you yell. I don't want to hurt you."

Tharon swallowed and looked down at Helm. "Is he going to be okay?"

Carl laid his palm on Helm's chest. "He's breathing steady. He'll have a headache tomorrow—least that's what them that lives has."

Carl picked up a roll of duct tape from the corner of the van floor. He tore off three pieces and covered each child's mouth. He held up a warning finger and said, "Be good," before closing the back doors.

Tharon and Kaid looked at each other with wide eyes.

Carl climbed into the front passenger seat. Burt slid open the side door and sat down in one of the two captain seats in the back of the van. He sat sideways to keep watch on the children and his face creased in a frown that rippled his graying stubble along his jaw.

Marty climbed in the driver's seat, threw the van into gear and sped down the road, spewing gravel in their wake.

A chill spread along Tharon's spine as they passed her home. She had to find a way to live. She couldn't die and let the last words spoken to her mom be in anger.

CHAPTER 4

Deputy Dana Donovan turned on her windshield wipers and cursed the powdery precipitation pelting her cruiser. Monday the temperatures had been in the sixties. Why couldn't the snow wait another week—even another day? So far it was melting when it hit the ground but if it kept falling this heavily... She gripped the steering wheel and sent up a silent plea: *Please don't let it destroy any evidence. And please help us find the children alive and well.*

A line of cars, trucks, and vans were pulled off to the side of the road across from the crime scene tape, which stretched for at least a quarter of a mile to a sturdy wooden bridge. She parked and walked the distance to the bridge. She observed the abundant personnel and felt like she was coming late to the party, giving her pause as to why she was pulled from her patrol at the other end of the county.

The technicians processed the scene at three sites: near a footbridge, a bit further at the side of the road, and at the wooden bridge which crossed the swollen creek. It was there that the body caught on a piling which kept it from washing down to the Eel River.

The entire scene was shrouded in gloom from the

overcast skies and the waning afternoon light.

Her heart fluttered when she saw Sheriff Simon Ellis, who stood head and shoulders above the cluster of people near the bridge. Only one man stood near his height—a farmer wearing brown coveralls and a dark knit cap, who had his arm wrapped around the shoulders of a very pregnant blond.

Dana approached the group clustered around Simon. She looked toward the bridge where Detective Max Stephens was knee deep in the current, helping the coroner and paramedics retrieve the body from the frigid waters.

Simon broke from the people as she neared. He looked tired. The sadness in his eyes aged his features. He said, "Deputy Donovan, this is Matt and Angela Harris, Doctor Walker and his wife Marilyn, and," he motioned to the tall farmer, "Tom and Lista Trace. And this is Maisy Baker, the Trace's...?" he looked between the Traces and Maisy, uncertain of their relationship.

Tom supplied the answer, "Close family friend and neighbor."

Simon continued, "It was their children who were taken. For the Amber Alert list them: Kaid Walker, age thirteen, Helm Harris, age twelve and Tharon Trace, age eleven—"

"Twelve," Lista said quietly. She cleared her throat as Dana looked up from the notepad she recorded the names on. "Tharon will be twelve tomorrow."

The mother's drawn face and the pain in her voice tugged at Dana's heart.

Simon continued, "Mrs. Trace said her daughter was upset and entered the woods shortly after the bus dropped her off—a little after three this afternoon. Mrs. Trace called Mrs. Walker and Mrs. Harris to find out if the boys knew where she would go. Both boys took off on their bikes to find her." He pointed into the woods. "Their bikes were found near a small wooden bridge. The Trace's dog was shot and is about fifteen yards past where the bikes are parked."

Dana took notes as he spoke, she looked at the distraught faces of the parents and tried to be as delicate as she could, "Sheriff, how do we know it was abduction?"

The Sheriff nodded to Tom, "Mr. Trace was the first on the scene. He heard three gunshots and followed his daughter's trail through the woods to that tallest tree at the top of the hill." He pointed to a tree that towered in the air high up above the ridge. "He believes they were in the crown of that tree and witnessed the murder."

Dana's eyes followed his pointing finger, as did the parents. Dana raised her eyebrows. "That—looks—tall." She bit her tongue before commenting on the wisdom of letting children climb trees like that when some of her own childhood antics flashed through her mind. She tapped the notepad with the end of her pen, "And what indicates abduction?"

Simon lowered his gaze to lock stormy blue eyes with Dana. "Mr. Trace found tracks of at least one of the children entering the back of a vehicle. From the wheel base where it spun its tires, it appears to be a mini-van."

Maisy bristled, "If Tom says they were put in a van, they were put in a van. The van I saw leaving around three-forty was white with partial picture of a golden snake on the side."

Simon said, "Donovan, get the Amber Alert posted," he turned to the parents, "She'll need pictures of your children if you have them."

He turned back to Dana, "Then I want you to go with Mr. Trace and get the dog's body. Take it to the veterinary clinic in Columbia City and stay with it until they extract the bullets for evidence. We need to know if the same gun that shot the victim, killed the dog." He bent close to her ear and whispered, "Tell the vet not to worry about the fee for disposing of the remains, I'll pay for that out of my pocket."

Dana nodded and turned away, feigning a coughing fit. Feeling Simon so close—his breath on her ear, the warmth of his cheek next to hers—left her flushed and a tad breathless. She hoped he thought her flushed face was a result of her fake coughing spell.

Simon touched her back with concern, "Are you alright?"

Warmth coursed through her and she choked out, "Fine. I just had a tickle in my throat."

Simon raised his voice loud enough for the parents to hear him, "I know you folks are upset and we're going to do everything we can to bring your children home safe. Right now I'd like for you to return home until we finish processing the scene. If you remember anything else that might help us, even if you think it is insignificant, call us right away. We'll keep you informed of our progress."

Matt Harris left his wife's side and asked, "Tom, how certain are you they were all taken?"

Tom frowned, "I'm certain Kaid walked to the back of the van. I think Helm and Tharon were carried there but I can't be positive." A worried look crossed his face as his gaze wandered from Matt to the rushing stream.

Matt frowned at the muddy waters, "You finish up what you have to do here. I'm going downstream to check and see if there are any signs of them." He turned to his wife, "Honey, you go home with Lista and wait for me there." He hugged her briefly, grabbed a flashlight from his car and took off.

Doc Walker patted his wife's arm, "You'd best get home and stay with Tracy. I'll go with Matt. If they did fall in...,"

Marilyn clutched at his coat. "There, there, I'm sure Tom's right but just the same..." he scurried down the road to catch up with Matt.

Dana turned to Lista, "Mrs. Trace, do you have any idea why your daughter was upset?"

Lista's face paled, "She grew up playing with Kaid and Helm. They were best friends. Today she found out that several months ago I arranged with the boys' mothers and Ginger Miller for the boys to stop spending time with her and for Veronica Miller and Tracy Walker to befriend her."

Tom snapped at her, "You didn't!"

Lista pleaded, "I'm so sorry. I only wanted her to be happy—to have a more normal life."

Even through Tom's perfectly groomed beard, Dana saw the hard set of his jaw. His brown coveralls and tall boots looked and smelled like he came straight from the cow yard to the woods. Yet despite his appearance he had a distinguished quality about him.

His blue eyes softened at his wife's bleak expression. "You and Maisy go home. We'll discuss this when Tharon is home safe and sound."

Angela pulled a picture from her pocket and looked at it for a long moment before she handed it to Dana, "This is the most recent picture of Helm. Please find him," she pleaded as much with her hazel eyes as with her voice.

Marilyn scrounged in her car and came up with a picture of Kaid, "He's taller now but still looks a lot like this picture." Her black, chin-length hair feathered around her face; her thin lips nearly disappeared in her solemn frown. "He's a good boy. Everyone likes him." Her blue eyes misted and she blinked rapidly. She repeated, "He's a good boy."

Angela and Maisy helped Lista into the car and the women left. Only Matt Harris's car remained parked with the official vehicles.

Sheriff Ellis turned to Dana, "Donovan, get that amber alert issued and then help Mr. Trace put his dog in your cruiser. I'm going to talk to Max and the coroner. I'll join you as soon as I can."

"Yes, Sir," Dana sensed the sadness in her boss. She'd grown skilled at reading his moods over the last four years. He'd lost his wife and two daughters to the influenza pandemic five years before. The same pandemic had taken her entire family along with nearly half of the world's population.

Both she and Simon were still grieving when she was hired to serve as his driver. In many ways their shared grief had been therapeutic for both of them. You can't daily witness someone else's sadness without learning to cope with your own. When one needed to talk the other listened. Their friendship grew quickly but for Dana it blossomed into a deep love.

She'd had no sign that Simon's heart reciprocated. If anything he'd become more detached from her and she learned to school her emotions around him. The only thing she imagined worse than him not returning her love was never seeing him. If the only relationship they could have was a working one, she'd content herself with that.

After issuing the Amber Alert, Dana stood by her cruiser and pondered the crime scene. The snow continued and began sticking to the ground but still melted on the roadway. She jammed her flashlight into her belt and was about to join Tom who waited by the footbridge. The crime scene technicians had collected all the pictures and evidence from the area and gave them the go ahead to get the dog's body.

Simon shook hands with the coroner and signaled Dana to wait for him. He pulled his SUV back down the road and stopped near her cruiser. He got out and walked to her side. "Did you get the Amber Alert issued?"

Dana's pulse quickened as it always did when Simon Ellis was near her. With practiced ease she kept her tone of voice void of emotion. "Yes sir. I scanned pictures of the boys but we still need a picture of the Trace girl."

Max Stephens pulled up in his truck and Simon bent to speak to him through the driver's window. "Stop by the Trace house and get a picture of their daughter and add it to the Amber Alert. And check with Miss Baker to see if she can give you a better description of the logo on the van."

He leaned on the truck and rubbed his chin. "Call Murphy and have her check every traffic cam in a hundred mile radius for white vans. That's our best shot at finding those kids," he took a deep shaky breath and lowered his voice so Tom couldn't hear him. "Max, the Trace girl is the same age my Cathy would be if she were still—," he blinked fast and his words were choked with emotion. "I don't think my heart can bear telling these folks they lost their children."

Max gave Simon a small two finger salute, threw the truck into gear and drove away.

Dana instinctively touched Simon's arm briefly, "We'll find them, Sheriff. We'll bring them home alive." She knew she shouldn't promise something she couldn't guarantee, but her heart twisted in knots knowing the pain and compassion he felt.

He covered her hand with his in a brief touch and the unspoken hope that she was right. He nodded toward Tom waiting by the footbridge. "This is a tough job I'm asking you to do. That man's had a rough day with his daughter missing and his dog killed. There's no one I trust more to handle the situation with sensitivity and compassion."

Dana's heart thundered in her chest and she snatched her hand away. "Yes sir."

He ran his hand through his short cropped blond hair, "Blast it, Donovan, I don't need the tough cop routine you've been playing for the past year. I need you to be the caring woman I've grown to—" he grasped for the right words, "—value and depend on."

For a tiny instant she thought he was going to say *love*. She turned away to hide her disappointment and murmured over her shoulder, "Don't worry, I'll do my job." She crossed and joined Tom at the edge of the road.

Tom studied the footprints again after the CSI team left. When Dana walked up he pointed to the bridge. "The only one I'm not sure about is Helm. His footprints just stop on the other side. I think the big man carried him across. The big man made two trips back to the van and on one trip his footprints are a little deeper than the other," he paused and looked down the stream. "At least I hope that's what happened. I'd hate to think of Matt finding his son's body down there," his voice caught, "or Tharon."

Dana asked. "You said you weren't sure about Tharon either?"

Tom stared at the impressions in the dirt by the side of the road, when he spoke, his voice was strained, "I didn't want to say much around my wife but I'm not that certain that Tharon made it to the van either."

Simon walked up behind Dana and stopped by her side.

Dana handed Tom her flashlight so he could show them the tracks. He pointed with the beam as he spoke, "It looks like she staggered there and the big man's tracks showed large strides to where she stood last. I'm going on the assumption and hope that the big man caught her as she fell," he looked from Simon to Dana and in a desperate voice said, "She just has to still be alive. I don't know how I could go on..."

Dana's heart was swallowed up in compassion for the desperate father. In a firm but gentle voice she said, "We'll do everything we can to find her, Mr. Trace."

Tom handed the flashlight back to Dana. "Please, call me Tom. If, heaven forbid, you have to bring us bad news, I don't want to feel like it's coming from a stranger."

Dana said, "Fair enough. You can call me Dana."

"And my name is Simon. Is there anything else, Tom?"

Tom looked across the stream to the deepening shadows, "I guess just getting my dog's body."

"I'm sorry." Simon said, "The last thing I want to do right now is cause you any more pain. We need to determine if the bullets came from the same gun that killed the victim."

Tom stuffed his hands in the pockets of his coveralls. "I understand. What will you do with his body?"

Dana spoke in a gentle voice. "I'll put a blanket on the back seat of my cruiser. I promise I'll treat him with the utmost respect. I'll take him to the veterinary clinic in Columbia City. We'll take care of disposing of his body."

Simon turned to leave but hesitated, "May I ask how did you come to know so much about footprints?"

Tom spoke absently, still staring at his dog, "I was raised in Canada by a survival expert. Part of his job was tracking people lost in the Canadian wilderness. He trained me."

Simon nodded his head, "Dana will help you get your dog into her car." He turned to Dana, "I'm going down the road to check on Mr.—on Matt and Doc. I'll be at the morgue after that if you need me."

"Yes sir." She didn't feel comfortable dropping the professional wall between them. She felt too vulnerable around him.

Dana and Tom crossed the footbridge, stepping carefully over the broken plank.

Tom knelt next to the body and gently stroked the still dog's head, brushing the thin layer of snow from his fur. A tear trickled down his face into his beard. His thick brown chin length hair twisted in the wind where it stuck out from under his knit cap. "He was a great dog. He loved Tharon—followed her everywhere. He sat by the road to wait for the school bus every day."

Dana fought to keep her own emotions in check. She didn't count herself a weak woman. She'd weathered and witnessed enough trauma, cruelty and horror in her job and in her own life to know she wasn't weak. So why did a single tear over a dog by this distraught owner—or a comment strangled with emotion from a strong man like Simon—make her eyes mist and her throat feel like she swallowed a golf ball?

Tom picked up the eighty pound dog's body with ease.

Dana led the way back to the creek. She steadied the dog in Tom's arms and guided him across the bridge. At the car she hurried to cover the back seat with a blanket she took from the trunk.

Tom hesitated, "Are you sure you don't want me to put Shep in the trunk?"

She nearly lost it when she heard the dog's name. Her late grandfather's dog was named Shep. Her eyes welled up with tears. She cleared her throat but her voice was still tight with emotion. "Absolutely not. Tharon's dog will ride in the back seat."

Tom gently laid Shep's body on the blanket and stroked his fur one last time. He shut the door and extended his hand to shake Dana's. He gripped her hand with both of his, and held it for a long moment. Tears spilled freely down his cheeks and disappeared in his beard. "Thank you for your kindness."

She said softly, "Do you want me to give you a ride back to your house?"

Tom ignored his tears and looked back at the stream with dread. "No, I'll catch up with Matt and Doc. I just hope..."

He couldn't say it any more than she wanted to think of them finding their children washed up along the stream. Dana didn't trust her voice to speak and merely nodded her head. She got in and started the cruiser. As she turned the car around and pulled away she saw Tom wipe the tears from his face, turn, and then jog down the road. She could hold back her own tears no longer. She wept openly now that she was alone.

Why did the dog's death hit her so hard? This was why she was alone. This is why she wouldn't let anyone or anything get too close to her. When she felt compassion for someone she did it with her whole heart—and she turned into a puddle of mush in the process.

Maybe she wasn't really in love with Simon. Maybe it was just her crippling compassion for his sorrow.

It only took a moment of reflection on the longing in her heart to realize that wasn't true. She loved him deeply. That's why she could never drop her professional guard around him. To hear him say he didn't feel the same would crush her heart to pieces. At least this way, she could be near him. If that was all she ever had, it would be enough. It had to be.

She wiped her eyes on her sleeve and was almost to the end of the road when she heard a sound from the back seat. At first she thought she imagined it and strained to listen. She heard it again. A soft whimpering whine—the most glorious sound she'd ever heard.

She turned on the siren and floored the accelerator.

Until she knew the dog would survive, this was a secret she'd keep to herself. It would be cruel to give the family hope and have them experience their dog's death twice. "Hang on Shep. You live and I promise I'll find Tharon and bring her home to you."

CHAPTER 5

Tharon tried to memorize which directions they turned and how long they drove, but Marty made so many turns that she quickly lost track. She figured they were taking back roads to Fort Wayne and her suspicions were confirmed when she saw a city bus ahead of them in traffic. Fort Wayne was the only city they could have reached that had buses.

"Carl, check the scanner," Burt scratched his jaw and sneered at her. "I want to know if they've missed these kids yet."

Carl touched the screen on the dash and the radio crackled to life.

The kidnappers are armed and dangerous. The three children are believed to have witnessed a murder and are considered to be in extreme danger. A white mini-van is being sought in connection with the abduction and murder. They were abducted by three men who we repeat are armed and dangerous....

Burt wiped his hands on the sides of his thighs leaving a damp swipe on his faded jeans. "That's enough, Carl, shut it off. Marty, get us off the main streets. We gotta stash these brats and hide the van. Go to the shop on Lake. We'll repaint the van and hide them in one of the vacant offices on the other end of the building. That'll give me some time to figure out what to do with them." His hands trembled as he held them flat in front of him. He knotted his fingers into fists and pressed them against his knees.

Tharon felt that icy ache in her chest while she watched Helm, who hadn't moved since he was placed on the floor of the van. A bump with a purple bruise formed above his left eyebrow. She glanced at Kaid whose worried expression matched her own. Twisting sideways, she lowered her ear to Helm's chest with her face turned toward his. Her head blocked Burt from seeing Helm's face. She felt Helm's chest rise and fall and searched his face. He opened his eyes and winked at her and then closed them again so quickly, if she'd blinked she would have missed it.

Burt's angry voice startled her, "Is that kid still alive?"

Tharon sat up and nodded her head.

Burt grunted, muttered something under his breath, and looked away. She winked at Kaid who sighed and released a measure of the tension in his shoulders.

She craned her neck to look out the windshield but all she could see were the tops of leafless trees, occasional stop lights and a few street signs which stretched over the lanes. She caught a few names that flashed past the edge of the windshield; white lettering on green signs: Elizabeth, Spy Run, Lake—but she knew she'd never be able to figure out where they were going, let alone how to get back home.

Her head was dizzy from the sharp, quick turns and her stomach rumbled. She swallowed bile that threatened to choke her since its most likely exit was covered with duct tape.

Marty stretched a long thin finger to the visor above him and clicked a garage door opener; the metal garage door rolled up and Marty pulled the van into a dark building.

After the metal door rolled down behind them, Carl opened the back of the van and hauled the children out. He draped Helm over his shoulder and urged Kaid and Tharon ahead of him.

Tharon blinked until her eyes adjusted to the dim light which filtered through gaps in the rough wood planks boarding up the two broken windows. Cold air blew in through the gaps plunging the temperature in the large auto shop.

The shop smelled of dirty grease, paint fumes, and cat litter in dire need of changing. The odor triggered Tharon's gag reflex and she tried to hold her breath to keep from smelling it but still sneezed twice against the duct tape, making her ears feel like they would explode.

Carl picked up a large flashlight from the bench by the door at the other end of the shop. He stopped by the closed door and juggled Helm as he held the flashlight under his multiple chins to maneuver the door open. He gently nudged Tharon and Kaid through and let the door slam shut behind them. "Just keep moving to the last door on the right before the lobby area. See that little bit of light down there? That's the lobby."

Kaid and Tharon kept their arms touching each other as they walked side-by-side down the long, dim hallway. Something large scurried past Kaid and brushed his leg in the darkness. He jumped, almost knocking Tharon over. She and Kaid trembled as they huddled up next to Carl.

"Don't worry. That's just Cat and her grown babies. They keeps the mice and rats out of here. Come on now, I needs to get you in a room before Burt or Marty comes lookin' for me. See I'm gonna hide you from Marty as long as I can. I's the only one with the key to this room. It's cleaner 'cause it used to be a doctor office."

With a gentle nudge from Carl, Kaid and Tharon started

forward again. As her eyes adjusted to the darkness she made out the dim light from the lobby.

"Stop here," Carl panned the flashlight beam along the empty hallway behind them. Again he fumbled with the flashlight under his chin as he palmed a key from his pocket and let the children into a waiting room.

The skeletons of metal chairs, minus some seats and backs, were piled in the corner. The strong stench of cat urine and ammonia assaulted Tharon's nose and burned her eyes. A pair of green eyes shown in the glint of the flashlight and a threatening hiss sounded from beneath the pile of chairs.

Soft mewing sounds protested when the mother cat stood up. Carl swept the beam of light around the room until it rested on a cat hunched over her kittens, "Cat, how'd you get shut in here? Did Marty lock you in here? That son of a—" he looked sideways at Tharon, "gun."

As Carl fumbled to unlock the inner door, the light from his flashlight reflected on a half open sliding window to the left of the door. Carl wedged the door open with his foot and caught the flashlight as it fell from his chin. "Go in the first room on the right. It should be clean and not too cold cause there ain't no windows."

Tharon pressed close to Kaid's side as they entered the room.

Carl prodded them forward to the center of the room. The flashlight beam was too weak to reach the dark corners. He gently laid Helm on the floor in the middle of the room.

Tharon looked around quickly while they still had light from the flashlight. The rectangular room was completely empty as far as she could see. The walls were white and bare except for splotches of mold on the lower half of the outside wall. Crumbled drywall littered the floor from holes in the ceiling and walls. She huddled up to Kaid with her right foot touching Helm and her toes pointed toward the door.

She tried to talk to Carl with her taped mouth but her words came out in a muffled pleading sound. After Carl gently peeled the tape from her face, she asked, "What's going to happen to us?"

The glow of the flashlight blinded her eyes but didn't reach Carl's face. She didn't need to see his face. She heard the concern and sadness in his voice. "See, I can't just let you go. Burt's my brother. I gotta try to protect him and you'll tell on him. But he's smart. If he can find a way for you to live and not tell, I gotta let him try. If I let you go free, Burt and me'll have to leave here and go on the run." He tipped the flashlight to look at Helm and light revealed sadness clouding his features. "But I promise I'll let you go before I'll let Marty or Burt hurt you."

The image of Burt shooting the man and dumping his body in the creek flashed in Tharon's mind. "What about Burt? Will he hurt you if you help us?"

Carl took a step closer and patted the top of her head, "No, Little Miss. Burt won't never hurt me. He's my big brother. Marty's a bad man, though. You watch out for Marty."

Carl returned the tape to her mouth and turned to leave. He took a couple of steps towards the door and looked back at Helm. "I'm sorry about your friend. It didn't feel like I hit him that hard. I hope he wakes up soon. I'll be back later when I finds out what Burt wants to do."

The light faded out the door. With a loud click the complete darkness fell like a thick cloak, intensified by the moist and musty air.

Fear gripped at Tharon's heart but she refused to surrender to the terror threatening to engulf her. She turned her wrists to overlap each other and slipped them out of the zip tab. She took the tape off her mouth and smoothed her hands up Kaid's arms to find his face and pulled the tape off his mouth too.

At first he flinched from her touch, "How'd you get free?" Kaid asked in a surprised voice.

"Shh! Not so loud," Tharon said. "We don't know if there are more people than them here." She squatted down next to Helm and felt for his face then pulled his tape off too. "Helm, are you hurt?" she asked as she helped him stand.

"Nah, I saw him throwing the punch at me and I kind of moved with the hit so he hardly hurt me at all. I figured they'd either leave me for dead, and I'd go get help, or if his hands were full carrying me that you two had a better chance of running away."

Tharon shook her head in the darkness, "Right. We'll have to remember that, Kaid. The next time he's passed out on the ground we should run off and leave him."

"Ha, ha," whispered Helm. "How did you get your hands free?"

Should she tell them the truth that she got beat up in the second grade and asked her dad to teach her self-defense? They were probably going to all die that night—did she really want their last mental image to be of her serving as Everett's personal punching bag? "Magic," she said.

Kaid snorted, "Right, no tell us, how did you do it?"

Ignoring his question she turned Helm's back to her. "Let me see if I can help you get loose." The total darkness unnerved her and her breathing became shallow. She tried closing her eyes so she didn't feel so disoriented but it didn't work. She held onto Helm and moved her hands down his arms to his wrists, "No, you overlapped your hands, the strap is too tight."

Helm jumped with excitement, "I have my pocket knife in the front right pocket of my jeans." He turned his pocket closer to her.

Tharon's hand traveled from Helm's wrist to his belt, feeling her way to slip her hand into his pocket, which was much deeper than she expected.

Helm sucked in his breath sharply and moaned.

She stopped with her hand still deep in his pocket, "What's wrong? Are you hurt?"

He breathed through his mouth and his voice cracked and strained when he spoke, "No. It's just—never mind."

Her fingers closed on the knife. She pulled it out and felt for the smaller blade. She turned Helm's back to her as she felt her way back down to his hands. "Hold still. I sure hope I don't cut you."

"Yeah, I'll second that," Helm said as he took a deep breath and held as still as a statue.

Tharon felt the cord slice like butter against the sharp blade. "Are you okay? Did I cut you?

"No. I'm okay. Thanks," Helm said.

She felt as if she were smothering. She had to hold it together till she cut Kaid loose. Holding out her left hand she said, "Kaid, where are you?"

"I'm here." Kaid's voice was close and to her left.

She felt into the darkness until she touched a jacket sleeve. "Is that you?"

"Yeah, I hope that's you, too."

She softly punched his arm, "Funny." Then she felt down to his hands and cut him loose.

"Thanks. I'm sure glad they didn't take time to search us," Kaid sighed with relief.

Helm kept a hand on Tharon's shoulder to keep track of her in the dark. "They were too busy arguing about whether to kill us or not."

Tharon closed the blade, "Helm, here's your knife." His touch on her shoulder calmed her but she still struggled with the panic welling inside her.

Helm moved his hand from her shoulder and slid it down to her palm. In the darkness she pressed the closed knife into his hand. He broke contact with her to pocket the knife.

Without his reassuring touch her senses heightened. Something skittered up her pant leg. She tried to stifle a scream and batted at her legs and arms, "Something's crawling on me!"

Hands grabbed her shoulders in the darkness. Helms voice sounded close to her ear. "Shh. It's okay."

Her breathing was rapid and shallow, blackness pressed in on her as she shook her arms and legs.

Helm unzipped his jacket and wrapped it around her as he put his arms about her and pulled her head to his chest. His hands rubbed her back, shoulders and smoothed over her head. "Is it gone now?"

She sucked in quick breaths of air, unable to speak, and nodded her head against his chest.

Helm spoke softly, his lips close to her ear, "Just try to breathe with me. Breathe in, breathe out. Close your eyes and imagine you're in a bright room but the darkness is only from having your eyes closed."

His soft voice soothed her. She closed her eyes and felt his chest rise and fall. She heard his heartbeat and got lost in its rhythm. At first her breathing was ragged but soon it became steady. She wrapped her arms around him too. Kaid's hand rested on the small of her back and she felt anchored to them both.

She didn't know how long they stayed like that but was grateful for the steady, calming strength she felt from them both. "Thanks," she whispered. Standing on her tiptoes, she reached up to kiss Helm on the cheek but his head was turned and she kissed him on the mouth. He kissed her back, just a little longer than the peck she'd intended and when she eased down again with her head against his chest, she heard his heart racing.

Kaid asked, "Are you okay now?"

"Yeah, there was something crawling on me and I freaked out. Sorry about being such a baby."

Tharon stepped a little away from Helm but still held his waist with both hands, "Thanks. How did you know how to help me?"

"My mom falls asleep on the couch and gets nightmares sometimes," Helm held her shoulders. "That's how my dad calms her down. I'm glad it worked for you too."

She became disoriented in the darkness and no longer knew which way the door was. She took another deep breath and felt her way to hold hands with both of them. "We need to stay together and find the door."

Kaid led the way, feeling along with his feet and free hand. When he came to the wall they all three flattened along it but found no door. Kaid led them to the left as they inched along the wall.

Tharon counted the corners and the steps for each wall. When she counted the fourth corner and thought of the number of steps on the opposite wall, she moaned. "Are you kidding me? We just went around the entire room. We started out right next to the door."

"Found it," Kaid whispered.

Helm pressed between them and felt for the door knob. He opened his knife again and said, "My dad locked the keys in the house once and he opened it with his—" click, "—pocket knife." The door knob opened in his hand.

Tharon felt the boys each grab hold of her shoulders as she led them into the hallway. She moved forward and felt until she found the opposite wall and then side stepped to the right until Helm whispered, "I found the next door."

Tharon heard Helm fiddling with the door. His knife kept striking metal. She touched his arm and moved his knife away from the door. "Let me check something."

She felt the frame of the door and found a square metal security plate overlapped the frame preventing them from using the knife to open the lock. She opened her mouth to suggest the glass window when she heard someone unlocking the door from the hallway. Voices filtered through a room to their right and the flashlight beamed through the glass window revealed a small room cluttered with overturned filing cabinets and rotting papers.

The children held still and listened to Marty, Burt and Carl arguing.

"They're in here ain't they?" Marty mocked. "You ain't got no imagination, Carl."

Carl scoffed, "No they ain't. I hid 'em good. I just heard Cat in here and knew she'd be hungry. You're an animal, Marty, leavin' the poor thing in here with no way to get food or water."

Marty sneered, "Serves her right. That monster bit me last week. You're lucky I didn't slice her open. The only reason I didn't was cause then I'd have put up with your whining."

Burt broke in, "Shut up, you two! Forget the stupid cat. We gotta figure out what to do with those brats. Carl, we either have to kill them or sell them. You ain't gonna like either option so decide now, which will it be?"

"Burt, we ain't gonna kill them! What do you mean sell them? Who buys kids?" Carl's voice sounded angry and scared at the same time.

"If they was babies we'd have lots of places we could sell them. Even just dump them off at a fire department. But they ain't babies. As long as they're in this country, then we got a problem. I've heard of a place in New York that'll take kids. This guy traffics kids overseas for sex slaves. He takes boys and girls. He pays good, too. The younger they are the more he pays."

Kaid and Helm tightened their grip on Tharon's shoulder.

Carl sounded wary, "I don't like the sounds of that. They're just kids. Ain't there anything else?"

Marty's gravelly voice gave Tharon chills. "I know a guy in Philadelphia. He takes in stray kids from the streets and sells them to a company that does genetic research. He figures if they survived the pandemic virus they might have immunity—might be able to stop another virus outbreak. Takes right good care of them, he does."

Burt sounded hopeful, "No foolin'? Does he pay good?"

Marty chuckled, "Yeah, he pays real good. And the kids is fed better than they ever was in their lives."

Burt slapped his brother's back, "There you go, Carl, sounds like a right good solution. Why don't you go find a box to put Cat and her kittens in? Marty and I will go call this guy and make the arrangements."

Carl's thudding footsteps retreated back toward the shop.

"What's the real story, Marty," Burt growled. "You know there ain't nowhere we can send those kids without worrying about them talking, unless we sends them overseas."

Marty chuckled, "That was just for Carl's benefit. You ain't the only one with a brother. My brother's in Philly and he do sell kids to a genetics company, but they gets cut up after they finish with them. My brother has a bit of a fetish though. He keeps some for himself. They don't last as long as the ones that goes to the company. He likes little girls. Recon he'd like that one just fine."

A new voice cut the air like a knife. He sounded younger than the other men and when he said a word with an s or z he made a slight whistling sound, "You morons. What the hell do you think you're playing at here? Don't you realize we have just two weeks before the plan goes into motion?"

"Well if it isn't our dandy police officer," Marty's voice dripped with sarcasm. "Careful, you might smudge those shiny boots of yours mingling here with us riff-raff."

The policeman sniffed loudly and sneezed, "The Hamron administration is targeting Indiana for a reason. This state has to be brought to its knees. Once we take the school bus hostage and claim the secessionist did it, the feds plan to save the day with a Homeland Security military strike force and Indiana will become the first police state in the Union. That will put an end once and for all to the secession movement."

Burt growled, "You ain't telling us nothing we don't already know. What are you doing here officer?" He said officer like it was a dirty word. "I thought we were supposed to keep a *respectable distance*—so today of all days you show up here? We found a spy and we took care of him, so what do you want?"

The officer made a short barking laugh, "*You* took care of him? Yeah, I heard how you took care of him. It's all over the news. I'm here because I got a call from the top to find out if you idiots thought to find out who hired him and what he told them?"

Burt sputtered. In his gravel voice, he grumbled, "We was askin' him but my gun's got a hair trigger an' it went off before we finished talkin' to him."

Marty snorted, "Hair trigger—you're going with that

excuse?"

"Shut up!" the officer shouted, "What were you doing out there anyway?"

"We was checking out the bus route," Burt grumbled, "That's how we found out Wil was a spy. We caught him using his phone. He was recording the GPS of the route. We stopped him before he could send it to anyone."

The officer's voice took on a more menacing tone, "What about the kids you took? Did you kill them?"

"Not yet," Burt growled. "My brother has qualms about killing kids. Marty and I was just coming up with a plan for them."

"Just as well. The boss wants the girl alive," the officer said, "but not the boys. Might be a good idea if you kill them and dump their bodies in one of the rivers to decoy searchers from looking for her elsewhere."

"Why do they want the girl and not the boys?" Marty's voice sounded suspicious.

"I'm sure I don't know and didn't feel inclined to ask. I got the impression the girl was always a target. That's why her bus route was picked and there was always going to be other kids who would disappear with her," the officer's voice was laced with contempt. "Your team wasn't on the need to know list."

"So if she's so important will we still take the bus?" Burt said. "I mean if we already got who they want, why bother with the hostage sham?"

"From what I gathered, taking the girl was to be a bonus. The plan is still a go. It has taken ten years but we have people in every level of government and law enforcement in this state. In one afternoon you put all that at risk. And Marty, I got to tell you, the boss expected better from you."

Tharon stood frozen in place it was only the grip each of

the boys had on her shoulders that kept her from screaming. *Why would anyone want me? I'm nobody.*

The policeman's sneering tone cut through her thoughts, "I have to know, how come you didn't look around to make sure the site was secure? Who was the first one out of the van?"

Marty grumbled, "It was me and Carl. But those kids had to be forty or fifty feet up in a tree way up on the hill. Who the hell expects to find kids up in a tree like that in freezing cold weather? It isn't natural." His voice dropped its usual scorn, "You can tell the boss not to worry. Those kids won't be talking to no one. Are you taking the girl now?"

"Don't be stupid. You're going to have to keep them under wraps until the heat dies down a bit. Might be a good idea to keep them alive for a few days, then kill the boys and dump them a couple hundred miles from here—maybe down on the Ohio River. That should take the pressure off the search here enough to smuggle her out to a secure government holding facility."

Kaid and Helm each squeezed Tharon's shoulder even tighter. She trembled and they inched closer to her.

The outer door creaked open wider and Burt said, "Who's going to kill the boys?"

Marty's cackle sent chills down Tharon's spine. "I'll take care of that. You don't have to hog all the fun."

Burt's voice moved back into the hall, "I think your brother ain't the only one in your family with a fetish."

Marty snarled, "I don't know if it's a fetish, but I got no qualms about nothing—no qualms at all."

The officer's voice faded into the hallway, "I'll report that you're taking responsibility then, Marty."

Marty's frightening chuckle faded as well, "I got no problem with that, no problem at all."

The heavy door closed with a loud thud as the locks clicked into place. Goosebumps prickled Tharon's arms and she broke out in a cold sweat. She whispered, "We've got to get out of here. Now."

CHAPTER 6

Maisy pressed and folded the bread dough on the counter in Lista's kitchen. She didn't expect anyone to eat it but she had to do something with her hands to keep hysteria at bay. The thought of sweet little Tharon in the hands of killers tore her heart to pieces. She brushed a tear from her cheek with the back of her hand, leaving a smudge of flour in its wake and punched the dough hard, wishing it was the kidnapper's face.

The front doorbell chimed. She heard Angela answer the door and a deep familiar voice from the foyer broke Maisy's rhythm and concentration. She strained to hear; when that didn't work, she silently tiptoed into the hallway and stood in the shadows of the dining room near the half wall behind the sofa.

Maisy saw Angela close the door behind Max Stephens, who stood at the edge of the foyer.

It had been a long time since Maisy had seen Max close up. His clothes were at least two sizes too big; the end of his belt had been trimmed and was fastened two inches past the regular holes; his pants were wet to above his knees. With his hat in his hands, he glanced down at the polished wood floors like a little boy waiting to be scolded for tracking mud into the house.

"Do you have a recent picture of Tharon we can put out with the Amber Alert? We've already collected pictures of the two boys from their parents."

Maisy sensed Lista's fragile emotional state. She slipped around the corner as Lista gulped for air.

Maisy's heart broke to see the panic and pleading in Lista's eyes when she looked at her.

Max stepped further into the living room, perplexed by Lista's reticence. When he spoke his voice became softer, more patient. "It's vital that we get pictures of the children circulated immediately. The more people who see their pictures, the greater chance we'll have of finding and rescuing them."

Maisy rounded the half wall and sat on the sofa facing Lista but angled her back to Max. She knotted her hands in her lap and when Lista locked eyes with her again, Maisy nodded to reassure her and smiled a bleak smile.

Lista perched on the edge of the oversized red floral chair in the corner by the fireplace. She cleared her throat, "Of course." With effort she stood and picked a frame from the mantle. The picture captured a happy moment of Tharon with her arms wrapped around Shep. Lista's lips curved into a sad smile as she studied the picture. "This is the most recent." Handing the picture to Max, she asked, "How far will the pictures be circulated?"

Max assured her, "The alert goes out to the local stations and of course the coverage areas include parts of Ohio and Michigan. But in all honesty, with social media, most amber alerts get nationwide exposure."

Tears filled Lista's eyes to the brim. When she blinked they spilled down her cheeks. She gave Max a sad smile as she handed the picture to him. "Please, bring my little girl home to me."

He touched her arm, "We'll do everything we can." He snapped a picture of the photo with his phone and handed the picture and frame back to Lista. He took a card from his shirt pocket and handed it to Lista. "You can call me any time, night or day, if you have questions or think of anything that might help us."

Lista absently placed the card on the stand next to her chair, "Thank you."

Max turned to Maisy, "Ms. Baker, you said you saw the van, can you describe it?"

Maisy tilted her head as she tried to visualize the van. "It passed very quickly but it was a white utility minivan. I couldn't tell what make it was but it must have been an older model because it had rust on the hood. The lettering was worn off but there was part of a golden rattlesnake painted on the side of it. There were only windows in the middle and front. There were no windows in the back." Maisy shifted uncomfortably under his penetrating gaze.

"Do you think you'd be able to describe it to a sketch artist?"

Maisy bridled at the thought of leaving Lista. "I think I can give you a fairly accurate sketch of it myself. Just give me a moment." She crossed over to the desk in the front corner of the living room next to the window seat. She pulled a piece of blank white paper from the printer and felt Max's eyes on her as she sketched the image with a pencil, erasing and redrawing until the drawing matched the image in her mind's eye.

While Maisy sketched, Lista said, "Max, I'm sorry, I'm so worried about Tharon I forgot to ask, how is Lucy doing? We've missed her the last few weeks at church."

Max's broad shoulders sagged a bit. He shifted his weight and seemed to not know what to do with his hands. He cleared his throat several times but his words were still choked with emotion. "That's kind of you to ask. She's having a hard time with the chemo treatments but, you know Lucy, she's smiles through it all."

Maisy finished the drawing. "Will this help?" she asked as she handed Max the sketch.

He studied the drawing, "This will give me a place to start and should help tremendously. Was there anything else that seemed unusual or that stood out to you?"

Maisy shook her head and looked out the window. "I could have sworn I glimpsed the profile of a man in a cowboy hat sitting in the back seat. I wish I could help more. It was moving pretty fast when it passed."

Why did he keep staring at her? She thought of Tharon and wanted him to leave and stop looking at her face. "You'd better get going, the quicker you get that out the quicker you'll find the children." She walked back down the hall to the kitchen but paused after a few steps and half turned without looking at him directly, "I'm sorry Lucy is feeling poorly."

CHAPTER 7

Tharon pressed her ear to the door again. The muffled mewing of the kittens were the only sounds she could make out. She gave up on the door with the guard plate and moved towards the open doorway to the right. She whispered, "We can't get this one open. I saw a glass window to the right of the door, maybe we can crawl out through it."

They huddled together to squeeze through the doorway into what was once a small office area. Each room they entered seemed to assault their senses. They shuffled their feet through mounds of what felt and smelled like soggy rotting paper and stubbed their shins against what felt like overturned metal file cabinets. The room smelled of mold so strong it burned Tharon's eyes.

Helm covered his mouth with his jacket and sneezed into it twice. "Sorry, I'm allergic to mold," he whispered. He pulled his t-shirt collar up over his nose and mouth.

Tharon held still and listened for any sounds rushing towards them. When she was satisfied no one was coming, she felt for the wall to the left of the door opening and found a counter-like ledge. It was too high for her to climb on by herself. "Can you guys give me a boost? I think there's a reception window above the counter."

They each lifted her under the arms and behind the knees and heaved her up so fast she hit one knee on the edge of the counter. She bit her lip to keep from crying at the numbing pain.

"Sorry," the boys whispered in unison.

Tharon felt the glass sliding window. The lock at the bottom was broken and she slid the glass open wider. It wobbled and snagged several times but she jiggled it free until the opening was wide enough for her to slide through. She felt for the top of the frame and hung on as she drew her feet onto the counter then lowered herself feet first out to the waiting room.

Helm came through next. He landed with a grunt and a thud but stood up quickly. Kaid launched himself through the opening head first. He tumbled onto Helm and Tharon and they all ended up in a heap on the floor.

Tharon was the first up and found the door. She whispered, "I found the knob, Helm, can you hand me your knife?" He pressed the knife into her palm and she opened the largest blade sliding it into the narrow gap between the frame and the door. She moved the blade downward until she met the resistance of the lock and breathed a sigh of relief when the latch clicked and she pulled the door open.

Nearby the stench of body odor hung in the air and fear clenched at her chest. Tharon held the knife behind her. Her worst fears were realized when a flashlight beam bathed her in light. She heard Marty's chilling voice say, "Gotcha. How'd you brats get loose? Carl went soft on you, did he? Well, we won't need to worry about you boys anymore, not since I caught you trying to escape and had to cut your throats."

The dim light from the lobby glinted on his sword-like

knife. She swallowed hard, convinced they were all about to die. The words her father told her when she was eight echoed in her head: *Don't let fear and danger rule your life.* She was afraid, more afraid than she'd ever been, but decided she wasn't going to let Marty see her fear. There was no way she'd let them kill her friends and keep her alive. Not without a fight. She gripped the knife and stepped forward.

Marty chuckled, "So what will it be? Ladies first? Sorry girlie, but someone has other plans for you. Which one of you boys wants to go first?"

Tharon gripped the knife with a firm determination to stay between Marty and her friends. If they wanted her alive then she was convinced she could shield the boys from harm. A soft voice to her right whispered, "I love you, Tharon."

Helm pulled her back and stepped in between her and Marty.

Marty's lips curled into a gruesome snarl and raised his knife to strike Helm. His arm made a sudden unnatural jerk backwards and behind his head. His bones cracked loudly when they broke and the sound of his shoulder popping out of joint made her shudder. His knife flew into the hallway behind him.

Carl's body blocked the light from the lobby as he picked up Marty and hurled him into the wall across the hall. He turned back to the children.

Kaid grabbed Tharon and Helm and pulled his friends past Carl.

Tharon stammered, "Carl, Marty was going to kill us." She didn't know why she felt she was betraying the big man by trying to escape. Kaid and Helm pulled her toward the lobby.

Helm scrambled to the boarded entry and found an

opening large enough for them to fit through. "I found the way out!" He pulled the blue plastic covering the opening back and the fading daylight flooded the lobby.

Carl's eyes were soft and sad. "It's okay, Little Miss. Run. Head west. Hurry before Burt gets here. I'm sorry—," his face contorted in a grimace. He fell forward with Marty's knife sticking from his back.

Marty crowed in agonized triumph, "You moron, too stupid to know you never turn your back on me. Only took me one arm to bring you down, big man."

Kaid dragged Tharon to the opening. He went through first and had almost pulled her through when Marty grabbed the hem of her coat and pulled her halfway back into the lobby.

Marty's face was twisted with pain and hatred. His greedy fingers kneaded their way up her coat, inching her back into the lobby.

Kaid and Helm tugged on her shoulders.

She forgot the knife was still in her hand when she batted at Marty's face, slicing him from below his eye all the way down to his jaw. Blood gushed from the slash onto her hand, leg and shoe.

He screamed and, with only one good arm, was forced to let her go as he pulled the tail of his shirt up to his face. "You little brat! You'll pay for this. Someday, you'll pay! I'll get you! I'm gonna kill you if it's the last thing I do! I don't care what they want with you! I'm going to kill you!"

Kaid and Helm pulled her the rest of the way out of the opening. She ran with them across the parking lot through the open gate and turned left toward a wooded area southwest of the building. At the edge of the woods they came to a wire fence and followed it west.

Tharon realized she still clung to the sticky knife. She wiped the blade on her jeans, closed it and shoved it in the pocket of her jacket.

In the neglected yard of a white frame house, a massive chained pit bull erupted into a frenzy of deep bellowing barks. Saliva dripped from his teeth as he yanked against his chain and lunged at them. They backed into the fence, being careful to give him a wide berth.

They'd no sooner crossed into another yard when a second dog picked up the barking chorus. When a third dog pitched in Helm said, "We've got to get away from houses or all these dogs will bring the killers right to us. Let's look for a break in the fence."

Two hundred yards further, they found a gate across a gravel road that entered a drainage area. They climbed over the gate and ran as fast as they could down a stretch of land between two angular ponds.

Kaid slowed after a hundred yards. "You know what this is? It's a water purification plant. That's why it's fenced in. I'll bet there's another fence up ahead. Let's hope there's another gate to climb over to get out."

Tharon nodded, too winded to say anything. The pain from the old broken rib she suffered in second grade was aggravated either from running or her scuffle with Marty, and the knee she banged on the counter felt hot but she was determined to keep up with Kaid and Helm.

Helm noticed her holding her side. "Are you hurt?"

She dropped her hand, "I'm fine. I just got a stitch in my side," she panted. "This is too open. We need to find some cover so Burt can't see where we are."

The boys kept running but slowed their pace so that she could keep up with them.

They cleared the drainage ponds and rushed through a wooded area with no underbrush and reached another fence, just as Kaid predicted. On the other side of the fence a paved walking trail followed the river on the north bank with trees on either side that would afford them enough cover to block the kidnappers from seeing them.

They followed the fence west until they came to a foot bridge which spanned drainage from the treatment plant to the river. Fortune smiled on them for the first time that day when they found a space under the fence where the soil had washed away either by rain or flooding.

Kaid went first and clawed some more dirt and rocks to fit through; Tharon went next and Helm shoved his backpack through and squeezed under last.

On the other side of the fence a cracked asphalt trail meandered along the edge of the river. Dried weeds sprang from the cracks.

Helm took her hand and together they tried to keep up with Kaid whose long legs quickly outdistanced them.

Kaid's relief at being sheltered by the woods evaporated when they rounded a curve in the trail and found the trail hugged the street with no trees or underbrush to hide them. On the other side of the street a neighborhood plastered with close set houses paralleled their path.

Kaid's throat felt dry and a cold fear clutched at his chest. "If he sees us, he could get us anywhere along here." He scanned every street and every car for a cowboy hat.

It occurred to him that he'd been looking for the cowboy hat but if Burt took it off he could get the drop on them with ease. Kaid searched for another way to escape if Burt found them, but the only choices were back the way they came or into the river. He looked down at the rapid muddy current and knew that in this weather, that would be a death sentence. He wasn't even sure any of them could swim. He only knew he couldn't.

As he wondered if the trees on the river bank were sturdy enough to hold them, an elderly lady came out of a little red brick house on the corner of the next street. She had a small white dog on a leash. He smiled at her and noticed the dog's fur was the same color as her white hair. She looked at them with a puzzled expression which grew to recognition and concern.

She crossed the street to the trail and Kaid opened his mouth to ask her for help when he saw a black sedan turn the corner and made out the cowboy hat on the driver. Burt had his head turned back the way they'd just come. Kaid stopped short; Tharon and Helm ran into him. "It's Burt," Kaid said. "Hide on the bank and hold onto the trees."

As he clung to the tree he looked at Helm next to him holding fast to a two inch tree and Tharon beyond him holding a large root with one hand and her other arm crooked around a five inch stump. His quick glance assured him they were all secure and hidden from view of the road.

Kaid strained to hear over the rushing water. The car engine purred in front of them. "Excuse me, ma'am, have you seen three children? My niece and two nephews wandered off and we think they were on the trail."

The woman's dog yipped frantically. "No, can't say as I have. You look familiar. Aren't you Burt Payne? You're that fellow that has the used car dealership off Illinois Road—the one with the rattlesnake on your ads. *We take the bite out of buying a car.* That's you, isn't it?"

"Yeah, that's me. I'm sorry about this."

"Sorry about what?"

Two shots rang out and Burt gunned his car engine and sped from the scene.

The second bullet hit the tree Kaid held onto. His grip slipped from the tree. He grasped at the roots and saplings which were too shallow rooted and gave way in his grip.

Helm grabbed his wrist and held him tight but the tree Helm clung to began to give way under both their weight.

Tharon reached out to Helm with one hand and grabbed the strap of his back pack.

Panic seized Kaid as he realized not only was he about to drown but he was going to take his friends into the river with him. He saw Tharon's hand slipping from the tree and Helm dug his toes and knees into the shale covered bank to relieve the weight pulling on her.

Kaid's foot hit a rock and he used it to push himself upward, stretching to grab another tree root and with Helm's help, he climbed back up to peek around a tree. "He's gone." His heart thundered in his chest. "He shot that lady and her dog."

As Kaid pulled Helm back up to the trail and reached for Tharon he said solemnly, "She saved our lives." He watched Helm put his arm around Tharon's shoulder and said, "You two stay here while I go check her." He felt for the lady's pulse the way his father had taught him, but felt nothing. He hadn't expected to find one after he saw the hole in her forehead.

He closed the woman's eyes and motioned Helm and Tharon forward. "Let's get out of here. At least we know what kind of car he's in now."

Before that day, Tharon had never seen a dead body. Now she'd seen two. She couldn't pull her eyes from the white haired woman.

Helm put an arm around her shoulder and blocked her view of the bodies, "The lady said he had a car dealership. I bet he goes and gets another one in case anyone saw him in the neighborhood."

Tharon snapped her attention from the bodies and pulled away from Helm. She began to run. "We better hurry then and get out of here before he gets back."

She slowed when the river and trail curved again. Street lamps along the streets flickered on, bathing parts of the trail in soft light. A spillway spanned the river ahead and before that to the left a bridge crossed North Anthony over the river. She craned her neck to the other side and saw a double railroad tracks on the other side of the river. "Let's cross here and follow the tracks. It will be harder for Burt to find us and one of them should take us close to Sandy Creek."

The boy's agreed. Tharon hoped Helm was right that Burt would go get another car. She had no idea how long it would take him and she wanted to get out of sight of the roads as quickly as possible. Shadows lengthened around them adding a new level of apprehension about walking through the city after dark.

As she approached the bridge she remembered the tracking code she and her father agreed on when she was eight. She paused at the edge of the bridge and scratched an arrow on the yellow paint on top of the curb at the edge of the bridge with the short blade of the knife.

Helm stopped next to her, "What's that?"

She was a little embarrassed, "It's a trail marking that my dad and I worked out. The right side of the arrow is the way we're going. I know it's stupid and he'll probably never find it, but I feel like I have to leave a trail for him to know where we are going. Do you mind? I'll just use the small blade but it will probably dull it."

Helm said, "I don't mind. You hang onto the knife and make all the marks you want to." He held her hand as they crossed the bridge.

The tracks crossed the road and ran parallel to the other side of the river. Tharon ran hard to cross the bridge and the street on the other side. The boys followed her as she scrambled to get out of the open area and headed for the cover of trees between the tracks and the spillway. She paused briefly to scratch her arrow on the curb of the intersection.

Soon she lagged behind them. She was tired and emotionally drained but she wasn't about to complain. The stitch in her side felt like a stab from a hot poker. She hated to admit it but she was running out of steam. She slowed to a walk and once they were hidden by the trees and a passing train, she dropped to the ground.

The boys stopped when they saw her and sat down on either side of her.

"I'm sorry, guys, I'm just so thirsty. Maybe if I rest for a few minutes it won't be so bad."

Helm slapped his forehead with his palm. "I can't believe I forgot. My mom sent some hot cocoa. She figured you'd be cold in the woods." He wriggled out of his back pack and poured some cocoa into the cup lid and handed it to Tharon.

She drank the rich chocolate milk. It wasn't steaming hot but was still warm and felt good going down. She drank a few swallows and handed the cup to Kaid. He took a couple of sips and passed it back to Helm.

Helm's stomach rumbled, "Too bad I didn't think to grab some food." He seemed to be mulling something in his mind and finally said, "So do you think we should try to get help from anyone else or just try to get home on our own?"

The bodies of the elderly lady and her dog flashed through Tharon's mind. "I don't think anyone would believe us that Burt is a killer. From what the lady said he must be pretty well known in Fort Wayne. Besides, I don't want to be the reason he kills anyone else."

Helm chewed on his lower lip, "Do you think Carl

would still keep Burt from killing us?"

Tharon swallowed the lump in her throat and sighed. "Carl's dead." The images of Marty streaming blood down his face, Carl with his glassy eyes, the lady and her dog lying dead by the street, the man Burt shot floating down the creek, and Shep lifeless in the woods, all took turns flashing through her mind. She stood up, took a few steps away from the boys and threw up next to a tree.

When she finished, Helm stood next to her with his palm on her back and handed her a tissue. "With my allergies, I always keep a small pack of tissues in my back pack."

She took the tissue and wiped her mouth and nose. "Thanks. Sorry about wasting the cocoa."

Kaid punched her shoulder lightly. "Don't worry about it. Let us know when you feel like you need some more and we'll take another break."

The last car of the train passed them heading east. Together they climbed up out of the trees and kept a wary watch to make certain no one took an interest in them. Buildings flanked the other side of the track; most were vacant as evidenced by their boarded and broken windows. Shadows lengthened around them and Tharon prayed that with the cold weather they wouldn't run into any vagrants or gangs who might attack them.

Helm held her hand and matched her pace instead of her struggling to keep up with them. "Come on," Helm said with an encouraging smile and a squeeze of her hand. "Let's go home."

CHAPTER 8

Max Stephens logged onto the department computer to search for company logos with a rattlesnake. He punched the keys with his long fingers and the computer made an offensive squeal in protest.

Penni Faulkner, the Sheriff's office manager, strolled to his side and peered over his shoulder. "Max, what are you trying to do?"

Max brandished the sketch. "I'm trying to find out where this logo comes from. It was on the side of the van we think the kids were snatched in."

Penni tucked a silver blond strand of hair back behind her ear. She frowned at the picture. "You don't need a search for that. Here," she nudged Max to the side. Her fingertips flew over the keys and pulled up a picture of the used car dealership on Illinois Road in Fort Wayne. Burt Payne sported a Custer style rim of blond hair under a black cowboy hat with a white band that gave him a pseudo cavalry persona. Penni turned up the sound.

"I'm Burt Payne and I want to be your last stand for used cars. So come on in to see us at Payne's Last Stand Used Cars where we take the bite out of the pain of car buying. Look for the sign with the golden rattler because we're shaking up a great deal for you!"

Max raised his eyebrows, "Kind of cheeky to drive your company van to commit a murder, isn't it?"

The stray lock of hair broke free and flopped down onto Penni's otherwise perfect fifty-five year old face. She pursed her lower lip in a futile attempt to blow the strand out of her eyes, then gave up and tucked it behind her ear again. She sat back with folded arms. "I don't imagine he thought anyone would see him out there in the sticks."

Max mulled that over, "Maybe it wasn't even him, just someone using his van." He picked up his phone and called his counterpart and friend in the Fort Wayne Police Department, Randy Bohman, to request they pick up Burt Payne for questioning in the murder of an unidentified man in rural Whitley County, and the abduction of three children.

Max's request was met with stone cold silence.

"Randy, are you there?"

"Is this some kind of joke, Max? Because if it is, it isn't funny," Randy said in a flat tone.

Max was confused and more than a little irritated. "Why would I joke about murder and kidnapping?"

"Burt and Carl Payne are volunteer police officers with the Fort Wayne PD. They provide security for the Three Rivers Festival and handle drive off complaints from gas stations. And they put on a banquet and fund raiser every year for the children of police officers killed in the line of duty. Hell, I play golf with them. So don't try to tell me those two are involved in murder and kidnapping, because I don't believe it."

Max leaned his elbows on the desk and propped his forehead with his empty hand. He needed Randy's help and couldn't afford to offend him. "Randy, we have a witness who saw a white van from his dealership. We have the footprints of three men at the scene. If they have an alibi, so be it. But I've got three missing children and a dead body. Can you at least bring him and his brother in for questioning?"

Randy muttered something under his breath. "Alright. But I've got a murder of my own to deal with. A little old lady and her dog were gunned down near the Maumee River greenway. The public's getting a bit edgy here."

Max tried to bridle his sarcasm. "You might want to see if the Payne brothers have any property in the vicinity—our criminals killed a dog, too."

The silence on the other end told Max he'd probably gone too far. After a long moment Randy said, "I'll get back to you after I have a talk with Burt and Carl." He hung up without waiting for Max to say goodbye.

CHAPTER 9

Shep was shot twice. Dana waited at the Veterinary Hospital until the bullets were removed from the dog. She bagged them for evidence and knew she should leave, but felt tied to the dog's side.

Dr. Roth tied off a stitch behind Shep's ear. She glanced at Dana and said, "Is there something else you need, Deputy?"

Dana pulled a card from her pocket. "The family doesn't know Shep is still alive. I don't want to get their hopes up. Can you call and let me know how he is and if he makes it?"

The vet motioned with her head for Dana to put the card on the counter. "Of course. Now get out of here and find those kids."

Dana couldn't help but pat Shep one last time for luck. "You hang in there, Shep. I'm counting on you."

She got in her car and for some reason was a bundle of nerves. She had that itching feeling like something ominous was about to happen and she had no clue what. Her mother used to call it woman's intuition but to Dana it felt more like an itch she couldn't scratch.

She drove to the Sheriff's department in Columbia City

and dropped the bullets off at forensics before she checked in with Max Stephens. "Any luck tracking our killer?"

Max grumbled, "I'm pretty sure I know who it is. Burt and Carl Payne have a used car lot in Fort Wayne." He opened the website for her to see then flipped screens to show pictures of the brothers. "The Fort Wayne PD wants to drag their feet. Turns out the brothers are volunteer cops—real upstanding pillars of the community. But guess what, there was a random killing today on the River Greenway of an old lady and her dog. Somebody doesn't seem to like dogs any more than he likes people."

The hair stood up on the back of Dana's neck and a chill ran down her spine. "Do they own any property in the area of the killing?"

"Little lady, you're gonna make detective one of these days. I checked and there's an old office building on Lake Avenue. Part of it has been converted to an auto shop. The Payne brothers store extra inventory there. I was thinking of driving over in my civilian clothes and have a look-see. Care to slip into something more comfortable and join me?"

"Absolutely." She felt like her heart was doing somersaults in her chest. Yep, time to scratch an itch. "How would you feel about taking Tom Trace along? He has quite an eye for tracking. He can recognize the children's footprints and might be able to pick up something that we'd miss."

Max paused. "That's a good idea, but you'd better run it past the Sheriff."

Dana paused and then asked, "Why don't *you* run it past the Sheriff?"

Max's eyes twinkled, "Because we want him to say yes."

CHAPTER 10

Tharon felt like every car that passed was watching them. What if Burt had other people out looking for them? She feared they didn't dare talk to any strangers. From what she'd heard before their escape, even the police couldn't be trusted.

She left trail markings wherever they changed directions but she was slowing them down. By the time they came to a series of elevated tracks over streets, darkness enveloped them. While waiting in the shadows to cross an intersection, Tharon recognized the street, "I think I know where we are. This is Spy Run Avenue. In the pioneer days spies kept watch for enemies approaching in the rivers and ran along this route to warn the settlers in the fort. The old fort is just north of here. We visited it for a school field trip in September."

"I guess after what we heard today, we're the spies now," Kaid said.

Tharon shivered as she thought of what they'd heard. "Why would anyone want me? I'm nobody."

Helm moved closer to her, "You're not nobody but I don't understand why they want you either."

When the traffic cleared Tharon ran across the road with the boys. She shoved her fears deep within her heart. The only thing that mattered was getting home. Knowing that her father would be the only one to recognize her markings, she knew he'd have realized she was following the tracks so she stopped making as many marks and picked up the pace. She had to get home. Her dad would protect her. Maybe he had some idea why someone was after her too.

She led the way following the tracks. When they were elevated, they walked below them. Whenever brush or trees clustered close to the tracks, they secreted themselves to travel deeply in the brush to hide from passersby.

The dark colors of the boy's coats helped them escape notice and for the first time, Tharon was grateful for the puffy black coat that was two sizes too big. Her mother found it in the resale shop and had paid next to nothing for it. She had replaced the zipper and planned to ornament it with white embroidery stitches and sequins on the collar and pockets. Tharon was glad her mom hadn't found time to do it yet; the white contrast moving along the dark streets might have sparked curiosity.

She wondered how long it had been since they were taken from the woods? What time was it? From the darkness, Tharon figured it had to be between six and seven o'clock. In the back of her mind was the nagging suspicion that there had to be something about her that made her unique but as she racked her brain to think of anything that would cause anyone to want to kidnap her, she came up with a big fat nothing.

After leaving the downtown area they came to a railroad bridge that spanned another river. The light from the streetlights on the nearby bridge over Main Street barely touched the railroad bridge. Hidden in the thick dried brush next to the river, Tharon's shoulders slumped as she peered at the double tracks over the water and felt her insides turn to putty. She couldn't make out a walkway and the muddy current looked as frightening as the other river. She moaned, "How many rivers does Fort Wayne have?"

She tried to swallow but her mouth felt like she'd been sucking on cotton balls. She looked wistfully at the sturdier Main Street Bridge. If they hurried across they might be lucky and Burt wouldn't find them. She pointed to the concrete bridge. "Can we cross over there instead?"

Kaid teased her, trying to lighten the tension they all felt, "Why? Are you afraid of the water?"

She was too tired and too scared to pretend to be brave about anything else. "I'm afraid of bridges over water. That bridge that goes to the Miller farm scares the crap out of me when the water is high. And this river looks a lot worse than the creek back home."

Kaid nudged her with his elbow, "You mean to say you can climb to the top of a tree but you're afraid to cross a river?"

Helm took the thermos out of his backpack. "Leave her alone, Kaid. You were just as scared as I was in that tree. Besides most of the girls we know would be crying their eyes out this whole time." He poured some cocoa and handed it to Tharon.

She took the cup and said, "Thanks," hoping Helm knew she was grateful for more than just the cocoa. She took a few sips and passed the cup to Kaid.

Kaid mumbled, "I didn't mean anything by it." He took the cup and without drinking passed it back to Helm. "I'm sorry if I hurt your feelings, Tharon. I'd never want to do that." He thought a moment, "If you're afraid of water, how come you crossed the footbridge when the water was high all those times?"

Normally she hated letting them or anyone know her weaknesses, but all the barriers she'd built around her heart came crashing down. "You never saw me cross it over high water."

Kaid tilted his head in thought, "Sure we did, lots of times."

Helm furrowed his brow. A slow grin crept over his face, "No, we didn't." His face lit with realization. "That's why you always wanted to race us and go through the woods?"

She shrugged her shoulders, "I usually won too." She sighed as she looked at the trestle. "I keep having dreams that I'm in a car and it falls off a bridge into a river. The car is filling with water and I wake up when my head goes under." She shivered, "It's the scariest dream I ever had."

A freight train sped west over the bridge, causing it to creak and groan. Tharon's eye's opened wide and she looked down at the muddy water. "And I can't swim."

A loud crack and pop from the bridge made them jump. "Me either," said Kaid.

Helm looked at the roiling river, "I can swim, but not that good."

Without another word, Helm stowed the thermos and rushed to the concrete bridge on Main Street. Tharon ran hard to keep up with him and heard Kaid close behind her. The boys seemed to have an unspoken understanding that they kept Tharon between them.

Tharon paused at the edge of the bridge to scratch a mark but the hard concrete would not yield to the blade. She glanced at the sandy dirt next to the side walk and scratched an arrow with her heel. She prayed if her father got this far he could follow her tracks.

They were half way across the bridge when a light green car slowed next to them. A pretty woman with skin the color of dark chocolate and hair graying at her temples rolled down her window. She wore a black dress covered in glowing blue-green sequins and had the same color of glitter dusted across her cheeks. Her wide bright smile captivated Tharon who sensed in her heart this was someone she could trust. The lady asked, "Are you kids in trouble? Are you the kids who were kidnapped from Whitley County?"

Tharon took a step toward the car but Kaid grabbed her coat and pulled her away. He said, "No. Our dad is waiting for us on the other side of the bridge."

The lady raised an eyebrow and followed slowly, "Are you sure? You can trust me. I'll help you get somewhere safe." In a tone that brooked no argument she said, "I won't let anyone hurt you."

Tharon believed the lady and trusted her kind face. She wanted to get in the car with her.

Kaid kept looking back down the street and urging the other two forward. "No, Ma'am. We're fine. You need to leave. You need to leave now!"

Tharon glanced past Kaid's shoulder and saw a black sedan several blocks away heading toward them. She broke into a run so fast the boys struggled to keep up with her.

On the other side of the bridge she saw a man with a hard hat walking across a dimly lit gravel parking area. He carried a lunchbox and walked toward a woman with bleached blond hair and dark roots who leaned against a dark blue minivan.

The lady from the bridge pulled into the parking lot behind them.

Terrified that Burt might be near and would kill them all, Tharon called out, "Daddy! Daddy!" The boys followed her lead as they clustered around the man, hugging him, and then ran to the side of the van as if they were getting into it.

Once out of sight of the street, Tharon peeked through the windows of the minivan and sighed with relief when the lady in the green car turned around and headed back onto the street. The black sedan drove past also. As it passed under the streetlamp she made out the outline of a cowboy hat.

The woman in the parking lot yelled at the man. "You have three kids? We've been married fifteen years you lying, cheating scum. Who have you been sleeping with?"

The man took the woman by the shoulders, "Baby, I swear to you, I've never seen those kids before in my life. There's nobody but you. I love you, Baby."

Her face turned red and she punched him in the nose so hard it sent his hard hat flying.

Kaid called out, "Sorry, mister, we thought you were our dad. Our mistake."

Helm grabbed Tharon's hand and pulled her to the alley at the back of the parking lot and around the corner of an empty garage with a sagging roof. At the corner of the next block they stopped behind a service station to catch their breath. Tharon peeked around the edge of the building. "I'm going to use the restroom," she announced and slipped around the corner.

In the weak light of the single CFL bulb Tharon studied herself in the mirror. Her brown eyes looked tired and her hair straggled around her face where it stuck out from her striped knit hat. Sticky blood covered the back of her right hand and she had a smudge of mud on her face and a stain of Marty's blood on her jeans and right shoe.

She washed her hands repeatedly, but they still felt stained. With a damp wad of paper towels loaded with soap, she dabbed, blotted and scrubbed her jeans, her shoe and the inside of her pocket to rid herself of Marty's blood. When she finished, her hand felt as stained as before. She scrubbed everything again before saturating some fresh paper towels with soap and tucking them in her pocket.

Next she opened all the blades of the knife and washed them, flushing the inside with hot soapy water. She dried it carefully and hoped she hadn't ruined it.

After she refastened her jackets she shook her head at her image in the mirror. As grateful as she was to have both coats, the puffy one made her look enormous. She smoothed her hands down the front of the jacket, accepting that it was better to be warm than look thin. Her hand hit a bulge in the contour of her puffy coat.

She unzipped the coat and dug a thick wad of folded money from the inside pocket. She clamped her hand over her mouth to keep from squealing in delight. With a smile on her lips she recounted her Christmas money which she had hidden in the inner zippered pocket to be ready for her annual Secret Santa shopping trip with her father.

A surge of hope coursed through her as she slipped out the door and met the boys behind the building again. She bounced on her toes and grabbed their sleeves. "I have money. I've got over forty dollars."

Kaid shook his head, "I don't know what good that will do us. We can't exactly go into a store without being recognized and someone calling the cops. That policeman is probably waiting for someone to call in a tip. He'll grab us and we'll be back in the same trouble we were before— maybe worse."

"Not if we're smart." Tharon tucked her pigtails up inside her hat and pulled it down low over her eyebrows. "Helm and I can go in the store. We might be able to find enough supplies to make a shelter and build a fire. And we can get some food. I'm sure they'll have stuff like beef jerky and bottled water."

Helm warmed to her enthusiasm, "Maybe we can find a lighter or some matches."

Kaid shoved his hands in his pockets, "How come you guys are going instead of me?"

Tharon blushed and was grateful to be in the shadows, "Because you're too good looking. Everyone always looks at you and yours is the face people will remember."

Helm's mouth dropped open, "Hey, what's wrong with my face?"

"Nothing's wrong with your face." She nudged Helm's arm with her shoulder, "But you and I are more average looking than Kaid. We'll blend in better. We just need to wait for a bunch of kids or a bus to stop before we go into the store."

"Fine." Kaid slumped against the wall, "Can you at least get some candy too?"

Tharon grinned, "Do you still like peanut butter cups?"

"Yeah, or licorice or crackers or chocolate or potato chips—oh, man, what I wouldn't give for a burger and some fries."

Helm touched both their arms, "Shh. Do you hear that?"

A bus of cheering students pulled into the gas station chanting, "We are the Lions, the mighty, mighty Lions!"

Tharon grabbed Helm's hand, "This is our chance, come on."

They eased around the corner and casually sidestepped around teenagers racing each other to the restrooms. She glanced at the bus driver who pulled a cable from the front of the bus and plugged it into the charging pump to flash charge the bus batteries. Inside the convenience store, she grabbed a plastic basket and handed it to Helm, "You get the water and some food while I check this side of the store."

She meandered down the aisle containing windshield wiper fluid, motor oil, bags of salt. Halfway down the aisle she found one rain poncho and three silver emergency blankets. A little further on she found flashlights and selected a multi-pack that promised bright light and included batteries.

Rounding the end of the aisle, she bumped into two cheerleaders who looked her up and down and giggled before turning away. She felt her face burn with humiliation. Even strangers thought she looked ugly.

Helm walked up behind her and whispered in her ear. "How are we doing?"

She dumped her items into the basket, "Pretty good. We need some matches."

"I saw some charcoal by the window, there might be matches over there." Helm walked by her side and whispered in her ear. "They weren't laughing at you."

She looked at his face, "What?"

He tilted his head towards the two girls, "I heard them giggling about some cute guy they saw."

Dread filled Tharon as she went up on her tiptoes and scanned the store. Kaid hovered in the last aisle near the fresh doughnut case with his back to the clerk. She snatched up a box of matches and said, "We better hurry. The bus is leaving."

She grabbed a permanent marker, two bags of beef jerky and several candy bars on her way to the cash register. She motioned for Kaid to stay back when he took a step toward them. She flinched when the tally took more than half of her Christmas money.

The attendant scanned her items and asked, "Will there be anything else?"

She looked around the counter, "Do you have any maps

of Allen or Whitley Counties?"

His fleshy hands rummaged beneath the counter and came up with a black and white map, "This one's on the house. The towing company that printed it for advertising has gone out of business."

Tharon handed him the money, "Thanks."

Once the money was safely in the register, the attendant said, "You kids better hurry, it looks like your bus is getting ready to leave."

Tharon stuffed the map in one of the bags and they rushed out the door. She glanced at the puzzled look on the attendant's face as she rounded the corner and hoped he would think they were running to use the restroom and not figure out who they were before they had a chance to get away.

Tharon ripped open the marker and stopped to draw an arrow on the side of the building, "Why didn't you wait outside?"

Kaid's face turned crimson in the pale streetlights. "Because two cheerleaders scared me half to death when they came around the back of the station to smoke a cigarette."

Tharon chuckled, "I guess what the other girls say is true."

Kaid wrinkled his brow. "What do they say?"

She grinned. "That you're a chick magnet."

CHAPTER 11

Dana found a semi-quiet corner of the station and called Simon. When his face appeared on her phone screen, she ignored her fluttering heart and said, "Sheriff, Max thinks he has a lead on the kidnappers. Burt Payne has a used car dealership in Fort Wayne that uses a rattlesnake logo. He thinks Burt's brother, Carl, might be the big man with him."

"Good. The Fort Wayne PD can pick them up for us."

Dana grimaced, "There's a bit of a problem. The Fort Wayne PD are dragging their feet to cooperate because the Payne brothers are also volunteers for their police department," she took a deep breath. "Max has a lead, well, more of a hunch, that he wants me to help him check out and he wanted me to clear it with you. I also thought it would be a good idea to take Tom Trace along. If the children aren't there he might be able to tell if they were and where they went."

The edges of Simon's eyes crinkled as he asked, "And *you're* asking instead of Max because...?"

Dana felt her face flush and cursed the technology that enabled Simon to see her pink cheeks. "Because we're going to be out of uniform and we'll be checking out a property on Lake Avenue in Fort Wayne."

Simon's eyes softened as he lowered his voice, "Dana, be careful. Do what you have to do. If you run into trouble you're operating under my direct orders. I'll take any flack that comes our way. Don't let Tom go after the Payne brothers. If it was them, we want to build a solid case and don't want them to get off on some technicality. And we don't want them killing Tom. Get those kids and bring them home. "

"Yes, sir." She hung up the phone.

Warmth flooded her chest and she whispered, "He called me Dana." She shook her head and muttered to herself, "Head out of the clouds, Donovan. Focus on your job and stop acting like a schoolgirl."

Penni walked up behind her, "Did you say something?"

Dana jumped, "Uh, no. Would you let Max know Simon—I mean the Sheriff, gave the okay to his plan and I'm going home to change. He can pick me up there."

Penni tried to keep a straight face. "You run along. I'll give him your message."

***

Simon held his phone a full minute after Dana disconnected and stared at the body in the morgue. Why did he feel like he was standing on pins and needles? He cleared the cobwebs from his brain. Still looking at the body, he asked Dr. Nelson, the Medical Examiner, "Do we have an ID on the victim yet?"

Dr. Nelson touched the flat plexi-screen on the desk which lit up with the victim's face on the screen. With a quick swipe the image became suspended on the glass window overlooking the hallway. "William Silar, aka Bill

Silas, aka Wil Silar. Something's screwy about this guy. Not ten minutes after I ran his prints I got a call from the Governor's office to keep them informed of all evidence pertaining to this case. Seems kind of strange the order didn't come from the BCI or the Indiana Department of Homeland Security. Anyway, his prints were flagged."

"Know anything else about him?"

The coroner's fingers flew over the surface with practiced ease splashing files onto the wall. "I just glanced over it. He was a pretty unsavory character. He got nabbed red-handed about eleven years ago in a bank robbery that resulted in the death of three people. It should have been death or at least a life sentence. That case was sealed and there's nothing much since then. Help yourself to the entire file." He spread his finger tips on the center of the table and pinched them together in one swift motion. The data splashed back onto the table screen and shrank to the size of a quarter.

Simon pulled a digital bridge—a paper thin clear plastic card the size of a driver's license—from a slot in the back of his phone. He touched the corner of the film over the image, which instantly appeared on the film then shrank to the size of a period. He tucked the film back into the slot, "Thanks. Have you found anything to indicate where he came from?"

"He's got grease stains on his fingers, fingernails and clothes so it's a safe bet he worked in the auto field on the old style gasoline powered or hybrid models. It's not much but it's a start."

"More than a start," Simon was grateful the information helped justify Max and Dana's investigation in Fort Wayne. "Thanks again and let me know what else you find."

Simon called Max as soon as he stepped outside the hospital. Max's face appeared on his phone screen with the

Sheriff's department in the background. "The identity of our victim is one William Silar. His prints were flagged so try to see what you can find out about him while you're in Fort Wayne. I transferred his file to the office with the digital bridge."

"Will do. Hold on and I'll see if I've got it." Max said.

After a few moments he said, "I've got the file."

Simon rubbed his jaw, "Might be a good idea if you use Nora's car. The keys are in my desk. It doesn't have any official logo or plates on it."

Max moved into Simon's office and found the keys. "Got them. Anything else?"

Simon scratched his chin, "Yeah. Take care of Dana. I don't know why but I'm edgy about her going along on this."

Max chuckled, "You don't know why? You're a bright boy, I'm sure you'll figure it out eventually. I just hope you do before some young buck sweeps her up for himself."

Max disconnected leaving Simon standing in the middle of the parking lot with his mouth open.

A man's deep voice behind him, drew Simon out of his thoughts, "Sheriff Ellis?"

Simon spun around, his hand on the gun at his side.

The man in a leather jacket held his palms out in front of him, "Whoa, I didn't mean to startle you. I'm from Governor Talbot's office. I need to talk to you. Can we take a little walk? And please leave your phone and all electronic devices in your vehicle."

***

Dana pulled into the drive of her ranch style house. The mums she'd planted around the front porch were dying back, giving the little home a barren loneliness that matched the interior. She put off going inside a little longer by calling Tom while still sitting in her cruiser.

He picked up on the first ring. "Hello?"

She knew he was hoping she had some good news for him. She played briefly with the temptation of telling him Shep was still alive but decided against it. "Tom, this is Deputy Donovan—Dana—did you find anything downstream?"

Tom said, "No. We followed the creek for more than a mile and there was nothing."

Dana took a deep breath, "I hate to get your hopes up but Max Stephens and I are going into Fort Wayne to check out a lead. We were wondering if you'd like to come along and maybe help look for signs that the children were there. I want to emphasize this is only a hunch and we've received no word of the children being there."

He didn't hesitate. "Where do you want me to meet you?"

Dana was distracted by her interaction with Simon and without thinking she rattled off her home address. She rolled her eyes at her breach in security. She'd never let a civilian know her address before. In fact having Max meet her here was also a first—the first time anyone had been to her house. Maybe that was why she gave Tom her address; she lacked practice in keeping it private because no one cared enough to ask for it.

She grabbed her mail from the cluster of mailboxes at the curb and hurried inside to change. The empty house was comfortable, but its furnishings were sparse and bland. No pictures on the mantle, nothing on the table or stands, no knick knacks. The only thing hanging on the walls was a musical clock she'd bought at a craft fair on the only vacation she'd ever taken.

Simon had insisted she take a long week after two years of volunteering for every overtime and holiday that came up. She traveled alone to Brown County for the fall colors, which were late that year—she missed them entirely. She stayed alone in a dingy motel; ate alone in restaurants where she felt hopelessly out of place among the happy couples and boisterous families; perused alone the shops and craft booths.

In one of the specialty shops she found the most magnificent clocks she'd ever seen. Every time a clock chimed the hour, gears opened around the face of the clock and played wonderful lilting melodies. The clock she picked played a different tune each hour. It cost her a half month's pay. She argued with herself about the cost but since there was no one else in her life who objected, she gave up and bought it.

On the plus side it gave her a story to tell about her vacation.

When she got home she looked for the perfect spot for the clock and finally settled on the living room wall above the lumpy thrift shop sofa. She felt good about her purchase, in fact it made her feel better about her home— until she tried to get to sleep the first night. The first two chimes made her smile, by the third she was counting how many hours of sleep she'd lost. By the sixth chime she got up and removed the batteries. She'd resolved to never again take another vacation.

Dana dressed quickly in jeans, and put on her snug white tactical shirt, complete with built in holster. Next she pulled on a loose-fitting, light-weight, powder blue sweater, and a black leather jacket that she'd bought specifically to help conceal her guns. Style might dictate wearing fashion boots or even high heels with her outfit but she opted for her favorite running shoes instead.

A glance in the mirror told her she still looked like a cop out of uniform. She pulled the low ponytail holder out of her hair, dug through the shelf of styling products she constantly purchased but rarely used, and selected one. She squeezed a quarter sized dollop of product on her palm, rubbed her palms together and worked the styling cream through her thick brown hair. She breathed in the tropical scent reminiscent of hot beaches and vibrant flowers which she'd never seen. Her long brown hair fell about her shoulders in thick waves.

She opened the vanity drawer and fished all the way to the back of it to find her makeup bag—a plastic sandwich bag holding mascara, two shades of lipstick and a small bottle of liquid foundation. She applied just enough foundation to even out the tones of her translucent skin. A few strokes with the mascara brush brought new vigor to her tired brown eyes. The rich wine colored lipstick made her lips appear fuller but left the tones of the rest of her face flat. She dabbed a little of the lipstick on her cheekbones and smoothed it in.

Her image in the mirror no longer screamed cop out of uniform. Instead she saw the hint of the woman she used to be and decided, at twenty-five, it was time to stop living like her job was her life and start having a life. Without being sure what that meant, she determined to figure it out after she found the children. Her mind wandered to Shep lying in the pet hospital. Perhaps she'd start by getting a dog.

She slipped her Sig Saur into the holster tucked under her left breast. She liked the shirt because the position of the holster left her arms unobstructed for running. She threaded her belt into the tabs of her jeans and clipped the custom holster for her Glock above her right hip. Both guns used interchangeable 357 Sig magazines; she tucked four magazines into the custom pockets she'd sewn into the inside of the jacket.

A final check in the mirror assured her the guns were well hidden beneath the jacket.

She'd barely finished changing when the doorbell rang. Tom stood on her front porch wearing a heavy jacket, open to his waist, and had a backpack slung over his shoulder. Instead of coveralls he wore blue jeans and a heavy sweater over a collared shirt. His hair was damp under a clean red baseball cap and the earlier odor of manure was replaced with the fresh scent of soap.

He fidgeted from one foot to the other and shoved his hands into his jeans pockets.

She raised an eyebrow at him. "You made it here rather quickly?"

He looked down at his hiking boots. "I didn't exactly follow the speed limit," he tilted his head sheepishly at the motorcycle parked next to her cruiser in the drive.

Max turned onto her street and parked in front of her house. He drove Simon's unmarked sedan instead of his truck. He jogged to the front porch and turned to Tom, "What are you carrying?"

Tom reached under his jacket and pulled a Glock from a shoulder holster and handed it to Max. He took a card from his wallet, "Here's my conceal carry permit."

Dana asked Max, "How did you know he was carrying?"

Max handed the gun and permit back to Tom. "Someone comes on my property, kills my dog and takes my daughter—I'm not looking for him armed with flowers." He turned to Tom, "That being said, I expect that gun to remain holstered at all times unless Dana or I instruct you otherwise. If we run across the suspects you are to remain absolutely silent. We don't want you to do anything that might jeopardize finding the children and getting a conviction. Do you agree?"

Tom nodded. "I just want my daughter home safe."

CHAPTER 12

Helm glanced at Tharon, unable to see in the darkness if she was suffering as much as he was. He locked his fingers as tight around her hand as their gloves would let him. Her firm grip and unflagging pace gave him comfort and courage. If she could do this, so could he.

He worried what to do for shelter for the night. The scrapes on his knees hurt and his feet were numb. He knew Tharon must be cold too, but if she was, she didn't let on. "What time do you think it is?" he asked, though he was making his own mental calculations.

Kaid slowed to a walk. "The clock in the service station said six forty-five," Kaid said, "and we've been running for at least fifteen or twenty minutes so it must be after seven."

Helm smiled to himself thinking that if he wanted a break from running, all he had to do was ask Kaid a question.

Darkness enveloped them so deeply that Helm only kept the trail by the feel of the gravel under his feet. He looked at the skyline; ahead in the distance streetlights marked another street crossing; on the right, warm windows winked at the night from houses crowded close together; on the left pine trees towered over them and stretched all the way to the distant crossing.

He knew Tharon must have been thinking the same thing he was when she said, "We've gone far enough to stop. Let's take a break for a few minutes to try to figure things out. We could rest and eat something and take a look at the map."

Helm was grateful for her suggestion. He didn't know about Kaid, but he was cold and hungry, and not about to whine about his discomfort as long as Tharon didn't complain.

They wandered deep enough into the woods to be hidden from view—at least they hoped they were hidden. Tharon sat down with her ankles crossed in front of her and leaned her back against a tree. Helm sat on her right and Kaid on her left. They scrunched up close to each other for warmth and heaped their purchases on the dried needles in front of them.

Tharon picked up the flashlights and looked for an easy way to open it. "Blast. It's one of those packages sealed so tight you need a blow torch to open it." She took the knife from her pockets, "Will one of you open it? I'm likely to get us all cut if I try."

Helm took the flashlights and the knife and slit open the package. He tested the small flashlight and handed it to Tharon before loading the batteries into the large flashlight, "Wow that is bright."

Tharon handed Kaid the peanut butter cups and opened a canister of potato chips. "Oh my goodness these taste good. I didn't realize how hungry I was." She offered the chips to Helm and spread the map out in front of her.

Kaid wolfed down the peanut butter cups and Tharon wondered if he even tasted them.

Helm poured the last cup of cocoa for them to share. "So where do you think we are?" he shined the large flashlight on the map as well.

Tharon traced her finger along the rivers until she found the bridge across the Saint Joseph River on Main Street. Next she found the railroad tracks. "I think we're here. I'm pretty sure the road up ahead is Lindenwood."

Helm picked up a stick and dug at the needles in front of him. "The thing is, no matter how fast we walk, we aren't going to make it home tonight. We need to start looking for a place to stay. It looks like a snowstorm is coming in. At least I hope it's snow. If it's freezing rain, I don't think we'll make it through the night."

The three were quiet. Tharon said, "I haven't been to Fort Wayne much. Do either of you know of a safe place to find shelter?"

Helm studied the map closer and pointed to a spot, then traced his finger back to where they were. "My parents took me to see the Korean War Veteran's Memorial on O'Day Road last Memorial Day. If we take the next railroad track that crosses this one it will take us close to it."

Kaid yawned, "Is there a picnic shelter there to get out of the rain or snow?"

Helm tapped the map, "Better than that—there's a building. We can break into it if it's locked." He looked at the map legend and estimated the distance, "It might take another hour or more to get there."

Tharon fought the yawn reflex and lost. She yawned wide and said, "That's sounds like a good plan." She opened the jerky and shared it with her friends before she loaded their meager supplies into the backpack.

While she munched she thought again about what they overheard. "No matter what happens, one of us has to make it home to tell about the plan to attack our friends and the invasion. But I want you both to promise you won't say anything about them wanting to take me."

She dragged in a deep breath before she continued, "And I want you to promise if we are going to be taken, that you will leave me and save yourselves."

The carpet of needles muffled sound, lending an eerie silence to the air. Helm played the edge of the flashlight beam to touch Tharon's face, "Didn't we just promise earlier today that no one would split us up again?"

She shrugged, "Yeah. But that was before we found out someone wants to invade the state. If we get taken, they will kill you. It would be better if we are going to be captured that you let me be taken alone. For some reason they want me alive. If that happens, you have to promise to leave me and tell my dad. He'll find me. I know he will."

Helm's firm and steady voice pierced the quiet night, "Then we'd better not get taken, because I won't ever leave you."

"Kaid, you understand, don't you? Tell him. You both have to leave. How could I live knowing you died just to keep a promise?"

Kaid shook his head. His voice caught in his throat, "How could we live if you were taken and we ran away?"

Helm stood up and held a hand out to Tharon. "None of us is going to die and none of us are getting caught."

She gripped his hand and he pulled her to her feet. "But—"

Helm whispered in her ear, "I will never leave you. End of discussion." He led the way back to the tracks.

In the quiet of the pines, Kaid heard the whisper. He had also heard what Helm said before he stepped between Tharon and Marty's knife. He followed them as they walked hand in hand, their silhouettes highlighted by the flashlight. It was obvious how much Helm liked Tharon. Did she like him as well? Had she chosen between them after all?

Blast Veronica and Tracy. If it wasn't for them the seed of moving beyond friendship might not have been planted in his head and his stomach wouldn't be churning.

Then again, the combination of peanut butter cups, cold cocoa and beef jerky wasn't helping either.

CHAPTER 13

Dana examined the building and grounds as Max drove past the property owned by the Payne brothers and turned around at the street's dead end. No movement. No sign of life. A single security light hung from a pole and bathed the building in more shadows than light. A closed sign hung lopsided on the door at the end of the building. Cars and trucks—some without tires, doors, hoods, engines—dotted the parking lot. The chain link fence sagged in places and no care was taken to gate the entrance to the parking lot.

Toward the front side of the gray pole building, a hodgepodge of boards were nailed over blue plastic on what must have been double glass doors at one time. A flap of plastic billowed at a large gap on the bottom right side of the opening. "I think I can get through there then open the door at the other end for you."

Max frowned, "You don't know who's in there. I can't let you go in there alone."

Dana pulled a small but bright flashlight from her pocket. "We can at least take a look. Why else did we come?"

Tom suggested, "I'll go in."

"No," both Dana and Max said in firm unison.

Max parked near the open gate. When they got out he told Tom, "Dana and I will check the entrance. You keep watch out here and tell us if you see anyone."

Tom pulled a flashlight from his backpack and slipped the pack's straps over his shoulders. He positioned himself inside the gate where he had an unobstructed view of the entire side of the building. With a turn of his head he could see traffic passing on Lake Avenue.

Dana pulled her gun and held it at her side as she followed Max to the opening.

Squatting down, he pulled the blue plastic aside and turned on his flashlight to look through the opening. A gray tabby cat burst out and swatted at his face. Max jerked away barely avoiding the claws. He lost his balance and crab-walked backwards. The cat arched its back, hissed and snarled with its tail pointing straight up. It bounced twice on the pads of its feet before running to the other end of the building, leaving bloody footprints in its wake.

Max managed to stand and brushed the dirt from his hands. "Blasted cat nearly gave me a heart attack. Shall we try that again?"

Dana panned her light along the foot prints, "Looks like blood. Be ready," she said as she anchored her stance and aimed her gun at the opening.

Max nodded as he again lifted the flap and shined his flashlight into the opening. "There's a pool of blood just inside the door." He bent lower and scanned the entryway with his flashlight beam. "There's a body in there. From the pictures I found online, it looks like Carl Payne."

Dana cast the beam of her flashlight in front of the opening. Even without Tom's practiced eye at tracking, she thought she recognized the bloody shoeprint as Tharon's. "Tom, come over here. There are some footprints here by the door I need you to look at. Stay to the side, some of them are bloody."

Panic seized Tom and he bolted toward the doorway. Max regained his footing in time to help Dana stop him from barreling through the door.

Dana tugged on his arm, "Tom, stop. Think. We have to protect the evidence."

His voice choked, "Evidence? I have to protect my daughter."

Dana shined her light on the footprints, "Look at this. I don't think she's in there. The prints are leading away. Is that from Tharon's shoe?"

Tom crouched and added his flashlight beam to the ground and studied it. "Yes, that's Tharon's. The boys were with her too. They were running." He stood and followed the prints out to the street. He paused a block away and called, "Are you coming?"

Dana frowned at Max, "Follow him or check out the blood? Your call."

Max watched Tom running down the street and made a split decision. "You go with him. I'll call this in."

Dana didn't like leaving Max alone—for all they knew the killers were still in the building—but she was less inclined to let Tom run off armed and alone, maybe to find three dead children on the trail he followed. "I'll let you know what we find." She took a few steps towards the road and turned back to Max, "Don't try to be a hero and go in there alone. Wait for backup."

Max nodded as he pulled out his phone, "You watch out for yourself. The Sheriff will have my hide if you get hurt."

Dana gave him a puzzled look and sprinted after Tom, who was already nearing the dead end. She walled off all feelings and thoughts of Simon in those safe and hidden corners of her heart and mind. The only thing that mattered was to bring the children home safely. She caught up with Tom at the wire fence at the end of the road.

He scanned the ground and followed his flashlight beam west along the fence and paused to study their trail. "The three of them were together. Look here, cowboy boots was about fifteen minutes behind them."

Sprinting to keep pace with him, she asked, "Can you tell how long ago they came this way?"

"It's just a guess but I'd say one to two hours ago, maybe more," relief flooded his features. "They were all three alive and together."

He tensed again when they came to a tube gate across the entrance to the water treatment plant. Tom swept his flashlight beam along the sandy gravel and studied the foot prints. "Cowboy boots—"

"We think he's Burt Payne. Max and I saw a body in the building back there. We think that was his brother Carl."

Tom nodded at the prints, "He followed them but came back out the same way." His jaw clenched, "Their tracks only go in." Tom vaulted over the gate and ran, easily following the trail through the dried weeds.

He paused by a tall maple tree then turned and followed their trail to a chain link fence which was topped with barbed wire. He ran, scanning the ground, until he reached the gap under the fence. He sighed, "They got out—all three of them." He shined his light on the trail outside the fence. "I don't see anything on the trail, but I'm certain they got through." He swept the beam in circles behind them to reassure himself. "Yes, there are no other tracks."

He pulled the backpack off and rifled through the outer pocket.

Dana raised an eyebrow, what was he doing? There was no way his wide shoulders could fit through the gap. "Look, I think I can fit under the fence if I take off my jacket. You can run back and skirt the fence to meet me on the trail."

Tom pulled a tool out of his pack and opened it. "I'll be able to fit through it, too," he said as he unfolded it into a set of wire cutters and cut the links to widen the opening. He bent it back to let Dana through and then squeezed through to join her on the other side.

He shook his head, "I still don't see anything on the paved surface but they should know to head west."

He ran with long strides.

As Dana struggled to keep up with him she was instantly grateful for her choice in footwear. In spite of her personal rigorous fitness routine, she found herself winded as Tom's pace never slacked. They rounded a curve and Dana quickly dodged to the right to keep from running into Tom as he came to an abrupt stop.

A section of trail was roped off with crime scene tape. The streetlight glow and portable spotlights lit up the half block of pavement. Blood stains covered the trail and a uniformed officer stood guard while a crime scene investigations van was parked on the street next to the trail. A technician dug a bullet out of a tree on the river side of the trail.

Tom's face blanched and his hard expression clouded his face.

Dana pulled out her identification. "What happened here, Officer...?" He looked young. She wondered if he even had to shave every day yet.

"Brandt," he supplied as he examined her credentials and said, "Whitley County. Aren't you a tad out of your jurisdiction, Deputy?" He stretched out the syllables of deputy with a note of disdain, as if she were nothing more than a cartoon character. His smooth cheeks were sprinkled with freckles and the gap between his front teeth gave his voice a slight lisp.

She snatched back her badge. "We're tracking three children who were abducted this morning from our county. The men who took them are armed and dangerous."

Brandt waived at the scene behind him in dismissal, "No kids here. An old lady and her dog got shot this evening."

Tom skirted the outside edge of the tape and examined the tree lined bank that dropped off steeply into the Maumee River. He dropped over the side clinging to a tree trunk and leaned out far enough to shine his flashlight where the children had hung. "Deputy Donovan, I found some tracks."

Dana, Officer Brandt and the technician rushed to the edge of the trail.

Tom pointed with his flashlight beam along the bank as he spoke, "Tharon was here, Helm there and Kaid over there," he paused and looked closer at the gouges in the bank. "It looks like Kaid slipped and Helm caught him. See where he shifted and dug his feet in. Tharon moved over too, and must have grabbed Helm to help keep the boys from falling in. It looks like Helm dug in with his knees and toes."

Officer Brandt sounded skeptical when he spoke, "You can tell all that just from looking at scratches in the dirt?"

Tom reached higher and swung up to the side of the trail. He towered over the youthful looking policeman and examined the dirt at Brandt's feet. "I can, as well as I can tell you that you wear a size ten shoe. You turn your left foot in as you walk and tend to walk on your heels. My guess is you're developing bunions or hammer toe."

Brandt's mouth dropped open. "I'll call this in and get more help for your search."

Dana touched his hand and stopped him from pulling out his radio, "You can't report anything about the children over the police channels. We've identified Burt and Carl Payne as persons of interest in the case. Burt was a volunteer policeman. He's probably monitoring the channels for information to lead him to the children."

Brandt looked perplexed, "Then what am I supposed to do?"

Dana was still annoyed by his initial pompous attitude. She said each word slowly, as if he were a touch dim witted, "Do—you—have—a—phone?"

She pulled out her own phone and rang Max, "Just checking in. We followed their trail to the river greenway. It looks like the kids might have witnessed another shooting, probably the one your friend Randy told you about. Tom and I are going to go on and see if we can find where they went. What's happening there?"

Max's voice sounded tight, "Randy's here with me. We found the brother, Carl, dead with a knife wound to the back. No knife on the scene, though. Someone else was cut by the door but there are no other bodies. We found the van hidden in the shop, half painted black. Look sharp, Donovan. I have a feeling Burt and the other man are out for blood."

Dana said, "You do the same. Let me know when you finish up there and I'll tell you where to meet us."

"It looks like our first victim worked for the Payne brothers. I'll check with the dealership and see what I can find out about him. I'll call when I'm done." Max said before disconnecting.

She put her phone away. Brandt had just finished his own call. He turned to the crime scene technician and said, "They need you pronto over on Lake Avenue." He turned back to Dana, "How can I help you, Deputy Donovan?"

Dana arched an eyebrow, "Do you have a phone number?"

He fished a card from his shirt pocket and handed it to her.

"I'll call you if I think of something," she said as she ran to catch up to Tom who was a full city block away searching for signs of the children. Dana ran to catch up with him as she stuffed the card into her hip pocket. She glanced back at Brandt who watched her with his head cocked to the side. He gave her a sheepish grin and a small wave before turning back to the crime scene.

Dana ran west following Tom until they came to the bridge on South Anthony over the Maumee River. She watched as Tom searched the trail and sidewalk until he found an arrow that seemed to be pointing back towards their right.

His mustache ruffled as his face broke into a wide grin. "This way. Tharon left a mark showing which way to go."

Dana hesitated. "But the arrow is pointing back there."

Tom excitedly motioned her to follow, "It's a code that Tharon worked out years ago. The right side of the arrow is the direction she's actually going. We used to play a wilderness scavenger hunt game together." Running across the bridge, he waved for Dana to follow.

Dana ran full out to keep up with him. She wondered how long he could maintain that pace—and worried even more how long *she* could maintain it.

On the other side of the bridge Tom found another mark on the sidewalk. "They're following the railroad tracks." He stepped off the curb and almost walked into oncoming traffic.

Dana grabbed his arm and the back of his jacket and jerked him to safety.

The passing motorist blasted his horn at Tom and flashed him the universal gesture of contempt.

Her heart raced and she gulped in air as she said,

"You're not going to do your daughter any good if you get yourself killed in the process. We'll find her but we need to stay safe, too."

Tom nodded, straightened his jacket and waited for the traffic to clear. "Sorry. I guess I got too anxious to look for a mark on the other side of the street."

While they waited for the light to turn green, Dana asked, "How did you know that about Officer Brandt's feet? Could you tell that from his footprints?"

He shrugged and his mustache ticked up on one side, "No. I just noticed his shoes had a wide roomy toe and figured he had bad feet." He glanced sideways at her, "I didn't like his attitude. I took a chance it would throw him off guard."

An amused expression curled her lips, "I didn't like his attitude either."

Across the street, he quickly found Tharon's mark on the other side of the intersection. He clenched his jaw when he saw where the children rested and the vomit in front of Tharon's footprints.

An increased sense of urgency pressed him forward, running when he could but always checking for Tharon's marks when tracks were lost on pavement. At first he checked over his shoulder often to make sure Dana was keeping up but her impressive stamina and determinations soothed his concerns and he focused on following the children's tracks.

Tom quickly saw the pattern in their movements, "Have you noticed they keep moving to the side of the tracks that is lined by trees?" He followed their trail into a wooded area that bordered the tracks to a metal trestle bridge over the Saint Joe River. The children's footprints stopped then turned towards the bridge where Main Street crossed the river. Tom found Tharon's mark in the dirt by the bridge.

Dana followed him, feeling edgy that Max didn't know where they were. She wanted to give him an update but it was all she could do to keep pace with Tom. Darkness enveloped them and the damp cold chilled her. She wished she'd dressed more for warmth than appearance.

She could see the tension in Tom's back and broad shoulders when he wasn't in sight of Tharon's marked trail or footprints. She admired the love he had for his daughter and was anxious to meet the resourceful girl.

On the other side of the bridge Tom stopped short. There were no markings anywhere in sight. With Dana trailing him like a puppy, he doubled back and scanned the bridge again. Nothing. He retraced their steps and started down the river greenway trail along the Saint Joe River. Nothing. He doubled back again and followed the sidewalk west to Cherry Street. He turned right onto the street and in the second block found Tharon's mark on the bottom brick of the corner fueling station.

He sighed in relief, "I found her mark. They went this way."

Dana looked at the mark and said, "She's quite a girl."

Tom's chest expanded and he stood a little taller, his face full of love and pride. He nodded his head, "That she is. Let's go find them."

CHAPTER 14

The tracks crossed an open field with no cover on either side. The street light of the next crossing illuminated a cluster of evergreens that bordered the track near the next overpass. Helm hoped the tracks were far enough from the distant parallel roads that no one would notice them. He said, "We'd better not use the flashlights. We'll need to stick together and feel for the gravel with our feet."

Kaid muttered, "Right, as long as I feel like I'm about to fall, I'm walking in the right spot."

Helm tried not to limp. He was glad he'd worn dark jeans so the blood stains on his knees didn't show, not that anyone could see them in the dark. His knees felt raw from where the fabric kept rubbing against the scratches he got when Kaid slipped on the bank.

Helm found it was getting difficult to keep moving fast and was content to lag behind Tharon and let Kaid take the lead. Every once in a while, Tharon stopped Kaid and they waited for Helm to catch up.

A lonely train whistle warned them of the train coming toward them from the west and they scrambled to close the gap between them and the trees. They dove deep into a thicket of junipers to wait for it to pass.

Helm didn't want to let the other two know about his knees but he had to see how bad they were. He hoped the evergreen foliage was thick enough to hide the light of the flashlight. He sat down and rolled up his pant legs and turned on the flashlight to look at them.

Tharon gasped when she saw the raw jagged cuts on his knees. "Why didn't you say something sooner?"

He frowned. Why was she scolding him for being hurt and not complaining? The railroad cars thundered by their hiding spot. He yelled over the rumbling roar of the train, "It's not like you could do anything."

She took the flashlight from Helm and handed it to Kaid, then pulled a wad of damp paper towels from her pocket and gently cleaned his knees. She had to shout to be heard over the train, "I took some towels from the restroom and put some liquid soap on them."

The boys looked at her with puzzled expressions, "Why?" Helm asked.

Tharon frowned as she cleaned his knees. "I cut Marty on the face. I didn't mean to, but I forgot I had the knife in my hand. I got blood on the knife and on my hand. I washed but I still feel like my hand has blood on it so I put a bunch of soapy paper towels in my pocket to clean them if I feel the blood again." She waited for a wise crack that didn't come. "I know. I'm weird."

Kaid touched her shoulder and said, "No you're not. You're smart. I wouldn't have thought to do something like that." He hovered over her shoulder, watching her movements but being careful not to block the light. The caboose thundered past and the roar of the train faded away.

"Does it hurt?" she yelled. She was so deep in concentration that she didn't realize the train was gone. The boys looked at her with surprise and they all three burst out laughing. It felt good to laugh.

"It doesn't hurt too bad; it feels good to get them cleaned. Thanks." He winced has she worked a tiny shard of shale out of his knee.

A trickle of blood flowed from the tiny hole the shard had plugged. She pressed the spot with the soapy paper towel to staunch the flow.

Helm sucked in his breath from the stinging soap.

"Give me your knife and I'll cut a bandage for you."

Helm dug the knife from his pocket and handed it to her. She cut into the fabric of the bottom of her t-shirt from under her sweater and ripped off two strips of fabric. She tied them onto each of Helm's knees. "Is that too tight? I don't want to cut off your circulation."

He shook his head and said, "It's fine," even though he figured the makeshift bandages would be around his ankles before he went a quarter of a mile.

She gently rolled his pant legs down so the bandages stayed in place. As she did she felt for more pebbles and picked two more shards from the fabric of each knee. She closed the knife and handed it back to Helm, "I washed it good but when we get home you may want to dry it in the oven so it doesn't rust.

"Thanks. But you keep it until we get home. You might need to make more marks."

Helm pulled out the map and traced his finger along their route, counting off the streets and roads they had crossed. "I think this is Hillegas Road." He looked to the north at the headlights traveling east and west, "I'm pretty sure that is Bass road over there. The railroad track that crosses this one angles up to Bass Road. It's just past the interstate and not far from where it crosses Bass is the Korean War Veterans Memorial. It's on O'Day Road."

The wind whipped up sending loose leaves swirling

around them. Tharon shivered and her teeth chattered. She pulled down her sweater and fastened her coats.

Helm opened an emergency blanket and draped it around Tharon's shoulders, tying it like a silver cape.

"You don't have to do that. I know how to tie a knot." She knew he was trying to be kind but she felt like a two year old having someone else dress her.

He unfolded the poncho and started to slip it over her head.

She stomped her foot. "I am not a child!" Snatching the poncho out of his hands she tugged it forcefully over her head and was grateful for the darkness to hide her blushing face. "There! Are you happy now?"

Helm blinked, "What did I do?"

She hit her fists against the sides of her legs, "Nothing. I just—I don't want to talk about it. I just want to go home."

Helm swung an arm across her shoulders and pulled her close. "We'll get home. I promise we will."

She sagged against him and leaned her head on his shoulder, embarrassed for her childish outburst, "I know. I'm sorry for snapping at you. I just don't like being treated like a little kid."

He whispered in her ear, "You know that isn't how I think of you. I didn't mean to make you feel bad."

She shrugged out of his arms and pulled the knife from her pocket. "It's okay. I shouldn't be so sensitive."

Tharon used the marker and wrote Korean War Veterans Memorial and a rough map of the intersecting tracks on the side of the underpass, they waited for a break in traffic before they ran across the next open field along the track. She had trouble running on the rough ground but desperately wanted to reach the cover. She felt vulnerable in the open, fearing Burt would pop up out of nowhere and shoot them. If he saw them from the road, he'd just have to drive to the next road, park and wait to kill them.

The thought spurred her on and she passed Kaid and ran ahead of the boys. At the junction of the tracks they planned to turn onto, she stopped to catch her breath. The new track passed under the double set of tracks they were following.

She dug a mark in the gravel with her heel to indicate the change in direction and fought to ignore the odds that her father would never see it. He had no way to know where they started. Still she took comfort in making the marks. Trying gave her hope. To do nothing invited failure. While she had a moment alone she whispered into the darkness, "Please, Heavenly Father, help my dad find me."

In answer the dark of the night deepened with thickened clouds. Rain pelted the ground in huge drops, clinging together forming tiny rivulets that streamed down the banks that sloped away from the tracks. A damp chill seeped into her bones. She peered into the darkness and strained to hear Helm and Kaid.

When the boys caught up to her, she took off the rain poncho and pulled out the small flashlight. "Here, Kaid. You put this on and we'll see if we can fit under it with you. You'll have to hold the flashlight too."

Kaid tugged the orange poncho on and poked his head out of the opening with the hood over his hat. He frowned at Tharon standing with rain streaming off her silver cape. "You should wear this."

"If I wear it you guys won't fit under it but if you do, Helm and I can walk by your side and we'll all keep pretty dry. You'll just be the only one who can see."

She lifted his right arm over Helm's shoulder and snapped the side shut around Helm; next she snapped the left side shut and ducked underneath. She pulled the emergency blanket tighter and wrapped her arms around Kaid.

Kaid adjusted the poncho over them and hugged her close to his side. Helm reached around Kaid and hung onto Tharon's arms and she held Kaid with one arm and Helm with the other.

Fighting the closed in feeling, she tightened her grip on Helm and said, "Okay, let's give it a try. Kaid, remember, this is where we take the other track."

"Got it. Just don't either of you trip me or we're all going down."

CHAPTER 15

Lista Trace sat by the fireplace crocheting a baby blanket. She and Tom refused to find out the baby's gender ahead of time so the blanket was predominately yellow and green with touches of soft pink and pale blue. Her hands worked mechanically as she stared at the freezing rain pelting the front bay window. Her hands stopped as she listened to the ping-pinging against the glass. It took a strong wind to drive the rain straight onto the porch.

In her mind's eye she pictured Tharon, dripping wet and exhausted fighting against the wind and rain. Fire crackled in the fireplace bathing the living room with the kind of steady warmth that fills one with bone deep comfort. She looked down at her handiwork and realized she'd dropped three stitches.

When Tom had returned from checking the creek he had stayed only long enough to let her know they hadn't found any sign of the children and to take a quick shower. He left on his motorcycle to search for them. Maisy promised to stay with Lista and he assured them that he would find Tharon.

He didn't kiss her goodbye. He was angry with her. He

tried not to show it, but the anger was there, like a massive wedge splitting them apart like splintered firewood. Tharon was angry with her too. In the perfect vision of hindsight, she was angry with herself as well.

What possessed her to deem it necessary to manipulate her daughter's life? She thought of her own manipulated childhood and adolescence. With a bitter laugh, she thought *the fruit really doesn't fall far from the tree.*

No matter how well intentioned, she vowed never again to interfere in Tharon's life. *Please, God, bring her home so I can keep that promise?*

She glanced at the clock on the mantle. Tom called at five-thirty to tell her he was going to Fort Wayne with Deputy Donovan and Max Stephens to follow up on a lead.

That was the last she'd heard from him. It gnawed at her insides that Tharon was angry with her when she ran to the woods. *This is all my fault. If I hadn't meddled in Tharon's friendships she wouldn't be in this danger. She would have happily come home and helped with dinner or gone to visit Maisy.*

Lista felt guilty she couldn't go with Tom; that her pregnancy kept her bound to the comfort of the living room. Was she choosing the safety of her unborn child over the safe return of her daughter?

She shook her head dismissing the thought. She loved her children, born and unborn. Remembering Tharon's stillborn twin brother and Lista's two middle-trimester miscarriages caused a lump to form in her throat.

Blinking back the tears she tried to reexamine her hand work and found more dropped stitches. Her eyes, blurred by tears, refused to focus on the pattern. She started tearing out the work she'd done, mindlessly wrapping the yarn around the yarn ball, pulling at the stitches she could no longer see.

The aroma of fresh baked bread wafted in from the kitchen. Maisy was busying herself, trying to keep Lista from seeing how worried she was.

Lista knew she should stay calm, not let herself get worked into frenzy, but something about the perfect comfort of her home made her snap. It was so alien to the torment and turmoil that roiled inside her. She felt as if she couldn't breathe.

She hated herself for her comfort; hated that she was confined to the house; hated the blanket for her mistakes; hated the baby—immediately she repented of the thought. Her guilt boiled within her—if only she hadn't meddled—if only she'd sent Tom after Tharon right away—if only she wasn't pregnant. If only...

Her frustration was more than she could bear. She wadded up the yarn, pulled the fireplace screen to the side and chucked the unfinished blanket, yarn ball, crochet hook and all into the flames. She closed the screen and watched the flames melt the acrylic yarn, igniting into a rainbow of hues and billowing thick smoke that worked its way up the chimney and spilled over into the living room.

Maisy rounded the corner from the hallway and stood holding a plate with a slice of fresh warm bread with melted butter. Her face was filled with sadness as she watched Lista.

Lista understood she was behaving badly. Was she being temperamental or immature—or both? She remembered Maisy had bought her the yarn and immediately felt another wave of guilt for destroying it. She took in a breath to apologize and inhaled a lung full of acrylic smoke which sent her into a coughing frenzy.

Maisy put the plate on the coffee table and rushed to her side. With one strong arm around her shoulder and the other holding her hand, she gently guided Lista toward the kitchen.

They rounded the half wall behind the sofa and stepped into the hallway when Lista felt a trickle down her leg. At first she thought she'd lost control of her bladder from coughing but the bloody flow told her otherwise.

She moaned, "Oh, Maisy! Not again. Not now."

Maisy half carried, half dragged Lista to her bedroom located in the front of the house across the foyer from the living room. After depositing Lista on the bed she ran to the bathroom for towels to put under her. She brought a glass of water from the bathroom and as she held the glass to Lista's lips, she fished her phone from her pocket and called Doc Walker. "Doc, Lista's water broke."

Lista took a few sips of the water and the coughing eased. She moaned, "This is my fault. I wished I wasn't pregnant so I could look for Tharon, too."

Maisy rushed back to the bathroom and wet a clean washcloth. She rung it out and hurried back to Lista's side, wiping her brow with it. "Hush, child. This isn't your fault."

Lista took the cloth and held it to her eyes to sooth her stinging tears. She tried to remember the last time she'd felt the baby move. Had it moved at all today? Had she felt it yesterday? She'd been so engrossed with preparing for Tharon's birthday, she'd failed to notice that the baby had stopped moving.

The guilt settled into a cold hard heaviness in her chest. No, her thoughts had not caused the miscarriage. She'd kept herself too busy to face the fact that her baby was dead. It had died two days ago.

She pulled the cloth from her eyes and clutched at Maisy's hand, "Don't tell Tom. He needs to focus on finding Tharon. There's nothing he can do. Promise me you won't tell him."

Maisy blinked at the tears welling in her eyes and nodded her head.

CHAPTER 16

It started with rain. Big dolloping drops fell and stung when they pelted Tom's face, as if the center of each drop held a tiny chunk of ice. He tried to tip his head forward for the brim of his baseball cap to shield him, but the wind was so strong he still got bombarded.

He ran harder, since a heavy rain meant he'd lose Tharon's trail. He glanced back at Dana and saw her slip and fall in the loose gravel next to the track. He hurried back to help her up. "Are you alright?"

She sounded annoyed when she answered. "Yeah. I'm used to running on paved roads and trails. Guess I need to add some cross country to my workout."

Tom took her by the elbow and picked up the pace again, shining his flashlight for both of them. Part of him wanted her to call Max to come get her and let him go on by himself. The other part of him was glad to have her along in case they ran into trouble. She'd been keeping good pace with him and he found something in her nature and bearing reassuring. It gave him comfort and hope to not be alone.

He looked ahead and said, "There's an overpass up there. We'll stop and see if Tharon left any messages."

Dana nodded and scrambled along by his side. When they reached the overpass she doubled over with her hands on her knees gasping to catch her breath. She straightened up and shivered involuntarily. Her jaws clenched and against her will, her teeth chattered as she spoke. "I didn't know farmers stayed in such good shape."

Tom held the flashlight so it didn't shine in her eyes as he looked at her. Her face looked pale; her lips blue. This wasn't good. "You're going into shock." He peeled off his jacket, removed his wool sweater and put his jacket back on. "Here, put this on," he ordered as he helped her out of her leather coat. He slipped the sweater on over her head and fed her shivering arms through the sleeves and then helped her struggle back into the wet leather jacket. He buttoned her coat up and pulled her into his arms and then wrapped his jacket around her and rubbed her back and arms.

After a few minutes her shivering subsided. Through chattering teeth she said, "Thanks. I guess I didn't choose my wardrobe too well after all."

"For what it's worth, you don't look like a cop if that's what you were going for." He continued holding her, feeling awkward. He'd never touched another woman besides Lista before. But if he didn't get her warmed up soon they couldn't go on.

"Thanks," she said, pushing free of him when she felt the worst chills subside. She pulled an elastic hair band out of her coat pocket. With shaking hands she squeezed the excess water out of her hair and twisted her hair into a wet ponytail.

Tom took his red baseball cap off and put it on her head. The hat sank down over half her face so he adjusted the strap in the back to fit her head.

Only when he was sure she was out of danger from

shock did he start looking for signs from Tharon. With the flashlight he scanned the concrete walls. He found the message she'd written on the concrete, "Do you have an idea where the Korean War Veterans Memorial is?"

She shivered as she studied the crude map and letters and said, "Yes. Let's head up to the overpass and see what road we're near and have Max come pick us up."

Tom noticed the dull and listless look in her eyes. "You stay down here out of the rain. I'll go find out and then you can call him."

He was only gone a few minutes but by the time he got back she was slumped against the wall of the underpass. He lifted her and wrapped his jacket around her again. He fished her phone from her pocket and found Max's number. "Detective, we're under the overpass over the railroad tracks on Hillegas Road just south of Bass Road. Hurry. Dana's taken quite a chill. Park toward the south side of the overpass and sound your horn when you get here. Hurry," he repeated, "I'm worried about her."

Dana tried to cling to consciousness. She thought of the children out in the same conditions and prayed they made it to shelter before the rain started. Through chattering teeth, she said, "Talk to me. Tell me something about your daughter."

Tom thought for a moment. When he spoke his deep voice rumbled in her ear. "When Tharon was seven, she noticed my apple picker didn't reach to the apples in the top of the trees and that I couldn't harvest them before they dropped. She asked if she could climb the trees and pick the apples. She wanted to sell them and have the money. I gave her permission and she climbed every tree in the orchard. You should have seen her. That girl loves to climb." Pride shined in his eyes.

"Lista and I thought she'd buy herself a doll or toys,

maybe a bike. Not Tharon. She saved her money. She'd heard Lista and me discussing a family in our church. The mother caught the flu during the pandemic and survived but she's never been the same. I guess it affected her heart. The father lost his job and had been out of work for over a year.

Tom smiled as he spoke, "Tharon had me take her shopping before Christmas. She didn't want anyone to see us. She made me promise to not even tell Lista. She brought the prettiest doll I'd ever seen. And she bought a new shirt and tie. She kept fretting about what size shirt to get. I asked her who it was for, thinking it was for me and she just didn't want me to know."

Dana closed her eyes and warmed to the deep timbre of Tom's voice.

Tom shook his head and his love and pride for his daughter was evident in his voice. "But she said, 'It's for Sarah Felger's daddy. He's out of work and I heard him at church telling the minister that he didn't even have a decent shirt and tie wear to an interview. I guess that's why he always keeps his coat buttoned up at church.' That's my Tharon. She had the minister give Ron Felger the new shirt and tie, and the doll for Sarah; and she gave him the rest of her money for Ron to buy presents from Santa for the rest of the family. She made Reverend Harper promise not to tell anyone it was from her because it might make Ron feel funny taking money from a child and she wanted Sarah to think the doll came from Santa," he paused and with a smile and his voice filled with love he repeated quietly, "That's my Tharon."

They heard Max blast his horn above them. Through her still chattering teeth, Dana said, "We'll find her, Tom. I promise we'll find her."

CHAPTER 17

Burt punched the steering wheel in frustration. He knew the brats had to be heading west but he'd crisscrossed every road and trail and he couldn't find them. He wondered if they'd already been rescued but dismissed that when the amber alert repeated again on the radio.

He'd tried to go back to his dealership to switch cars after he killed the old lady and her dog, but police seemed to be everywhere he went.

That big detective, Bohman, kept calling him, but he knew better than to pick up. It was stupid to take the dealership van, even the old one, to check out the bus routes, but how was he to know Wil Silar was a spy? It wasn't like he planned on killing him.

It was all those kids' fault. What in the heck were three kids doing in the top of a tree in freezing weather?

And Carl, big, dumb Carl whose heart was ten times bigger than his brain—Carl was dead. That was them kids' fault too. Because of them the whole operation would have to be scrapped. Ten years of planning down the drain. His life was in ruins.

All evening, every time he heard the scanner announce a possible sighting of the kids, the police beat him to the location, and the kids were nowhere in sight. He could tell from the calls they were heading west. He'd zigzagged through every street and neighborhood since the report on the Main Street Bridge. The only thing he could figure was they were heading west along the railroad tracks.

He checked the map on his computer tablet and picked a crossing he knew they couldn't have reached yet. He planned to hide his car and wait under the overpass for them to come to him. He fondled the gun in his pocket. If it was the last thing he did, he'd kill those kids, and then he'd find Marty and kill him, too—kill him for Carl.

The rock hard resolve of revenge steeled his body against the cold. He chugged whiskey from a flask, whose permanent address was his inside jacket pocket, and thought of his poor soft-hearted and soft-headed brother. Carl wouldn't want him to kill the kids, but Carl wasn't around anymore to stop him. Nothing mattered anymore.

Burt knew he was a dead man. If the cops didn't kill him, Hamron's goons were sure to. Either way, he was bound and determined to get those kids first.

He smirked to himself. His one chance to get out of this with his skin intact was getting the girl back. If that didn't work, he'd kill her too.

He blew his nose into a handkerchief and turned up the police scanner to listen for any news on the brats.

CHAPTER 18

When Max saw Tom carrying Dana up the embankment he scurried out of the car and helped Tom wedge her into the front passenger seat. Tom climbed in the back but Dana refused to let them take her to the hospital until they checked to see if the children were at the memorial.

Max knew where it was and lead footed it to O'Day Road.

Rain poured steadily and darkness pressed around them; Tom knew there'd be no tracks to see and no path to follow.

Dana sat in the front seat with the heater blasting on her, but the chills still shook her body.

Max and Tom exchanged a worried glance in the rear view mirror.

Tom hoped they'd find the children and be able to get all of them quickly to the hospital. He jumped out of the car as soon as Max pulled into the Korean War Veterans Memorial.

Max turned to Dana, "You stay put and get warm." He grabbed the flashlight from the cup holder where he'd stashed it.

Tom ran to the side door of the oblong building at the

edge of the parking lot. "Tharon, Kaid, Helm! Are you here? Tharon, it's Dad! Are you here?" He banged on the door facing the parking lot, then joined Max as he shined the flashlight in the windows. They checked every door and window in the building but found no trace of the children.

Tom ran to the pavilion and checked every inch of it. He found no sign of Tharon or the boys. He checked the out buildings while Max searched the memorial. The children were not there. They hadn't been there.

Tom's shoulders sagged as he slumped into the back seat, "They must still be on the track. Can you drop me off and I'll backtrack to find them?"

Max was somber. "Tom, what do you think your daughter would do?"

Tom thought a moment. "If she couldn't make it here for some reason, she'd find a farm and call me. But my phone hasn't rung."

"Do you have any messages?"

Tom pulled out his phone and slammed his fist against his thigh. "The battery's dead."

Max frowned, "I hate to say this but we have to do what takes priority. Dana has to get to the hospital; I'm worried she's going into shock." He took a deep breath and said, "And there's something you need to know. Your wife didn't want you to be told, but I have some bad news for you. Doc couldn't reach you and he called the Sheriff. Your wife is in the hospital. I'm sorry to tell you, she lost your baby."

Dana gasped and tried to speak but her words were strangled in shallow gurgling coughs. Tom got out and opened her door. He slid her seat back as far as it would go and lifted her onto his lap as he sat down in the passenger seat. He pulled the door shut and turned his face to the side window.

Max cranked up the heat and whipped the car around in the parking lot. He floored the gas pedal as he sped toward Route 30 to Whitley County Hospital on the east edge of Columbia City.

Dana felt Tom's warm tears drip on the side of her face. She cuddled into his warmth as he rubbed her back and arms. All she could work out of her tense jaws was a ragged, "Sor—ry."

Max called Simon to let him know they were bringing Dana to the hospital with possible hypothermia.

Tom kept rubbing Dana furiously, hoping that at least *she* would live through the night. He realized in that instant that he had not said one prayer for Tharon's safety. He didn't care what Max and Dana thought of him as he prayed aloud, begging for the Lord to save the children and Dana. He couldn't speak aloud the loss of his unborn child or the anguish he knew he shared with Lista.

When Tom ended his prayer, Max whispered, "Amen."

CHAPTER 19

The distance to O'Day Road took much longer than they anticipated from the map. Every muscle in Kaid's back ached as he struggled to see through the driving rain. When he crossed the tangle of tracks near Yellow River Road, he was nervous to see all the small houses lining the road. Most were boarded up or dark, some with the entire structure gone except for the foundation. He wondered if this was the path the tornado had taken the year before. It had wiped out a newer subdivision in Sandy Creek and he'd heard that its destruction extended all the way to Fort Wayne.

He stopped to shine the flashlight on the street sign and found a rusted metal sign next to it with an arrow to the Memorial. "I see the memorial," Kaid said after he steered Tharon and Helm onto O'Day Road. Their progress had been agonizingly slow and he was grateful to be breaking into a run as Tharon and Helm burst from beneath the poncho. As soon as they entered the parking lot the security lights flickered on.

The main building looked more like a house with a brick facade on the front and Kaid searched for any signs of light or life in the building but saw nothing. He searched the homes across the road but they too were darkened and devoid of any signs of life. All the houses they passed had the dried remnants of tall weeds and grasses in their yards.

Helm tried to jimmy the lock on the door facing the parking lot.

Kaid felt exposed in the bright security light. When Helm shook his head at the deadbolt lock, Kaid picked up a rock and broke the door window to reach in and unlock the door.

Inside he found the thermostat and cranked up the heat. In the meeting room he huddled up next to Tharon with Helm on her other side, as they warmed their feet at the same heating register. After a small meal of jerky, candy bars and water, each retreated into their own thoughts.

Helm broke the uncomfortable silence. "Tharon, I think Kaid and I would be dead by now if it wasn't for you getting us free. You have to be the bravest girl I know."

Tharon hid her face in her knees. "Me brave? Ha. I was so scared I couldn't move. If Kaid hadn't dragged me out of there, I'd have died with Carl." She nudged Kaid with her elbow, "Thanks for saving me."

Kaid tucked a loose strand of hair behind her ear. "I hate to think where we'd be if you didn't bring that money with you. Can you imagine walking through that freezing rain without the poncho? How come you had all that money in your coat pocket anyway?"

Helm dipped his head to look her in the eyes, "It's your Secret Santa stash, isn't it?"

Tharon's eyes opened wide, "How do you know about that? No one is supposed to know. It's a secret."

Helm shrugged his shoulders. "I saw you the first year you came to my parents' store to Christmas shop with your dad. I've watched you every year since."

"What Secret Santa stash?" Kaid was beginning to feel

like the odd man out. He didn't like it.

Tharon wrapped her arms around her knees and held her hands over the forced air of the register. "Do neither of you know the meaning of the word secret?" She lay down and pulled the silver blanket up to her chin.

The boys lay down next to her. They were quiet for what seemed like a long time when Kaid said, "Speaking of secrets, what do you make of what we heard those men talking about?"

Helm bent his right arm behind his head, "We have to tell someone what we heard, but who can we trust?"

Tharon chewed on her lower lip, "We can trust Detective Stephens. His wife is Maisy's best friend. Do you think he'd know who to tell?"

Helm turned on his side and propped himself on his elbow to face Tharon and Kaid, "I've heard my dad talk about Governor Talbot. He says he's a good man. We need to get word to him somehow."

Kaid turned on his side and faced Helm, "What if they push up their plans because of us? They could take our friends hostage tomorrow before we can even tell anyone."

Tharon chewed on her lower lip, "I still don't get why anyone would want me but since they don't have me and I'm not home yet, maybe they will wait. What we have to do is find out who wants to kidnap me and why." She poked the air with her index finger as she spoke. "How can we trust any police? We have to trust someone and we have to tell them soon. Who do we trust more than anyone?" she thought a moment. "I trust my dad. He'll know what to do."

"I trust your dad and I trust my dad too," Helm said. "He understands politics and government. What about you, Kaid?"

Kaid thought before speaking, "I trust both your fathers

too. I think we should tell them and let them decide what to do."

Tharon searched Kaid's face, "What about your dad? Don't you trust him?"

Kaid rolled onto his back. "I trust him as a doctor—but something like this?" He shook his head, "I think it's beyond him to know what to do."

They all laid on their backs under the blankets, still in their coats and damp shoes. Kaid took hold of Tharon's left hand and Helm found her right as they snuggled together for added warmth.

She smiled and sighed then whispered out loud. "Thank you for helping us get here tonight, Heavenly Father. Please help us get home tomorrow. Amen."

The boys each squeezed her hands and said, "Amen," then fell into the quiet of exhaustion.

Kaid turned his head and studied Tharon. Her eyelids drooped like she was on the edge of sleep when he asked, "Will someone tell me about the Secret Santa?"

She yawned, "I pick the apples in the tree tops and my dad lets me sell them. I use the money to help someone in need have a nice Christmas..."

Kaid raised his eyebrows and looked at Tharon. His dimples accented his grin, "That's cool."

He laid back and stared at the ceiling thinking. After a long pause he asked, "Does anyone want to talk about what was said right before Carl attacked Marty?"

"No!" Tharon and Helm said in unison.

Kaid's dimples danced in his cheeks and he let go of a tension in his shoulders he hadn't realized he was holding. Maybe she was still choosing not to choose. The thought filled him with a small measure of hope.

CHAPTER 20

Simon waited outside of the ER with an orderly and an intern. Max pulled up to the entrance and Simon's face blanched when he saw Dana. He opened the door and lifted her out of Tom's arms, ignored the orderly with the wheelchair, and carried her straight past reception into the ER suite. "I've got the hypothermia case here, which room does she go in?" he barked.

"In here, Sheriff," a tall thin nurse, with a long strawberry blond ponytail and a badge emblazoned with the name *Gretchen*, ushered him into an ER room. She was joined by another nurse who immediately started to cut Dana's clothes off of her. Simon lingered by the doorway, his focus locked on Dana, in that instant he acknowledged what he'd refused to recognize before: he loved her. He deeply and completely loved her. The thought of losing her twisted his gut into knots.

Dana flailed at the hands with scissors cutting up her pant legs. She took a deep breath and with all the energy she could muster choked out, "Simon!"

Simon muscled the nurses aside and rushed to Dana as the nurses tucked warm blankets around her. "Dana, Honey, I'm here. What do you need?"

Dana squirmed beneath the blanket. With a quivering voice and quirky grin she said, "Simon, Honey—" she pulled her hands from beneath the blankets and held her side arms in front of him, "could you hold onto my guns for me?"

Simon took the guns and tucked them in his pockets. His face turned a deep shade of crimson.

Dana took his face in her trembling hands, pulled him close and gently kissed his lips. Color flooded back into her face. She held up her shivering index finger, "One more thing," her hands dove back under the blankets and squirmed around again. When she brought them back out she handed him four clips of bullets and her shield. She shoved them into his coat pockets.

Simon leaned close to her lips again and said, "Have you got any idea how incredibly hot you are?"

Gretchen said with a smirk, "Do you two want us to leave and give you some privacy?"

Simon gave Dana a lingering kiss and backed away smiling at her. "Sorry, ladies. I'll be in the waiting room." His eyes remained locked on Dana. He backed into the door frame. "We'll talk later." He walked backwards out the door and when he turned he bumped into a cart knocking a tray of instruments to the floor. His blush deepened "Sorry," he said again.

After Simon left, Gretchen took Dana's temperature again. "You're a cute couple. How long have you two been together?"

Through chattering teeth, Dana said, "About two minutes now." She couldn't stop smiling.

Gretchen grinned wide. "Well, I think you two have found the perfect cure for hypothermia. Another two minutes with him and your core temperature will be back to normal. We do need to get you out of those wet clothes though."

Dana stuttered, "Okay, but can we not cut off my tops, one of the sweaters isn't mine and the tactical shirt is my favorite holster."

Gretchen shook her head and laughed. "Well, that's a sentence I'd never thought I'd hear, let alone understand."

CHAPTER 21

Tom spoke to Doc before he found Lista's room. He took a moment to compose himself before entering. He shook his head in embarrassment at how he'd let his emotions run amuck all day. Lista didn't need that. She needed him to be strong.

He had no delusions about where the strength in their family resided. Every child they lost seemed to break his heart to pieces but it turned Lista into a boulder. Not that she was in any way hard-hearted. She was as tender-hearted and compassionate as the day he'd met her. But she had a rock hard strength in her core.

He knew she drew part of it from her faith, which was so much stronger than his own—but she also harbored an innate sense of survival—something he only acquired after years of training—a drive that no matter how bad things got they'd get through them. He hoped and prayed that Tharon got that quality from her mother. She'd need it if she was going to survive this night.

He sighed and pushed the door to his wife's room open. Lista lay asleep on the bed. Her hair spilled onto the pillow in a tangled nest of blond curls. Maisy sat by the window watching the snow. She turned to him with hopeful excitement but he shook his head no.

She slumped back in the chair, and then she got a good look at him. She whispered, "Come sit down, I'm going to find some scrubs for you and get your clothes dried. Then I'll find something hot for you to eat even if I have to make it myself."

Tom was too tired to argue. "Can I borrow your phone? My battery died."

She handed it to him as he sank into the chair next to Lista. Maisy touched his shoulder and he reached up to hold her hand for a moment. Then she left to find some scrubs.

Lista stirred and opened her eyes. "Where's Tharon? Is she alright?"

Tom leaned forward and took her hand. "Tharon and the boys escaped this afternoon. She left a marked trail for me to follow and I thought I knew where to find her but she wasn't there." He kissed her hand, "Dana, Deputy Donovan, was with me and she developed hypothermia so we had to bring her to the hospital." He rubbed his thumb gently over her knuckles, "Max told me about the baby. So here I am."

He smoothed her hair back from her forehead. "Do you understand what happened?"

Her face scrunched up in sadness, "Our baby died. I don't remember anything since the time we got to the hospital. What happened?"

He kept stroking her knuckle, "Doc had to do a C-section and when he did he found a tumor. He thinks he got it all and he thinks it was benign. He's pretty sure that was why you've had so many miscarriages."

"You mean we still might be able to have children?" her voice betrayed the depth of her pain.

He touched her face and with a sad smile said, "I'm sure

we will."

Lista emerged from her anesthesia fog and wrinkled her brow. "When are you going back out?"

"I'm going to call Matt Harris to go with me. I'll leave as soon as he gets here." He pulled out Maisy's phone but stopped and shook his head. "I don't know his number and our phone has a dead battery."

With no small measure of irritation, Lista said, "Angela's number is on there. Use it."

Tom bristled at her tone. He tried not to let his hurt sound in his voice on the phone.

After he finished talking to Matt, Maisy reentered the room holding a steaming mug and carried a set of blue scrubs under her arm. "It's chicken noodle soup. Sorry that's all I could find. Here, slip into these and I'll take your clothes to get them dry."

He stood up. "No, I don't have time. Matt will be here soon. Give the soup to Lista. I have to go."

Lista pleaded, "Tom, wait! I'm sorry I was abrupt. I'm just so worried about Tharon."

He rounded on her, even as he spoke he knew he shouldn't, but her edgy comment dug at him like a thorn in his side. "Do you think I'm not worried about her? I know exactly the elements she's facing. I saw them almost kill an adult woman. Our little girl is out there with wet feet, wet clothes, and no hot food and still she's marking a trail for me. For *me*! No one else on earth could read her markings."

He caught himself before he accused her of being to blame for the children being abducted. "So no, I'm not going to sit here in this warm room and sip hot soup and wait for my clothes to dry. I wanted to keep looking for her on my own and the only reason I came back was because..."

Maisy's face was filled with sadness. She touched his arm and said, "Because you love your wife and thought she might need you."

Lista held her arms out to him, an IV line dangling from her left hand. "Tom, I love you. I'm so sorry I can't be there with you. Please don't be angry with me."

He moved back to her side, sighed and gently kissed her lips. "I'm not angry. I had to see that you were all right. I couldn't be out there worrying about both of you. But now I'm going to check in on Deputy Donovan and then I'm going to find Tharon. I won't come home without her."

CHAPTER 22

November 10, 2056

Tharon lamented that her beating at the hands of Everett Edwards no longer ranked as her most terrifying experience. She fell into a restless sleep. In her dreams spiders and centipedes crawled across the floor, beneath the silver blanket and up her legs. She kicked and screamed, "Get them off me! Get them off me!"

Helm grabbed her in his arms and pulled her to a sitting position. He locked his arms and around her cradled her as he had done in the dark room, "Shh. You're safe. See? Open your eyes. See? Breathe with me. We're safe."

She blinked and looked at the security light filtering through the narrow slits in the blinds. She closed her eyes and sank into Helm's arms and felt his breathing, listened to his heartbeat. She slowed her breathing to match his and opened her eyes again to look at the blinds. "Isn't the security light triggered by movement?"

The beam of a flashlight flickered in through the window at the far end of the room and started moving toward them, one window at a time. Avoiding the flashlight's beam, they rushed to gather their belongings as quickly as they could; to don their hats and gloves as rapidly as they could; to hug the wall as tightly as they could. The scrambled ahead of the light and headed for the back door through the kitchen. Tharon grabbed the poncho and the emergency blankets and stuffed them into Helm's pack as she ran.

"Come on, you brats! You're only making this harder on yourself. I will find you—best to get it over with now—no place else for you to run." Burt's voice bellowed as he neared the door with the broken window. "Listen, I only need the girl. Let me have her and you boys can leave."

Kaid unlocked the kitchen door and eased out first, Tharon next and then Helm. Helm took the back pack from her as she passed in front of him and slung it over his shoulder.

She hit the ground running as the entry door crashed open and Burt's angry roar split the quiet night.

Though the rain and snow had stopped, the night was long from over. Clinging to Helm's hand, she plunged across O'Day Road, over the narrow wooded corner and across Yellow River Road. Speeding through a small woodlot, they ran until they came to the railroad tracks and then turned west, or whatever direction it was, away from where they'd been.

Burt stumbled through the woods, his flashlight flailed through the darkness searching for them.

On the other side of the tracks they slid down a steep bank. At the bottom a tall dense hedge bordered a large yard whose security lights were too far away to cast even a shadow on them.

Tharon pulled the boys to the hedge. They tucked themselves deep between the dense crowded columns of the evergreen. She pressed snugly in its branches and breathed in the scent which reminded her of the arborvitae bush by the back corner of her house. The familiar scent filled her with a pang of longing for home: for Dad, Mom, Maisy and Shep. Her chest tightened at the thought of poor Shep, killed trying to protect her. Against her will, she let out a quiet strangled sob.

Helm pushed all the way through the shrub and pressed into the other side of the bush she was hiding in. She heard the rustle of the soft flat leaves as he pressed into the tight space behind her. He wrapped one arm around her waist and gripped her arm. She crossed her arms to cover his hands with hers and sank back into him standing perfectly still.

Burt stomped along the tracks above them. He slipped on the gravel and the flashlight hit metal and skittered along the rail.

Tharon turned her head and buried her face in Helm's chest. She prayed silently that Burt wouldn't find them.

Burt let loose a flurry of curses that made Tharon blush; she didn't understand most of them, but, from his tone, she knew they were things she didn't want to understand.

A man's deep voice boomed from far away in the yard. "You out there with the flashlight. I've called the Sheriff and I've got a rifle so get the hell out of here or I'm going to shoot you."

Burt dug his pistol out and fired three shots at the man.

The man shot three times towards Burt's flashlight.

Tharon felt Helm lose his balance for a moment and then right himself as he squeezed tighter on her hand.

Burt's flashlight shattered and he dove for the other side of the tracks cursing with greater fury. He wrapped his hand in a white handkerchief and muttered, "Forget this. All I gotta do is wait where the track crosses the next road.

That's what I'll do. Then I'll put an end to them brats."

Tharon heard him stumble back through the woods toward the memorial. She stayed still for a long time and the boys didn't say anything. Tharon had a horrible thought, what if the bullets hit Kaid or Helm? She whispered, "Are you guys hurt?"

Kaid's voice hissed from her right, "Shh. Listen."

The engine of Burt's car rumbled to life and faded away down Yellow River Road. Kaid whispered, "I think we can go now," he said as he reached in and pulled her free of the shrub.

Helm didn't emerge from the bush behind her. She frowned, "Helm? Are you hurt?" When he pushed through the bush she sighed with relief.

Helm took her hand, "Come on, we need to find a place to hide before daybreak. We need to find some nice big woods." He walked slowly, and she thought how kind he was to make sure she didn't get left behind in the dark.

She clung to his hand, unwilling to let go of him. For some reason when he held her hand, she felt less afraid. Together they walked side by side as Kaid led them along the tracks in the darkness.

She felt like they'd walked twice the distance between her farm and the Walker farm when Kaid said, "Look, there's some woods to the left. We can hide there and rest till the sun comes up."

Tharon continued to hold Helm's hand but something was different. His grip on her hand seemed weaker and the rhythm of his footsteps was off. He dragged his right foot and slowed down. She could no longer make out Kaid's shape ahead of them. "Helm, what's wrong?"

"I think one of that man's bullets hit me—the man from the house." He started to sag next to her.

She cried out, "Kaid! Helm's hurt!"

CHAPTER 23

Dana huddled under the warm blankets and waited for Gretchen to return. She hated that her poor wardrobe planning led to getting the chills and the useless rush to the hospital. All she could think about was getting back out to help Tom find the children. She hoped he hadn't left without her but she wouldn't blame him if he had.

Simon rapped on the door and leaned against the door frame. She smiled but was a tad nervous, given their last encounter, to know if he'd just been caught up with concern for her safety. "Hi. Come in."

He rolled a stool over to her side, and asked, "So where do we go from here?"

She smiled sheepishly. "Well, as soon as Gretchen gets back, I'm going to find Tom and Max and we're going to go back out and bring those children home."

Simon leaned closer, "You know that's not what I was asking."

She pulled a hand from beneath the blanket and touched his face, traced the strong line of his rough jaw, looked deep into his blue eyes. She'd longed for this connection with him, yet her drive to finish the search overrode all personal feelings. "You know me. Do you think I can indulge in my joy until I find those children? Can you?"

He sighed as he took her hand and kissed her palm. "No, I guess not."

There was another knock on the door. They looked up to find Tom and Max filling the doorway. Warmth coursed through her when Simon continued to hold her hand.

A wide grin plastered Max's weathered face.

Tom hated to interrupt but he was itching to resume his search, "Simon, I just wanted to check on Dana and let you know Matt Harris is meeting me in a few minutes and we're going to look for the children."

Dana saw Gretchen returning. "Can you wait for me? I really want to go back out with you."

Gretchen pushed past Tom and dropped an armful of warm dry clothes on the bed.

Dana picked up Tom's sweater and tossed it to him. "Here, you'll need this. Now you men scoot out of here and let me get dressed."

Simon stood up to leave but Dana grabbed his hand, "Simon, Honey, I believe you're holding onto my favorite fashion accessories." She batted her eyes at him.

He grinned from ear to ear and emptied his pockets of her guns, ammunition and badge. "I'm beginning to see how things are going to be."

She pulled him to her and kissed him tenderly. "Any complaints?"

He devoured her with his eyes. "Not a one."

Gretchen shooed him out of the room, "Out, we have children to save."

Simon left and Dana threw off the blankets and rubbed her hands together, "So what did you find?"

"We spread the word through the whole hospital and everyone wanted to help. We have thermal underwear— the kind that die-hard runners wear, jeans, socks, running shoes, a down jacket, hat, scarf, gloves and hand warmers."

Dana was in awe of all that was donated to her. "I can't tell you how grateful I am." She quickly pulled on the thermal underwear, followed by her tactical shirt. She continued to layer her clothing. When she finished tying the shoes, she stood up, "I owe you. If there's ever anything I can do for you, just name it."

Gretchen smiled a crooked smile, "You bring those kids here when you find them. We'll be ready for them. And one other thing, I want an invitation to the wedding."

Dana checked her guns, slipped them into her holsters, and pocketed the magazines, "Oh, I don't think we're ready for that yet."

Simon peeked around the corner. "Are you ready?"

"Absolutely, Sheriff." Dana smiled as she clipped her badge on her belt.

Simon gave her a puzzled look, "Are we talking about the same thing?"

"I think so." She grinned at him, "We're going out to find those kids, right?"

Simon smiled back, "Right." He bent and kissed her lightly and then slipped his arm around her waist as they walked to the waiting room.

Tom, Matt and Max huddled in the corner pouring over the map Matt had brought with him. Tom drew a line along the track to the Memorial. "I figure we'll head back to the Korean War Veterans Memorial. If the kids still aren't there, we'll back track until we find them. We can take two teams and one can start at Hillegas Road and the other from Yellow River Road."

Simon's phone rang. He listened for a moment, "Thanks for letting me know, Penni. Are you going to keep listening?" after her response he said, "Let me know if you hear anything else."

He disconnected. "Penni has been monitoring the Fort Wayne police channels. There's been a report of a prowler with a gun near the Memorial. Shots were fired."

Tom and Matt didn't wait for instructions. They ran out to the parking lot to Matt Harris's vintage Charger. Dana caught up with them and climbed into the back seat.

"Let's go get those kids." She and Tom nodded to each other. She turned to Matt, "Do you have a gun with you?"

Matt glanced in the rear view mirror at her, "Yes. I've got a .22 in the trunk."

Dana sat back, "Good."

Simon floored his SUV and still had trouble keeping up with Matt. He used his flashing lights but kept the siren off, and imagined the cars they passed thought he was in pursuit.

He saw the sedan fishtail when it turned onto O'Day and tried to suppress the niggling worry for Dana's safety. She was a good cop. He knew he couldn't protect her or change her assignments, or the way she did her job. It was one of the things he loved about her. He smiled, thinking of the wild ride their life together was going to be.

Max sat next to him and saw his smile, "It's about time you woke up to see what you had right before your eyes."

Simon rubbed the stubble on his chin. "I guess I have been a bit self-absorbed."

Max said softly, "Sure, who wouldn't be after what you lost. Doesn't mean you have to give up a happy future because you lost a happy past. Dana's a good woman and a good cop. She's not the same kind of woman as Nora, but she'll make you just as happy if you let her."

Simon scratched his head, "I know. I just hope I can make her as happy as she deserves to be. Do think Penni will be too bent out of shape if I have her rework the schedules starting next Saturday so Dana and I can go on our honeymoon?"

Max barked out an amused laugh, "Man when you fall, you fall hard! No, I don't think Penni will mind the inconvenience one bit. What's the hurry? Are you afraid she'll change her mind?"

Simon grinned wide, "No. I just want to spend the rest of my life with her and I don't want to waste another minute."

CHAPTER 24

When Dana got out of the car, Officer Brandt sidled up to her before she even had the door closed. He stood far inside her comfort zone. "Deputy Donovan, when I heard about the shooting, I wondered if you might be involved. I thought I'd see if you needed anything."

Dana still hadn't forgiven him for his earlier slight. "I need to find three missing children. Have you seen them?"

Brandt stepped back, "Well, no."

Dana wasn't ready to let him off the hook, even though she was anxious to catch up with Tom and Matt who were rounding the corner of the building with their flashlights. "Officer Brandt, aren't you outside your jurisdiction out here?"

Brandt took another step back, "Well, I—you see—"

Dana hurried away from him, "Look Brandt, I've got a job to do. Why don't you see if there's a crime scene you can guard." She glanced back at him as she hurried to catch up with Tom and Matt. Brandt was looking at her backside with his head tilted to the side, his mouth hanging open.

Simon observed the exchange between Dana and

Brandt. The younger man's leering expression stirred a level of ire that Simon struggled to contain, "Officer, is there a reason you're staring at my deputy's backside?"

Brandt snapped to attention, "No, sir. I mean," he grinned sheepishly, "I enjoy a good view."

Simon frowned and leaned down until he was inches from Brandt's face, "In my county, that could be easily construed as sexual harassment."

Brandt's eyes popped open wide. "I think I need to check in with my supervisor." He hustled into his cruiser and drove away.

***

Dana caught up with Tom and Matt on the other side of the road. Simon joined them before they plunged into the dried undergrowth.

"Did you find any tracks?" Simon hoped they'd found justification for searching in the neighboring county.

Tom scowled at the ground as he swept it with the beam of his flashlight. "The kids and cowboy boots entered the woods but only cowboy boots came out." *Again.*

Max joined them at the edge of the road. "The Allen county deputies answered the shots fired call and saw the door broken at the Memorial. It looks like the kids made it here and Burt found them."

Simon put a hand on Tom's arm, "Maybe you and Matt should wait here and let Dana and I look for the children."

Tom still studied the foot prints. "I know what you're thinking, but I know my daughter and she and the boys have been tough and resourceful to get this far. I know my daughter is alive. I'm going to find her." He plunged into the woods following Tharon's footprints.

Dana called over her shoulder as she ran, "I'll go with Tom and Matt. Why don't you and Max drive the roads bordering this area and see if you can find Burt Payne? I'll keep in touch and you do the same."

Simon nodded his head and bit his tongue to keep from saying something trite like *be careful* or *stay safe*. He reluctantly returned to his SUV with Max.

Tom trailed the footprints to where the children hid in the bushes then turned west following their path along the tracks. He squatted next to the footprints, dabbed his finger to the ground and examined it under the flashlight.

Dana recognized the now familiar tension in his shoulders, "What is it, Tom?"

He stood and wiped his hands on his handkerchief. He put a hand on Matt's shoulder. "One of the children is bleeding. I'm sorry, Matt, it's Helm."

Matt had to ask, even though he knew the answer. He'd hunted with Tom enough to know his skill as a tracker. "Are you sure?"

"It doesn't look like a lot of blood, but it is Helm." Tom resumed tracking, this time running along the railroad tracks. Every fifty yards or so, he'd stop to make sure he hadn't lost their trail. The sky began to lighten behind them and soon burned with vibrant shades of orange and gold.

Matt's face was hard and grim. He kept pace with Tom and carried the .22 in his hands, as one accustomed to running with a gun.

Dana struggled to keep pace with them. She wondered at their stamina as the light from their flashlights shrank in the distance ahead of her. What kind of background gave farmers and store owners such military-like skills and bearing? She tucked away a mental note to find out when this was all over.

The fickle clouds had wavered between snow and freezing rain all night. At last they made a final decision: snow. Dark, thick clouds poured across the sky dimming the sunrise. Large, heavy, wet snowflakes dropped thickly, shrouding the ground in a blanket of white. Thinking it far better than the freezing rain, Dana tugged the zipper of the down jacket as high up to her throat as it would go and silently sought a blessing on all those who donated the warm clothing to her.

With the stark, white backdrop she easily saw Tom and Matt ahead of her, frantically scanning the ground. She didn't need to be a skilled tracker or even to catch up with them to know what had happened. In the thick carpet of new snow they'd lost the trail.

CHAPTER 25

Deep in the center of the woodlot Tharon cradled Helm's head in her lap as he drifted in and out of consciousness. Kaid helped her make a bed of sorts from leaves covered by the poncho. Once they positioned Helm on it Tharon covered him with an emergency blanket.

Kaid took over cleaning and dressing Helm's wound while Tharon held the small flashlight and tried to keep Helm still. With the strips of fabric from Helm's knees Kaid used one to press on the wound and tied the other around it.

Kaid finished dressing the wound and took the flashlight from Tharon. "I think I've got the bleeding stopped." He played the flashlight beam across Helm's features. "He looks weak."

Tharon gripped one of Helm's hands and felt his face with her other hand. "Kaid, we have to build a fire. I don't think Helm will make it till morning if we don't. Maybe none of us will. It's awfully cold."

"What about Burt?" Kaid looked around fearing he might even now be watching them. "He might see the flames and come after us."

She considered the danger Burt posed but couldn't bear

to see Helm suffering. She remembered Helm holding her and helping her to be strong all day—from helping her breathe in the dark to holding her hand most of the day. There was only one answer for her. "We can vote. I vote to build a fire to help Helm."

Through clenched and chattering teeth Helm managed to say, "No. Not safe."

Kaid only had to hear the weakness in Helm's voice to know Tharon was right. "We build a fire. We live together or we die together. But we don't sit down and freeze tonight. Not after everything else we've done today."

She squeezed Helm's hand, "All for one and one for all. Just like the three musketeers."

She fit an emergency blanket over Helm and listened to Kaid stumbling around the woods breaking twigs and gathering sticks. Her eyes began to make out his form as he moved about even without the flashlight. Dawn must be coming soon.

Her teeth chattered and she felt the damp cold seep into her, but she wasn't worried about her own safety or comfort. Helm's shallow breathing frightened her as much as anything that had frightened her all day. His skin felt cold and clammy to the touch. She gripped his hand, "Helm, can you hear me? If you can hear me, squeeze my hand."

It took a moment for him to process her words; he gave her hand a gentle squeeze.

"That's it. Keep holding my hand and don't let go. Don't you dare let go of me, Helm Harris."

Kaid finished arranging the wood like a teepee, "I've got the matches and the fire is ready but I couldn't find any dry tinder."

Tharon was quiet a moment. There was only one thing she could think of to use. She pulled out the knife, opened the larger blade and pulled down on her braids. After cutting them at chin length, she closed the knife and with tears running down her cheeks, she handed the braids to Kaid, "Use these, they should catch quickly."

Kaid's mouth dropped open as he watched her, then turned his back to start the fire.

She crawled under the blanket and snuggled next to Helm to keep him warm and bury her head in his shoulder.

He touched her cheek and felt her hair, "I can't believe you did that for me."

She found his hand and held it tight, "*I* never stopped being *your* friend." She didn't mean to say it with accusation. Against her will and reason, the hurt in her heart was still raw.

He whispered, "I'm so sorry. Your mom thought we were too old to spend time with you. In my heart, I never stopped caring for you."

She heard the effort it took for him to speak and touched his lips, "Try to rest." She held him close and couldn't help but ask what had been gnawing at her heart for months. "Was it because I'm just a little kid to you?"

He barked a short laugh that turned to a sputtering cough. When he was able to catch his breath he wheezed, "Never. I know you'll grow up eventually," he gave her a playful squeeze. Then with sincerity he said, "The rest of us need to catch up to you. It takes someone very special to come up with something like Operation Secret Santa all on their own."

She heard Kaid strike the match. "I never wanted anyone else to know. It's supposed to be a secret."

His breathing wheezed as he spoke, his breath felt warm against her forehead, "I was picking apples with my parents the first time you talked your dad into letting you climb the trees. That Christmas when you went shopping with your dad, I was in the store. I followed you and heard you tell your dad what you were doing. That was when I started to like you. That was when I knew I wanted to be your friend."

Tharon felt warmth course through her. "You might have known about the apples, but you couldn't know about the gifts when everyone was mean to me because I wore my work boots to school. That was when I started feeling like you were my friends."

He was quiet for so long she thought he'd fallen asleep. When he spoke he whispered in her ear, "I like you more than as a friend. You're the first and last girl I ever want to kiss. If I don't make it—I just wanted you to know."

Kaid whooped, "I did it! We have fire!" Within minutes he had a blaze going that he kept feeding. When his pile of gathered wood was about exhausted he said, "I'm going to get some more wood."

Helm drifted off to sleep. His face felt warmer but his breathing remained shallow.

Snow drifted down on them as the sky lightened and the bright glowing skyline filtered through the trees. Tharon studied the trees and saw one she thought she could climb. By the time Kaid returned with an armload of wood, the sun was up enough to take a good look at Helm.

"I think the bleeding has stopped. That's good," she said.

Snow drifted through the trees, sticking and blanketing the ground. Kaid built the fire back up, "Yeah, but he can't walk and we can't stay here. What can we do?"

She nodded to the tree with low hanging branches, "I could climb up and see if there is anyplace close by where you can go get help. And I can check to see if Burt is around."

Kaid frowned. He took off his hat and scratched his

head. "Okay. I'll give you a boost."

She tucked the blanket around Helm and touched his cheek. As she and Kaid walked to the tree she said, "You have to leave us if Burt shows up. One of us has to tell someone about what we heard." She looked up at the tree at the edge of the woods.

Kaid took her by the shoulders and bent to look in her eyes. Daylight bathed her features. "There is no way I'll leave you and Helm. If only one of us is to survive it has to be you."

She smiled and touched his face, "One of us has to live. You know I'm right. And you know I'll never leave Helm."

He clenched his jaw, "All of us have to live. I won't leave you." He let go of her and interlaced his fingers to boost her up. "We'll talk about it after you take a look around."

CHAPTER 26

Before it disappeared, the children's trail followed the railroad tracks. They decided to continue following the tracks, which veered to the right to skirt around a large section of woods.

Dana ran as fast as the rough ground permitted, but could barely keep up with Matt and Tom. She cursed her short legs as they cleared the far side of the woods and she was still several hundred yards from it. The smell of burning wood slowed her pace.

Dana scanned the landscape. To her left, a half mile or more away, she saw a black car parked along the road with a Fort Wayne Police cruiser behind it. She wondered if Officer Brandt had made himself useful after all.

Smoke drifted up from the woodlot ahead and left of the tracks. As she looked for the source she saw something in the trees. She shook her head in amazement and her heart surged when she saw the waving arm and heard Tharon's faint cries in the distance calling out, "Daddy! Daddy!"

She cupped her hands and yelled, "Tom, there she is! Up in the tree! Do you see her?" Dana left the tracks and headed straight for Tharon and the smoke. Tom and Matt did the same. She was closer and knew she'd reach the children well ahead of the fathers. A wave of anticipation bordering on guarded relief swept over her. But she couldn't shake that unsettling feeling that had plagued her since yesterday. She drew her Sig from her chest holster and spurred forward with a burst of adrenaline.

Dana crashed through the woods and reached the tree just in time to see Kaid catch Tharon when she dropped to the ground. "I'm Deputy Donovan from Whitley County. Where's Helm?"

Tharon pointed through the woods to the smoky fire and ran toward it. She dropped down by Helm, whose face was pasty white. "Helm, help is here. Your dad and my dad will be here any minute."

Helm held her hand in a feeble grasp. "Burt?" he rasped out through cracked lips.

Tharon said, "His car is parked near the end of the woods. There's a police car behind it."

Dana shifted her gun to her left hand. She took out her phone and called Simon, "I'm with the children. Helm is in pretty bad shape, we'll need an ambulance. We're in a woodlot. You should be able to see the column of smoke rising from our position."

"Great news!" The happiness in Simon's voice tugged at her heart, "I see it. Are you secure?

Dana hesitated.

Simon's voice lost the smile. "Dana?"

She spoke out loud to order her thoughts, "Something feels off. I'm not sure—oh, no."

She turned her phone as she spoke to capture for Simon the image of the two men moving toward her. Burt Payne pointed his revolver at the children. Walking in stride with Burt was Officer Brandt. His gun targeted Dana's chest.

Her only concern was for the children. After all they'd endured during the past day; she would not let this be their end. She would not let Tom come into this clearing to find his daughter dead. If talking didn't work, she'd draw both their fire until help arrived. *Please, don't let it be too late.*

"Officer Brandt? What's going on?" As she spoke she positioned herself between the children and the two men. Tharon shielded Helm with her body and Kaid knelt by the fire between Burt and his friends.

Brandt sneered at Dana, "Deputy, I see you found the children. Too bad for you."

Burt's gun hand started to shake, "Deputy? I didn't sign up to kill no cop."

Brandt snapped at the man who was old enough to be his father, "You want to shoot little kids but you don't want to kill an adult cop. Don't you get it? It was a cop you killed yesterday that started this mess. You idiot, you're dumber than that stupid brother of yours." Brandt made a whistling noise when he spoke the s sound.

Tharon and Kaid looked at each other with wide eyes. They recognized the voice of the officer from the dark building.

Burt's voice turned hard. "Nobody talks about my brother like that."

Brandt scoffed, "*Everybody* talks about your brother like that. Now focus. We got orders to take the girl but you can kill the boys."

Tharon stood up and clenched her fists at her side. She yelled angrily, "Who ordered you to take me where?"

Even Dana was stunned by the intensity of her outburst but it gave her the split second distraction she needed to drop her phone and pull her second weapon from the holster at her hip and aim it at Burt. Her movement had the desired effect of both men now aiming their guns at her.

Tharon shouted again, "Who ordered you?"

Dana took a side step away from the children. The guns followed her.

Brandt said, "Kid, shut up and walk over here to me."

Tharon's anger ramped higher, "Or what?"

Dana took another step.

Brandt fired the same instant Dana pulled both triggers.

Brandt took the bullet in the midsection and her other shot grazed Burt's right shoulder.

Burt's bullet went wide but Brandt's hit her hard and she felt like someone punched her in the chest. She flew backwards against a tree with her head snapping back with a thud. She sank to the ground still gripping her guns. Fog crowded at her consciousness and an excruciating pain throbbed on the top of her head.

Burt half hobbled, half ran away toward the road. Dana's bullet threw Brandt flat on his back. He recovered before Dana's head cleared. "You dim wit! Too stupid to notice I'm wearing a bullet proof vest?"

Dana saw two Brandts. She raised her gun to aim between them and laughed, "You think a hick deputy doesn't wear tactical gear?" she hoped she was aiming at him and that he didn't call her bluff.

Shots rang out from her right as two Toms and two Matts ran into the clearing toward the children.

The two Brandts staggered but managed to keep their footing as the bullets hit his vest. He lunged for Tharon to pull her in front of him as hostage and shield.

In the midst of the gunfire, Tharon pulled the knife from her pocket and opened the large blade. When Brandt grabbed her coat, she sliced his gun hand. Blood spurted from his wrist. He let go of his gun and Tharon as he gripped his bleeding wrist.

When the officer dropped his gun, Kaid picked up the

unburned end of a two inch branch from the fire and wacked Brandt in the face and head with the hot embers which also ignited his hair and dropped down inside his shirt and vest.

Brandt dropped to his knees. He screamed in agony as he slapped at his face with his bloody hand and rolled in the leaves.

Tharon grabbed the gun and ran to her father. She hugged Tom and said, "Oh, Daddy! I'm so glad to see you," she handed him the gun then tore from his embrace to run back and drop to her knees next to Helm.

Kaid continued to beat Brandt about the head with the branch until Tom put his hand on Kaid's shoulder and said, "You can stop now, son, I think he's had enough."

Matt Harris knelt next to Helm's other side and targeted his rifle on Brandt. "Helm, wake up. It's Dad, I'm here."

Helm opened his eyes and gave his dad a weak smile and poked the air with his right thumb.

Dana still held her gun poised in the direction of the two Brandts and only relaxed her hand when the double Toms approached her. "I'm really glad you two joined the party," she said. She heard Simon's voice calling her name. Was that her phone or was he nearby? "Simon," she breathed his name as darkness closed around her.

CHAPTER 27

A flurry of reporters, photographers and cameramen greeted the ambulances outside the Whitley County Hospital Emergency Room.

Tom pulled his hat brim low over his eyes and draped his jacket over Tharon's shoulders but she refused to let go of Helm's hand. A photographer captured the image of Tharon and Helm clinging to each other with Kaid's hands on her shoulders. The heart wrenching picture was splashed on the front page of every newspaper in the country and went viral on social media.

Angela Harris's petite frame shouldered a reporter out of her way and rushed to Helm's side as soon as the paramedics lifted him from the ambulance. She gasped at the sight of his pale face.

The paramedics hurried them inside, straight past reception. Marilyn skirted behind the throng and ran to her son. When she reached Kaid she hugged him fiercely.

Before Doc Walker examined anyone he pulled Kaid into his arms and hugged him tight. After a quick check for injuries he tousled his hair and passed him back to Marilyn.

Teams of nurses and doctors spirited each child into an

exam room and worked quickly to assess their condition, warm and clean them. As hands removed her clothing and tucked warm blankets around her, Tharon looked around and wondered why her mother and Maisy weren't there too.

Dana's stretcher wheeled in close behind Helm's. Sheriff Simon Ellis hovered over her. He stepped out as the nurses went to work on warming her and cutting away her clothes. With a quick pat to his pockets, he made sure he'd recovered both guns and all of her bullet clips, badge and phone. He took a moment to seal her phone in an evidence bag.

A reporter and his cameraman forced their way past reception into the ER. A graying woman in her early sixties rushed after them, "You can't go in there. I've called security, you have to leave."

The reporter shoved a microphone into Simon's face, "Sheriff, can we get a statement on the condition of the children. Who found them and was anyone injured? Did you catch the kidnappers?"

Simon struggled to check his fury at the intrusion into the private reunion of the families and the blatant security breach. He was spared having to respond when Nurse Gretchen rushed forward with her hands on her hips.

Gretchen hissed at the newsmen, "If you don't get out of my ER and out of this hospital, I'm going to have the Sheriff arrest you. Then you can ask him all you want from inside the county lockup. For now get out of my ER!"

Gretchen motioned the hospital security guard to escort the reporters back outside.

Simon called his office for Penni to send more deputies to help with security at the hospital. "Dana has a head injury and is still unconscious. One of the children has a bullet wound to the leg but the other two seem relatively unharmed."

"Back up—Dana's still unconscious?" Penni couldn't mask her concern, "How bad is she hurt?"

Simon closed his eyes. "I don't know." He passed his hand over his face and his voice shook a little when he spoke. "What if I lose her?"

He could hear the smile in Penni's voice, "So, you finally opened your eyes. It's about time. She's a tough woman. You're not going to lose her unless you slip back into stupidity. So don't. Call me and let me know when she wakes up."

Tharon's hand stretched out for Helm as they wheeled him into the exam room next to hers. A gasp escaped from her throat when she saw his face even paler; his lips bluer. She couldn't lose him. She just got him back.

A whirl of activity flowed in and out of his room. The cramped space forced his parents to wait outside his room, watching the nurses and doctors work on their son. Angela strangled a sob and buried her face in Matt's chest.

Tharon dangled her legs off the side of the bed and sat up. As she slid to the floor she said, "I need to be with Helm. I'm not hurt."

Tom lifted her back up and covered her with the warm blanket the nurse gave her, "The doctors are helping him now. Let the nurse check you and after the doctor says we can, we'll go see him. I promise."

Reluctantly she let the young nurse named Ellen help her out of her clothes and into a hospital gown. Tharon winced when her socks were peeled off and welcomed the warm blankets tucked snuggly around her.

Nurse Ellen said, "Honey, I'm going to get another nurse to look at your feet. You stay here and I'll be right back."

A nurse with strawberry blond hair entered. Her face was bright with a crooked grin. "Hello, Tharon, I'm Gretchen. I'm just going to take a peek at your feet." She lifted the end of the blanket to examine Tharon's feet. Gretchen blinked rapidly as her eyes glistened with tears.

Tharon's feet were swollen and covered with blisters, several were broken open. She looked straight up at the ceiling without blinking.

Gretchen cleared her throat, "Oh, sweetie, you must have walked a long way. Are you in a lot of pain?"

Tharon kept looking at the ceiling; she gave a quick shake of her head.

"Nurse Ellen will bring you some special medicine to help your feet," To Ellen she said, "The doctor will probably want to keep her in for a day or two for observation and to make sure no infection develops."

Gretchen moved to Tharon's side and patted her arm, "You're a brave girl, but if you are in pain, you need to tell us. You're safe here and we want to help you feel better."

Tharon grabbed her sleeve as she turned to leave, "Can I see Helm yet? How is he?"

Gretchen patted her arm again, "Honey, don't you worry, we're taking good care of him. He's in the room right next door. Give us a few minutes to get him stable and then you can see him, but not until after the doctor sees you." She smiled and left the room.

Doc Walker came around the corner from Helm's room. He spoke to Gretchen, but his voice was too low for Tharon to hear what he said. She noticed the cloud of concern that passed over Gretchen's features.

Tom came back into her room and stood by her bed.

Tharon watched Doc Walker join Angela and Matt. He spoke to them in low tones but Tharon was able to pick out a few words: *knees, infection, septicemia, transfusion, amputation.* She looked up at her father who had been listening too; his face filled with sadness.

Doc touched Angela's arm and said, "He needs you both to be strong for him."

Angela nodded. Matt kept his arm around her shoulder as they entered Helm's room.

Doc washed his hands in the sink by Tharon's bed and said, "Helm and Kaid tell me you were very brave and that it was because of you that the three of you escaped and got rescued," he looked squarely into her eyes. "Thank you doesn't begin to express my gratitude."

Tharon shrugged, "We all saved each other. How's Helm?"

Doc frowned. "You and Kaid did a wonderful job dressing his wounds, but it was very dirty in the woods. I'm afraid Helm has a bad infection and he's lost a lot of blood. We can't risk surgery until he's more stable."

Tharon sat up, "I didn't lose any blood. You can give him some of my blood. I never get sick."

A gleam lit in Doc's eyes but then he shook his head, "You're much too young. I'm certain there will be plenty of blood donors wanting to help Helm."

"I want you to give him my blood," she said firmly.

Tom touched her shoulder, "Honey, you heard Doc. You're too young. I know you don't understand—"

She was adamant, "No, you don't understand. It should have been me that got shot. We were hiding from Burt and I was thinking of Shep and I didn't mean to, but I made a crying sound and Helm squeezed in the bush behind me to comfort me. That bullet should have hit me instead of him."

Doc was deep in thought and seemed to be considering her offer.

Tharon clutched at her father's sleeve. "Daddy, tell him. I never get sick so my blood might help make Helm better."

Doc studied Tharon's face then looked at Tom and shrugged. "It isn't a bad idea." He paced around the small room talking more to himself than to them, "We could try a small fresh whole blood transfusion. It's a proven safe and effective practice in the military. Not enough to endanger Tharon. We can compensate for her loss of fluids with an IV." He tapped his chin with his index finger as he spoke.

He stopped abruptly, enthusiasm in his eyes, "We could try. I promise there'd be no danger to Tharon. And if it doesn't work..." he shrugged his shoulders.

Tom and Doc exchanged a long look, and then Tom nodded his head. "If Doc says it's safe for you, you can donate a small amount."

Tharon relaxed back onto the bed and said, "Good. He'll get better. I know he will. When can I go see him?"

Doc gave her a warm smile and patted her arm, "First let me make certain you are in good enough health to donate. And we'll have to check your blood type and cross match it with Helm's."

Tom smoothed her hair back and kissed her forehead. "You're a remarkable girl."

Doc probed her belly and she winced when he touched the tender place where Everett had kicked her. "How long have you had this pain?"

Tharon glanced at her father, "It happened when I was eight. It hasn't bothered me for a long time but when we were escaping and running it got a little sore."

Doc continued to gently probe her sore rib, "How did it happen?"

Tharon stared up at the ceiling, "Someone kicked me in

the side." As though it made a difference, she repeated, "But it happened a long time ago."

Doc looked from her to Tom. "You should have come to me when it happened," he nodded to Ellen, "I want to get an image of her rib to make sure there's no danger. Then you can bathe her and clean her feet."

The nurse came back in and handed him a small device with a rounded end. Ellen squeezed a small amount of a clear gel onto Tharon's side.

Doc smeared the gel with the smooth rounded end of the device, "This is an ultrasound. It lets me see inside you without opening you up. Just hold still. That's good." The image appeared on the white screen above the bed.

Doc's brow furrowed then smoothed as he watched the screen and moved the device over her rib. "Your rib tip healed crooked. I don't see any immediate need for surgery. There is no sign of internal bleeding. Let me know if it continues to bother you."

The nurse pressed some tissues into her hand and she dried the gel off her ribs, "Do I have to stay in the hospital?"

He examined her hands and feet. He frowned at her white toes and the open blisters. "Any numbness? Can you feel all your toes?" he asked as he touched her feet.

"All but the two middle toes on my right foot," she resumed staring at a fixed spot on the ceiling

Doc raised an eyebrow. "How about pain?"

She wasn't fooling him. "They hurt more now that they are warming up. Please don't keep me away from Helm, he needs me."

Doc shook his head, "I'm going to have the nurse clean your feet and fit you with a special sock. Even when you walk it takes all pressure off your feet and we can control the temperature so your feet will re-warm without too much pain. They look like duck feet. We call them happy feet. Once we get you and Kaid fitted with them, you can visit Helm and I'll set up a small direct transfusion."

He moved back to her side and patted her arm. "I want you and Kaid to stay in the hospital for a day or two, until I'm sure your feet are healing and there are no other complications. We can put you near your mother's room, if you want."

"Why is Mom in the hospital?" Tharon looked from Doc to her father.

Tom gripped her hand. "Mommy's here because—"

"The baby died, didn't it?" she said softly. Tears welled in her eyes.

Tom smoothed her hair back, "Yes. I'm sorry to give you bad news."

"Oh, Daddy, I'm sorry too." Tears spilled down her cheeks. The last time she saw her mother, she was angry with her. Did she cause the baby to die? She cried for the unborn child; for her parents; for her own loss of the brother or sister she'd been so excited to love.

CHAPTER 28

Max showed his badge and passed through security. He paused outside Dana's ER room to ask Simon "Is she awake yet?"

Simon shook his head and folded his arms. "No. Doc called in a neurologist to take a look at her. He asked me her history. I haven't a clue if she's ever had a head injury before." He scratched his jaw, "Did you know she listed me as her emergency contact?"

Max raised an eyebrow, creating a wrinkled arch in his forehead, "I'm sure that's because she's got no family. She's practically married to her job, so I guess that would make you her next of kin."

Simon's head snapped up, "You think that's all it is?"

Max rested his hand on Simon's shoulder, "My friend, the only two people who didn't know how you felt about each other was you and Dana. Of course that's not all it is. She's crazy about you. And we all think pretty highly of her, so don't hurt her."

Simon leaned against the door frame again, "I don't intend to. Where's Brandt?"

"He's in surgery at St. Joe Hospital, getting his wrist and shoulder sewn up. His face and neck got burned pretty badly so he'll end up in the burn unit." He grinned and shook his head, "I wish I could have seen Dana and those kids take him out."

Simon frowned. When Dana dropped her phone it landed at an angle that he saw her get shot. He tried to scrub the image from his mind. "Any word on Burt Payne or the third man?"

Max scrunched his weathered face as he surveyed the bustle of the ER. "Still not in custody. Burt must have hidden near the road and left right after we entered the woods. The third man is Marty Phillips. His prints were found at the shop where the children were held captive. Detective Bohman thinks it was his blood inside the door. The gun that killed the lady near the trail matched the one that killed our victim and the Trace's dog yesterday morning."

Kaid overheard them from the room next to Dana. He poked his head out from behind the curtain of his exam room. Wrapped in a warm blanket, he padded out to them wearing thick webbed socks on his feet. "That's because Burt shot the man by the creek and he shot the lady and her dog, too. She didn't tell him that she saw us. If she had, he would have killed us there by the river. She helped save us," his voice cracked with emotion.

Marilyn tried in vain to get Kaid to lie back down.

Max and Simon looked at Kaid. Max's voice was gentle when he asked, "You saw him shoot her?"

Kaid thought a moment. "I saw Burt turn the corner in his car a few streets away. We scrambled down the bank and held onto some trees. The lady recognized Burt. I heard her call him Burt Payne. Then he told her he was sorry and he shot her and her dog. One of the bullets hit the tree I was hanging on and I slipped and almost fell into the river. Helm caught me and when he started to slip,

Tharon grabbed him. We managed to get back up to the trail after Burt drove away. After that we were afraid to ask anyone else for help."

Max swallowed a lump in his throat.

"Thank you," Simon said gently. "You and your friends have been very brave and your information will put Burt away for a long time."

Tom and Tharon walked out of her exam room. Her feet were wrapped in the same bubble-like footwear as Kaid. She saw Kaid talking to the Sheriff and said something to her father before she walked over to Kaid. "Did you tell him yet?"

Kaid shook his head, "I wasn't sure who to tell."

Tharon turned to Max and Simon. "How long have you been in the Sheriff's department?"

Simon looked at her with a puzzled expression, "Fourteen years, but I've only been Sheriff the last six years."

Max said, "Twenty-five years. Why do you ask?"

Tharon and Kaid looked at each other and nodded. Tharon looked around nervously to see if anyone was listening. An orderly stood counting and recounting things on a cart; a man from housekeeping paused his mopping to watch them.

Simon noticed her hesitation and the way both she and Kaid looked nervously around. "Why don't you both come in here and we can shut the door to talk." He ushered them into Dana's room.

Tharon breathed a sigh of relief as she took her father's hand and pulled him into the room with her.

Kaid turned to his mother, "I'll be back out in a minute." She opened her mouth to protest but he shut the door behind him before she could say anything.

Simon pulled up a chair and a stool for the children to

sit on and said, "What did you want to tell us?"

Tharon exchanged a worried look with Kaid. She turned to the Sheriff, "Before we escaped we heard Burt and Marty talking to that officer who I cut. We recognized his voice in the woods. They said that they were going to take our school bus hostage. They were going to claim the people wanting to secede were behind it."

Kaid nodded his head. "Yeah, but it's supposed to be a trick. The government is behind the kidnapping and they want to make it look like they're coming to the rescue, but it's just an excuse to keep Indiana from succeeding."

Tharon corrected him, "No, from 'seceding', from leaving the Union." She looked the Sheriff square in the eyes, "They said President Hamron wants to make an example of Indiana and that he will make Indiana the first police state. That man that we saw Burt kill was some kind of police spy. They were trying to stop him from telling about the hostage plan."

Simon weighed what they were telling him. The representative from the governor had told him an invasion was coming but the hostage plan was new information. Silar hadn't been able to let authorities know any details of the plan. "Did they say anything about when the invasion is to happen?"

Kaid snorted, "Yeah, Thanksgiving is when Hamron wants to invade. I guess he wants us to be thankful he comes to save us."

Tharon leaned forward and said, "Officer Brandt said if word got out about the hostage plan that they'd go to plan B. He said a lot of their own people would die with that plan."

Simon squatted down in front of them, "Did they say anything more about this other plan?"

Tharon and Kaid looked at each other and shook their

heads.

A worried look crossed Simon's face, "Did they know you heard them talking?"

Tharon shook her head, "I don't think so. We escaped right after that. But Officer Brandt and Burt were talking about it in the woods."

Simon scratched his chin, "I heard that much over Deputy Donovan's phone." He stooped to eye level with them. "You children have done a great thing in giving us this message. You may have saved a lot of lives. But I'm afraid if people know you told us you might be in greater danger. Will you trust me to notify the people who need to know?"

Tharon looked up at her father who nodded his head. "Okay." She looked up at her father again, then back to the Sheriff. "Did you find Burt and Marty yet?"

Simon touched her shoulder, "Not yet, but we have all of law enforcement focused on finding them."

"That might not be enough." Tharon held the Sheriff's gaze, "That Officer Brandt said they've spent ten years putting their people in every level of law enforcement and government. That's why we wanted to know how long you worked here."

Kaid's eyes got big and he whispered to Tharon, "What if they recruited people who worked there longer too?"

A suspicious expression clouded her features. She looked the Sheriff square in the eyes. "How do we know we can trust you?"

"You can trust him," Dana said in a weak voice. "I swear to you on my life he can be trusted."

Simon spun around and with a sigh of relief said, "You're awake," he stood next to the bed and took her hand. "You had me worried."

While Dana had the adults' attention, Kaid whispered,

"Should we tell them about someone wanting to take you?"

Tharon shook her head and whispered, "I think they heard that in the woods."

Tom opened the door and motioned for Tharon and Kaid to follow him, "Come on, Helm's waiting for you."

Kaid touched Tharon's shoulder as they left the room, "Have you been crying?"

She shrugged, "A little. My mom's baby died. She's here in the hospital."

Kaid gripped her hand. "I'm sorry."

"Let's not tell Helm. He needs to get stronger and I don't think me crying will help him."

"Unless he's really out of it, he'll know something's wrong. You just watch." He nudged her with his elbow, "You know I'm your friend too, don't you?"

Tharon gave him a light punch on the shoulder. "I guess. I missed you, jerk. Don't ever dump me like that again."

He said in a serious tone, "I won't. I promise. I'll always be your friend."

She smiled, "Me too."

Together they said, "All for one and one for all."

Max nodded to Tom and watched Tharon and Kaid as Tom took them to Helm's room. Max shook his head and muttered, "I don't know whether to be impressed with how calm they are after what they've been through, or worried that they're not more upset."

"I think they are three incredibly resourceful, brave children." Simon said, "Call Penni and have her get Murphy and Jackman down here to help guard these kids—and make sure Fort Wayne has a guard on Brandt." He clenched his jaw, "I don't want anything to happen to him before we get a chance to question him."

"If what those kids said is true," Max raised an eyebrow

to Simon, "how do we know who to trust?"

"We don't. We'll just have to keep our eyes open." Simon watched Dana's features go slack. He pressed the call button and held her hand. He sighed when he felt her pulse. "We can't let distrust and suspicion cripple us. One thing we'll do for sure is get the word out that we know about the hostage plan. That should at the very least discourage them from endangering children. We'll just have to make sure we're ready for whatever else they may have planned."

CHAPTER 29

Matt pulled the curtains back and made room for Kaid and Tharon. Marilyn pushed a wheelchair into the room but Tharon and Kaid stood next to the bed.

Helm lifted his head off the pillow. His skin still looked pasty and he had dark circles under his eyes but his smile made it all the way to his eyes. "Hey, are you guys okay? My dad told me what you did for me. Thanks. I guess I was pretty out of it."

"We're okay, we just got these cool duck feet now," said Kaid, slapping his feet on the floor.

Tharon drew her blanket around her shoulders and stood next to Helm. "I'm so sorry you got shot. That should have been me. If I hadn't almost cried—"

Helm tried to reach for her hand. She saw how weak he was and closed her hand around his.

Helm squeezed her hand weakly and said, "I think the only thing worse than getting shot would have been seeing you get shot."

She thought for a moment, "I guess it would have been better if Kaid was the one who got shot."

After a moment of stunned silence the three burst into laughter. Helm's chuckle turned into a cough that wracked his body and left him gasping for air.

Nurse Ellen put some oxygen tubes in his nostrils. "This will help him breathe better."

Tharon and Kaid stopped laughing and drew closer to his side. Tharon drew his hand to her and laid her other hand on his chest, "Breathe with me. Slow and steady."

Helm locked eyes with her and, except for a few mild coughs, matched Tharon's breathing. "Thanks. That helps a lot."

When Helm calmed his breathing, Kaid said, "That was a funny joke, Tharon."

Tharon gave him a teasing smile, "Who said I was joking?"

They all grinned but tried not to trigger another fit of coughing from Helm.

Helm studied Tharon's face, even after the laughter; he saw the trace of sadness in her eyes. "You've been crying. What's wrong?"

Kaid nudged Tharon with his elbow. "Told you."

Tharon tried to brush him off, "It's nothing for you to worry about. Doc said you need to get strong for surgery."

"Just tell me or I'll worry even more."

Tharon took a deep breath, saying it was even harder than hearing the news and she was surprised it was more difficult to tell Helm than Kaid. Her voice broke with emotion as she spoke, "My mom's in the hospital. Her baby died."

He gripped her hand weakly and said, "I'm so sorry. This isn't a very happy birthday, is it?"

She shook her head and gave him a bleak smile. "I forgot it was my birthday. You know what that means? We're the same age now."

Helm coughed again. When he caught his breath he said, "Only until January ninth, then I'll be a year older than you again."

Nurse Ellen and Doc Walker came back into the room. Nurse Ellen spoke quietly to Tom, Matt and Angela and had each of them sign the consent for the transfusion on the electronic tablet she showed them. She lifted the blanket to check Helm's legs. Angry red spokes radiated from his knees. His legs showed marked signs of swelling.

Doc put his hands on Tharon's shoulders, "Are you sure you want to do this?"

She glimpsed the marks on Helm's legs and nodded her head.

Helm lifted his head off the pillow. "What is she going to do?"

Matt and Angela stood on the other side of the bed.

Doc said, "Helm, you need a blood transfusion and Tharon insists on giving you some of hers. We checked both your blood types and Tharon can donate some blood to help you get strong enough for surgery."

Helm looked from Doc to Tharon and back to Doc, "Will it hurt her?"

Doc patted his arm, "No. We are only going to take a little and she'll be just fine."

CHAPTER 30

"Dana, wake up. Can you hear me?" Gretchen snapped her fingers by Dana's ear.

Dana wrinkled her brow and blinked at the bright lights. "Gretchen, is that you?"

Gretchen sighed and with a lopsided grin said, "Yes. You had us pretty worried, kiddo. Glad to see you coming around."

Dana blinked and tried to lift her head but a neck brace immobilized her and a blinding headache for such minimal effort, made her sink back onto the exam table. "How are the children?"

Gretchen gathered up the clothing that had been cut off Dana, "As soon as I throw this stuff away, I'll find out. Right now, there's someone who's been anxious to talk to you."

Dana closed her eyes.

Gretchen snapped her fingers again, "Stay awake. You have a concussion and you are not allowed to go back to sleep. Understand?"

Afraid to try another head nod, she gave Gretchen the thumbs up sign.

Gretchen pulled the curtain aside to reveal Simon who

stood at the foot of the bed.

He pulled a stool up next to her and took her hand. "You scared the daylights out of me. When I saw Brandt shoot you, I nearly lost my mind."

Dana squeezed his hand, "Children?"

Typical Dana Donovan—barely conscious and her first concern is the welfare of others. Simon ran his free hand over his short cropped blond hair, "The Walker boy and Trace girl—,"

She gave him a wry look, "Kaid and Tharon."

Simon remembered their promise to treat the families as friends, "Right. Kaid and Tharon are in pretty good shape physically. Their feet are pretty raw. Maybe a little frostbite but from what I've been told, neither will lose any fingers or toes."

"What about Helm?" she hadn't seen Helm move or say anything in the woods and she braced herself for bad news.

Simon held her hand with both of his. "He took a bullet to the back of his leg. They're trying to get him stabilized for surgery. He lost a lot of blood and I heard Doc say he's septic. Plus his core temperature is pretty low. They put a call out for his blood type and there's a line a block long of donors. Guess who was first in line?"

"Tharon," Dana said with a smile.

Simon tilted his head at her, "How could you know that?"

She took a deep breath and let it out slow. "I saw how she looked at him. She looked at him the way you've been looking at me."

He raised an eyebrow and looked thoughtful, "Is she thinking about all the paperwork involved if he died?"

Dana raised an eyebrow in return, "You know if you want an out, I won't hassle you."

Simon leaned over and whispered in her ear, "I want all

the hassle you've got in you," he kissed her ear; her forehead; her cheek; her lips.

Gretchen rushed into the room and turned the sound off on the rapidly beeping heart monitor. "Sheriff, can you restrain yourself, please?" her tone was more amused than angry.

Dana blushed and brought the subject back to their jobs, "What happened with Brandt?"

Simon sat back on the stool but kept holding her hand. "He's in surgery in Fort Wayne. Some hot embers dropped down his shirt and burned his clothes and skin under his vest. Those kids did a pretty good number on him. He darn near bled out at the scene. Swore he'd cooperate if we helped him. So we helped him. Well, the others helped him. I was prepared to let him bleed out."

Gretchen checked Dana's vitals and shined a small light in her pupils, "The doctor said she's to be kept calm." She scolded Simon, "Don't you think she's done enough for the day?"

Dana raised her index finger, "Just one more question: Did you get Burt Payne?"

Simon shook his head, "He slipped past us when we ran into the woods after you and the kids."

A petite blond bubbled into the room. She was decked out in high heels, pearls, and round dark-rimmed glasses that made her look like a giant insect. Her chin length brown hair was both practical and stylish.

Without any obvious movement she wedged Simon out of her way and loosened the neck brace. "Dana, I'm Dr. Goodwin. I'm glad to see you awake, young lady. Your x-ray looks good so we can take this neck brace off. Your partner here didn't know if you have any history of head trauma. Can you fill in the blanks for me?"

"Um, when I was a child I got into a fight with a bully

and he slammed the back of my head against the concrete. I had a pretty bad concussion. My parents told me I was unconscious for a day."

Dr. Goodwin checked her pupils with a pen flashlight. "Anything else?"

Dana shook her head and moaned at the throbbing pain.

The tiny doctor clicked her heel and frowned at Dana. "Who do you have at home with you?" she glanced over her shoulder at Simon and arched her eyebrows.

Before Dana could answer, Simon said, "She has me."

Dr. Goodwin turned back to Dana and clicked her heel again. "Good to know. That being said, I still want you to stay in the hospital overnight. We'll see how you are tomorrow and if you don't show any complications, I'll let you go home, with specific restrictions and the understanding you are to call me night or day if any symptoms arise."

Dr. Goodwin stepped into the corner of the room to talk to Gretchen in hushed tones and key instructions into her tablet.

Dana pushed the button to raise the head of her bed. She looked past her toes across the ER bay to Helm's room. She wrinkled her brow when she saw Doc monitoring the transfusion. Tom stood next to Tharon who sat on a tall stool beside the bed. She held Helm's hand.

Marilyn hovered near the door to Helm's room behind a wheelchair holding a sleeping Kaid.

A thick voice boomed from the entrance to the ER. "Everybody listen or this granny will be dead." Burt's gritty drawl silenced the ER. The only sounds came from the beeping monitors.

Simon fished in his pocket and slipped one of Dana's guns under her blanket before he moved to the doorway and peered around the corner.

Dana closed her hand around the familiar handle of her Glock and clicked off the safety. The lazy drawl of the voice sent chills down her spine. She looked at the exam room across from her and saw the fear on Tharon's face which confirmed she was right—Burt Payne had forced his way into the ER.

Dana saw Doc remove the tubing from Tharon's port. He pulled a vial from his pocket which he filled with her blood and pocketed before removing the needle from her arm.

Burt's voice drawled, "You, big man by the door, move out here to the far end of the room."

Simon moved out into the ER bay, drawing Burt's attention away from Dana.

Dana slowly eased her feet over the side of the bed and sat up. Gretchen and Dr. Goodwin opened their mouths to chastise her. She held her index finger to her lips with a stern warning look that hurt her head to make, but forced silence on the two women.

She pulled the monitor leads from her chest and silently dropped to the floor. She pressed around the end of the bed to the far edge of the door frame, carefully staying hidden. Across the room, Tharon crouched behind her father. She took Tom's gun from his shoulder holster, and placed it into his hand.

Tom readied his gun at the side of the bed; he made eye contact with Dana and gave her a slight nod.

Burt eased further into the ER. He dragged the grandmotherly receptionist, with one arm around her neck and the other hand holding a gun to her temple. Blood trailed down his right arm and his voice slurred when he spoke. "Them dang brats are the reason my brother's dead and my life's ruined. Ten years it took us to set things up.

Ten years and they screw it all to heck in one day! Either them or me is dying today."

Tharon's clear voice rang through the beeping monitors, "I'm sorry about Marty killing Carl. Carl was nice."

Burt wrinkled his brow in confusion and sadness. He glanced at Tharon peering at him from behind Tom. His features got hard as he tightened his hold on the receptionist. "Carl was a stupid idiot. He was soft. He let some doe-eyed brat get him killed. If anyone's dying here today, it's you, brat.

The receptionist's arms went limp and her eyes rolled upward. As she sagged to the floor Burt lost his grip on her and the barrel of his gun pointed harmlessly at the ceiling.

Dana raised her gun and Burt turned his gun on her.

Three shots rang out. Tom's bullet ripped into Burt's chest, and Dana's hit him in the forehead. Burt's bullet hit Dana in the right shoulder. She fell backwards onto the bed, wondering if she or Tom killed Burt. Either shot looked fatal.

Time seemed to slow down as she slid to the floor. Gretchen and Dr. Goodwin lifted her onto the bed. She was surprised how strong the little woman was. Simon hovered over her. She stared at his mouth trying to make out his words. Her shoulder burned like fire. What was Simon saying?

Doc Walker ripped the gown away and started working on her shoulder. "Who's the surgeon on call today?"

"Dr. Anderson," Gretchen replied.

Doc barked, "Have him meet you in the OR." He patted Dana's hand, "You're going to be just fine. He's an excellent surgeon."

She blinked and finally made out Simon's words, "Dana, hang on. Do you hear me? Don't let go. Don't you dare leave me." He kissed her lightly on the forehead.

She smiled and in a weak voice said, "What a girl has to do to get your attention."

Gretchen elbowed Simon out of the way. Wheels rolled into the room and someone counted to three. She felt her body slide onto a narrow gurney. Rails locked in place at her sides. Someone poked a needle into the hand Simon had been holding.

"Let's get her to surgery," Dr. Goodwin said.

She passed worried faces: Simon, Max, Tom. As though she was tuned to Tharon's voice, she heard her asking Tom, "Will she be alright, Daddy? She saved us twice today."

Tom's answer touched her heart, "She's a strong woman so I'm sure she will, but it might help if we prayed for her too."

Dana closed her eyes thinking *no one has ever prayed for me before—not even me. Maybe it's time I start.*

***

After thirty minutes the ER returned to its normal level of chaos. Doc entered Helm's room and was amazed at how much color had returned to his face. He lifted the blanket from Helm's legs. The angry lines already faded to a pale pink.

He patted Angela's shoulder. "He's going to be fine. We'll check his blood work again in an hour and as soon as he's in the normal range we'll get him into surgery."

Angela breathed a sigh of relief. She and Matt stood next to the bed and hugged each other.

Helm woke up, "Is Tharon okay?"

Doc smiled, "Yes, yes. She's just fine. She keeps asking about you. She'll be glad to know you're awake. You try to rest and we'll get that bullet out of you as soon as we can."

As Doc Walker left the room he patted the vial in his pocket and smiled.

CHAPTER 31

November 11, 2056

The sun streamed in through the hospital window and warmed Dana's face. She pressed her eyelids closed against the brightness and turned her head. The dull headache was at least tolerable compared to the pain from before...before what? What was the last thing she remembered? Simon. His worried face hovered over her because...she'd been shot.

Someone mopped the far end of the corridor outside the open door. The rhythmic swishing of the mop, the smell of disinfectant and the soft shuffle of feet helped her orient herself. She wasn't out in the cold trailing children; she was in a warm clean hospital.

And she'd been shot. Again.

She opened her eyes and looked around the room. An enormous arrangement of red roses and small white chrysanthemums filled a cart near the window.

Simon sat in a chair by her bed. His head drooped forward and his soft snoring made her smile. Her right arm lay at her side with the palm facing up; his left hand covered her palm. She watched him for a few glorious moments. His strong, usually clean shaven jaw bore at least two days of stubble. His close-cropped blond hair sported a higher hairline than when she'd joined his department. His broad shoulders tapered to the slight love handles at his waist. She squeezed his hand.

He took a deep waking breath and sat up, blinking, "You're awake. How are you feeling?" He reached for the call button and pressed it.

She tried to speak but her throat hurt; her mouth felt like it was filled with cotton; her lips were cracked and dry.

Simon filled a plastic cup with ice water from the pitcher on her tray. He stuck a straw in the cup and held it to her lips.

The cool liquid felt good on her throat. She tried to sit up, but winced from the pain in her shoulder and head and lay back down. In a husky voice she asked, "Children?"

Simon smiled and pressed the control to lift the head of the bed. "They're fine, thanks to you." He sat back down and took her hand again.

"How long?" her voice croaked and she swallowed again.

"You've been asleep for twenty hours. I was starting to get worried," he squeezed her hand again.

She smiled and whispered, "I thought your snores sounded concerned."

Simon lifted her hand and kissed her palm. "So I snore. Is that something you could live with?"

She touched the side of his face with her palm and in a husky whisper said, "It's something I can't live without."

Happy tears welled in the corners of her eyes as Simon leaned in to kiss her.

Right before their lips touched the nurse burst into the

room, "Good, you're awake."

If there had been a loaded bedpan nearby, Dana would have hurled it at her.

The short and solid nurse changed the IV bag, took a year to adjust the flow and another ten years to explain how to use the call buttons and which button to push to get more morphine.

When the nurse finally left, Simon leaned toward her again. This time their lips barely touched when there was a soft knock on the open door. Dana moaned.

Simon sat back and said, "Come in."

Tom supported Lista's arm and pushed her IV pole as they walked, Maisy and Tharon followed them into the room. Tharon rushed to Dana's side, "Thank you for saving us. I'm sorry you got hurt."

Dana nodded her head and squeezed Tharon's hand. In a hoarse whisper, she said, "I'm so glad you like to climb trees. I hate to think what might have happened if I hadn't seen you and reached you when I did."

Lista smiled warmly at her, "Tom told me how much you helped him, and how you saved Tharon. We can't begin to express how deeply grateful we are to you."

Dana looked from Tom to Lista and said, "I'm glad I could help. I'm so sorry about your baby."

Both Dana and Lista's eyes glistened.

Simon broke the uncomfortable silence. "We just got engaged. At least I think that's what we agreed." He cast a worried look at Dana who smiled and nodded in agreement.

Tom shook Simon's hand and Lista expressed her congratulations to them both. Lista detected the looks between Dana and Simon. "Oh, my. We're interrupting them. We need to get going but we want to invite both of you to Thanksgiving dinner with us. Please let us know when the wedding is. We'd love to be there if it's not intruding."

"I was thinking this Saturday, if she feels up to it," he looked at Dana who nodded in agreement, tears of joy now streaming down her face.

Lista herded her family out of the room. "Dana, I'm at the other end of the hall. Perhaps we can make a few laps together when you feel up to it. And if you don't have a church, we have a lovely chapel in Sandy Creek. Maisy and I would be thrilled to help with the arrangements."

Simon said, "That'd be kind of you. Neither of us has any family left." He again looked to Dana who nodded in agreement.

Tom shook his hand again, "Oh, yes, you do. You're part of our family now."

Maisy and Tharon clapped their hands together and smiled with excitement lighting up their eyes.

Dana said, "Be careful of the wet floors. I heard someone mopping."

Tom looked puzzled and stuck his head out of the door. "That's odd. The mop and bucket are in the middle of the hall but there's no one around."

Dana grabbed Simon's hand, "The third kidnapper."

Tharon gasped and backed away from the door. "You mean Marty?"

Dana tried to get up.

Simon pulled one of her guns from the pocket of his coat which was slung over the back of the chair and gave it to her. He said, "You ladies and Tharon stay with Dana. Tom, let's check the boys."

Dana pulled the leads off her chest and wheeled the IV pump to the doorway to take position between the women and the hall. She leaned on the door frame for support.

Simon and Tom re-emerged from Kaid and Helm's

room with Matt Harris. "The boys are fine," Simon said. "I'll check with security. I wish I had a description of the guy."

Tharon peeked around the corner. "Marty has stringy chin length brown hair. He's a little shorter than my dad but is real skinny. His eyes are light gray and he has a new cut on his face from next to his eye down to his jaw." She drew the cut on her own face with her finger.

Simon asked, "Did you see him here in the hospital?"

She shook her head, "No. That's what he looked like the last time I saw him."

"How do you know the cut on his face is new?" Simon asked.

Tharon looked sheepishly from her mother to her father, "Because I cut him when he was trying to catch me to cut my tongue out."

Lista's hand flew to her mouth in horror.

Tom touched his daughter's shoulder and said gently, "How did it happen?"

Tharon tried not to look in his eyes but he tipped her chin up and she had no choice. "Kaid and Helm were pulling me out of the opening in the door. Marty was pulling me back in. I forgot I had Helm's pocket knife in my hand and when I hit at Marty's face, I cut him. I didn't mean to."

Tom kissed her forehead, "You didn't do anything wrong. Sometimes you have to fight and this was the right time for it. You did good."

"Thank you, Tharon," Simon said. "With that description, it will be a lot easier to find him." He pulled out his radio and gave the description and instructed that Max be contacted and search area doctors and hospitals for anyone treated for a facial laceration.

A short man in his late fifties got off the elevator. He

ambled down the hallway to the mop and bucket and resumed mopping.

Simon barked at him, "Were you mopping here earlier?"

The housekeeper swallowed hard, "Yes, sir."

"Why did you leave the bucket in the middle of the hall unattended?"

The man swallowed and had a guilty look on his face. He said in a low voice, "Please, don't report me. I need this job. I know it's supposed to be a smoke free campus but I've been smoking since I was a kid and can't seem to break the habit. I ran to the woods and had a quick smoke. Please don't tell."

Simon and the others breathed a sigh of relief. Simon grumbled, "Just don't let it happen again. It's not safe to leave a bucket and mop out like that."

Tom and his family left the room and Simon helped Dana back to bed. As she lay down he took her gun and put it in the bedside table.

She blushed, "Sorry about the false alarm. I guess I'm paranoid."

A wide grin spread across his face, "No problem. It's better to be too careful. Besides, I enjoyed the view."

She eased back onto the pillow, "What view?"

He leaned over her and touched the side of her face. "Your gown was open in the back."

Her eyes opened wide and her lips parted but before she could say anything he smothered her mouth with a deep passionate kiss.

The nurse came in and tried to interrupt them with a loud *Ahem* sound but Dana held up the index finger from her good hand before she wrapped her good arm around Simon and pulled him closer.

CHAPTER 32

November 12, 2056

Dr. Anderson studied his tablet at the nurse's station. "These results can't be accurate. Run the blood panels again. I've never heard of anyone recovering this quickly from septicemia." Dr. Anderson entered his orders on the tablet. He muttered to himself, "Either this is a miracle or Walker misdiagnosed him in the first place. And I don't believe in miracles."

✦✦✦

Sunday afternoon, Dr. Anderson spoke to Angela and Matt outside the hospital room. "I can't explain it. I've had his blood work repeated three times in the past twenty-four hours and there's no sign of infection and his wounds are healing more rapidly than I've ever seen. His rate of recovery is nothing short of miraculous, and believe me, I don't use that term lightly."

Dr. Anderson folded his arms. "I can't justify keeping

him in the hospital after tomorrow but I'd like you to bring him in to see me toward the end of the week, sooner if you detect any signs of infection or he starts running a fever. The pharmacy will have a pain prescription for you to pick up before you leave. It might make him drowsy. And regardless of the results, I still want him to complete the full course of antibiotics as well."

Angela looked into the room where Helm and Tharon sat side by side on the bed with the head raised as high as it would go. Helm read a book out loud to her while she rested her head on his shoulder. "What about Tharon? Is she going home too?"

Dr. Anderson frowned, "I don't see why not. But that will be up to Dr. Walker. He's rather proprietary when it comes to her care."

CHAPTER 33

November 14, 2056

Dana and Lista took turns walking to each other's room several times a day and quickly developed a strong friendship. This was a new experience for Dana who had been so absorbed with her job that she had no close friends in the area.

On Tuesday morning Dana walked to Lista's room. "Care to join me for a race around the hallway?"

Lista edged her feet off the bed and into her fuzzy slippers. She sat for a moment to let a wave of dizziness subside. "You're on, but I don't think I'll be giving you much competition today. I didn't sleep well last night."

They shuffled down the hallway, each woman pushing her IV pole by her side. Dana felt well enough to move at a brisker pace but she sensed Lista needed to take things slower so she let her new friend set the pace.

Dana was nervous but also desperate, "Were you serious about helping me plan the wedding?"

Lista's face lit up. "Oh, yes. Please let me help. I so

need something positive to occupy my thoughts."

The tension eased from Dana's shoulders. "Do you think Saturday is too soon to get married?"

Lista observed her worried expression. "How long have you and Simon been dating?"

Dana shook her head, "That's just it. We've never dated. We've worked together for four years, but we've never dated." She looked sideways at Lista, "How long did you and Tom date before you got married?"

Lista chuckled, "Oh my goodness, don't make any decisions based on our marriage."

Dana persisted, "How long did you date?"

Lista stopped and tilted her head to the side, "You know we never have been on a date. We'd known each other two weeks when we got married."

Dana's mouth dropped open, "Two weeks?"

Lista patted her arm, "You can't measure love by time. How long have you loved Simon?"

Dana thought for a moment, "That's hard to say. I guess I started loving him soon after we met. He was so devastated by losing his wife and daughters to the pandemic—I think he'll always grieve for them."

Lista smiled and nodded her head, "It's good that he's opened his heart to love again. He's probably been in love with you for a long time too, but felt he was betraying his first wife by having feelings for you."

They reached the end of the hallway and made a wide u-turn with their IV poles. Dana was thoughtful, "So you don't think we're being reckless by getting married so soon?"

Lista thought a moment and studied Dana's concerned expression. "If you know you love someone, you'd be reckless not to marry and spend as much of this life together as you can."

Tension drained from Dana's face, "Thank you. That eases my mind." She thought a moment and said, "I just have two requests for the wedding. I was wondering if Kaid and Helm could be our ring bearers and if Tharon could be my flower girl. I know they're a bit old for it, but I don't have any family and the only friends I have are from work. Not to diminish what the children went through, but if it wasn't for them, I don't know if Simon would have ever admitted his feelings for me."

Lista's face broke into a wide grin, "I know Tharon will be thrilled and I'll talk to the other mothers. What else do you need?"

Dana's face felt hot and she knew it was turning all shades of red. "I know I'm a cop and I could get married in my uniform, but I was wondering if you have a dress I could borrow. It wouldn't have to be white, it's just that, well, even though I carry a gun and Simon knows all my rough edges, I want to look and feel more feminine when we exchange our vows. Does that sound vain?" She released an exasperated sigh, "I don't even own a dress."

"Of course that's not vain. What size do you wear?"

Dana shrugged her shoulders then winced at the pain the movement caused to her wound. "I think I'm a size four."

Lista appraised Dana's size. She was taller and slimmer than Lista. A few women close to her size came to her mind, "You leave it to me. Even if Maisy and I have to make one, you'll have a dress to wear for your wedding."

Dana's gratitude was genuine. "Thank you. You don't know how much this means to me."

Lista touched her arm, "What are friends for anyway?"

"This is all new to me," Dana shook her head. "Outside of work, you're the first real friend I've made here."

Lista's eyes glistened. "I'll do my best to be a good one then."

They were almost back to Lista's room when Dana shook her head and said, "Two weeks?"

CHAPTER 34

November 16, 2056

Lista went home Wednesday morning and, in spite of Maisy's near constant hovering, both women relished diving into the wedding preparations.

Thursday morning they still had not found a suitable dress. While Lista reached out to everyone she knew to find someone who might have a dress or an old wedding gown that would fit Dana, Maisy drove into Sandy Creek on a mission. She circled the block past Lucy Stephen's house to check for their private signal: the blinds over the kitchen sink were open Lucy was alone. Maisy parked around the corner and walked down the alley to the backyard gate.

Lucy waited for her by the back door. When she ushered her friend inside she threw her arms around her and said, "I thought you'd never come. I've been watching for you for two days. Have you found a dress yet?"

The spark in Lucy's eyes warmed Maisy's heart. "No, that's why I'm here. Our brave officer is a size four. It seems to me I recall another blushing bride who wore that size."

Even the light in Lucy's eyes couldn't mask her ashen skin tones or hide the toll the treatments took on her energy. "Oh, it's been many years since I was a size four," she poked a withered finger skyward, "Fortunately the dress hasn't changed with my figure. I'm afraid I'm going to have to impose on you to dig it out of the attic and have it cleaned and pressed."

Maisy clapped her hands, "This will be such a treat for Dana." She saw the struggle her friend was having standing. "Why don't you go sit down in the living room and I'll make us some tea."

"That would be lovely." Lucy made her way to a cushioned rocker in the living room, leaning for support on every counter, chair and door frame along the way. She eased herself into the chair with a sigh. "Having Dana wear my dress will be a treat for me and Max too. I never had a daughter to hand it down to and, well, my three daughters-in-law had their own mothers to help them with their gowns. I just hope it isn't too old fashioned for her."

Maisy spoke loud enough for Lucy to hear her from the kitchen, "I don't think Dana is the kind of woman who worries about fashion trends."

Lucy closed her eyes as she rocked. "Max was always talking about Dana and Simon and how blind they were to each other's love. I'm so glad they got their eyes open." She lowered her voice, "Life is just too darned short."

Maisy carried two mugs of tea into the living room and watched her friend take a tentative sip, "How long have you been in this much pain?"

Lucy opened one eye and looked up at Maisy, "You always could read me. It got worse after the last treatment. And don't even think about talking to Max about it. He can't afford to take any more time off from work."

"Do you really think you're fooling him?" Maisy scoffed. "He is a detective, you know."

Lucy chuckled, "Some detective, he still hasn't figured out who you are."

Maisy sat quietly and looked out of the window at the last crimson leaf on the maple tree in Lucy and Max's front yard. It twisted in the wind until it wrenched free of the branch. The wind buoyed it up in the air briefly before it floated gracefully to the earth. "It's better that he doesn't figure it out. The girl I was is gone. I had a great life with my husband and he sacrificed everything, including me, to give me back to this place and this life with Tom and his family. They mean the world to me."

Lucy's rocker stopped, "I'm so grateful we found each other again. There's something important I want you to do for me." She leaned forward. "I can't bear the thought of Max being alone when I'm gone." She looked at Maisy and nodded her head, "I want you to marry him."

Maisy choked on a mouthful of tea and spewed the hot brew all over her shirt. "You what?"

"You heard me. After I'm gone and a respectable time for mourning has passed, I want you and Max to marry. Neither of you should be alone."

Maisy fingered the locket hanging from the gold chain about her neck. "You're forgetting I have a husband."

"So you say, yet when was the last time you heard from him."

Maisy didn't hesitate, "Twelve years, three months and twenty-one days ago."

Lucy's voice grew weaker, "Sounds to me like you have grounds for abandonment. Whatever his or your reasons are, you shouldn't be alone. You have so much to offer a man. You deserve to be happy." She yawned and closed her eyes.

Maisy's voice softened, "My friend, let me help you to your bed so you can take a nap. Just tell me where the wedding dress is and let's celebrate the happy couple instead of trying to figure out our own futures."

Lucy sighed as Maisy helped her to her feet. "I don't want you to feel you have to marry Max. I just want you to know, if you two should fall in love, you have my blessing."

Maisy supported Lucy as she leaned heavily against her, "And I want you to know, I'm not in the market for your sloppy seconds. Besides, I'm not ready to let go of you and I expect you to hang on for a long, long time."

She eased Lucy onto the bed and covered her with a crocheted blanket. "Now, tell me where the wedding gown is so I can get out of here before Max comes home."

CHAPTER 35

The most accurate description of Indiana's weather was unpredictable. Temperatures rose again and rain made a comeback.

Dana watched the water cascading down the window of her room. Her mood matched the gloom outside. She'd heard enough of Tharon and Kaid's conversation with Simon to know he had more urgent things to worry about than to babysit her. He'd made at least two trips to Indianapolis already and hinted he was gearing up for something big, but didn't want to discuss it where they might be overheard.

Before Lista went home, her companionship had kept Dana from brooding on her insecurities, but with Lista gone, that old demon Doubt kept whispering in her ear that it was all too good to be true. Simon was bound to realize she didn't hold a candle to Nora, and he'd break off the marriage plans.

The next day was Friday and she was due to be released from the hospital in the morning, the day before they planned to marry. Simon had been MIA all day. He'd left before she woke up and it was nearly midnight; there still was no sign of him. He hadn't even called to check on her.

Every time she closed her eyes to try to sleep she imagined him breaking off the wedding.

She was in the midst of picturing a particularly painful scene when she felt him hovering over her. Her eyes whipped open and she said, "Where the heck have you been?" *That was harsh. What am I doing chasing him away?*

Simon's face traveled between shock, pain, realization, and amusement. His lips curled into a grin, "I've been preparing a surprise for you." He kissed her pouting lips until they surrendered to his affection. He drew back to look at her, "What did you think I was doing?"

She traced his rough strong jaw with her thumb, "I imagined you came to your senses and were trying to figure out a way to dump me."

He shook his head, "Nonsense. You should know me better than that. You know I'd never lie to you. Haven't I already told you that I love you?"

She thought a moment and shook her head, "Not in so many words."

He fingered the button to raise the head of the bed, "How many words would it take to convince you?"

She was nearly upright, "Three ought to do the trick."

"How about seven?" He pulled a ring from his pocket and dropped to one knee. "I love you. Will you marry me?"

Tears welled in Dana's eyes and spilled down her face. She touched her lips with her fingertips. Her heart filled to bursting with love for him and that perfect moment stretched out, making time seem to stand still—she was completely overcome with emotion.

Simon shifted uncomfortably. With uncertainty he asked, "Dana, will you?"

She blinked when she realized she hadn't answered him, "Oh yes. I love you. Yes."

He sighed in relief and placed the diamond on her finger. His kiss lingered on her lips. Then he trailed kisses along her cheek to the nape of her neck. His hands caressed her curves through her hospital gown. His touch ignited a hunger deep within her as his mouth found hers again and he kissed her with an intensity that made it clear, he shared her hunger.

He reined back the fires of desire and said in a husky voice, "That should seal it for you. Would I risk a harassment suit if I wasn't sure?" his hands lingered at her hips and he rested his palm on her flat abdomen. He groaned, "I can hardly wait for Saturday."

She didn't realize she'd grabbed a handful of his shirt fabric until a button popped off. They laughed and she said, "I guess I can't wait either."

He fingered the controls until she fully reclined again, and gave a look of dread to the recliner he'd called a bed every night that week. "At least this is the last night I have to sleep on that torture device."

Dana caught his hand and pulled him to the bed as she scooted over to make room for him. "Sleep with me."

He kissed her hand, "Are you sure?" He kicked off his shoes and lay on his side facing her.

She grinned, "You don't take much persuading, do you? Just mind those hands or you'll be starting something I won't be able to stop."

He draped his left arm around her waist and pulled her close, "How's that? Too much?"

She kissed his lips lightly and cuddled into his embrace, "Perfect. Good night."

Simon answered with the soft snore she'd already grown to love.

***

Dr. Anderson checked her wound during his Friday morning rounds. "You're healing nicely. Not as remarkably as your young friend, but you're healing just fine."

Dana looked from the surgeon to Simon, "What young friend?"

Dr. Anderson lifted her arm to the side, "Hmm? Oh, the Harris boy. I never saw such a rapid recovery. I doubted the initial diagnosis until I verified it with the nurse. One for the record books," he said absently.

Dr. Anderson tested the grip of both her hands with a dynamometer. He frowned, "You're right hand dominant?"

She nodded and half held her breath. She didn't need a device to tell her she'd lost some strength in her right hand. "How bad is it?"

He typed into his tablet, "In your line of work, it could be an issue. I'm putting an order in for a physical therapy evaluation. Can you shoot with your left hand?"

She grimaced remembering how wide from the mark her shot at Brandt had been. "I can but I'm not as accurate."

Simon shook his head, "Don't let her fool you. She's ninety-eight percent accurate with her right and eighty-five percent with her left. That's nothing to sneeze at."

Dana shook her head, "It was bad enough that it enabled Brandt to get his hands on Tharon. If it wasn't for her and Kaid's courage and quick thinking, we could be looking at a terribly different outcome."

Simon sat down next to her and placed his palm on the small of her back. He asked, "Can she go home today?"

The doctor looked up from his tablet. "Yes. But I'm not clearing her to return to work quite yet." He turned to Dana, "No driving until you're off the pain meds and no shooting with the right hand until you're completely healed. In the meantime you might try increasing the strength of your right hand. The nurse will have a series of exercises for you along with a list of restrictions. No heavy lifting. Also, as long as you're still on the pain medication, we advise that you refrain from making major life decisions. This isn't a good time for you to go out and buy a new car."

Simon's expression clouded. When the doctor left them alone, he said, "Perhaps we're rushing the wedding. I don't want to take advantage of you."

Dana pulled him to her, "No. This simply means that I'm going off the meds until after the wedding. That way you can be certain the only reason I'm marrying you is because I love you. You'll also be able to decide if you still want me once you see what a wimp I am when I'm in pain."

***

While Simon picked up her prescriptions, she opened the bag holding the clothing Simon had picked up for her; she smiled and flushed with embarrassment. Her soon to be husband not only had discovered her weakness for fancy lingerie, he'd picked out her favorite black lace panties and matching holster bra.

She fumbled to put on the bra and double checked the safety on her Glock from the bedside table before slipping it into the holster. Thankfully Simon had picked out a knit jogging outfit in a pale pink and gray which was easier to don than the under garments.

They left the hospital and by the time they got the marriage license, picked up a few groceries, and drove to her house—Dana was beyond exhaustion and her shoulder felt like it was on fire.

Simon unlocked the front door to her house and the aroma of fresh bread and something Italian wafted from the kitchen. "You fixed dinner? When did you have time to do that?"

He blushed and with great self-deprecation said, "All in a day's work."

Penni rounded the corner from the kitchen. "Ha! And whose work would that be? Don't you let him start putting on airs. If it wasn't for frozen pizza he'd never eat."

Simon gave Penni a playful sneer, "You were supposed to be gone when we got here."

Dana grinned then looked around her home, "Something's different. What did you do, Penni? It feels—oh..." She continued to scan the room. A newer, less worn, burgundy version replaced her lumpy sofa and brought with it a companion chair and a leather recliner. Flowers brightened end tables and accent lamps made the room glow with warmth. A big screen TV adorned the wall opposite the sofa. Below it a shelving unit hosted an impressive array of electronics.

Dana continued to the stone fireplace in the corner of the great room. Half the mantle was now home to pictures of her family: her parents, grandparents, younger brother and sister, and younger images of herself. On the other half resided images of Simon with his first wife and his daughters.

Penni nervously waited for her reaction. "We can take it all out if you don't like it, I hope you're not upset that we came in and gave the place a makeover."

Dana delicately touched a picture of her younger brother. "How did you find these? I never unpacked them?"

Simon brushed a lock of hair behind her ear, "I remember you telling me, when you first started working with me, that you couldn't bring yourself to even unpack your family's pictures."

Her eyes misted, "You remembered that?"

He nodded, "So last night, after we finished moving in the furniture, I took the liberty to find them. They're a part of you, just like my family is a part of me. Is it okay?"

She looked at the mantle as tears threatened the edges of her eyes, "No."

Penni gasped and covered her mouth with her fingers.

Simon's countenance fell.

Dana rearranged the pictures on the mantle creating a space in the center. "There should be a wedding picture of you and Nora here with our wedding picture next to it."

Simon sighed in relief and gathered her in his arms, being mindful of her wounded shoulder.

Penni shrugged on her coat and, with tears in her eyes, said, "I'll leave you two alone and see you tomorrow at the wedding."

Dana broke from Simon's embrace and turned to Penni. "Thank you for everything." She looked around the room and made a sweeping gesture, "I'm sure you had a lot to do with this and I love it, all of it." She swallowed and hoped she hadn't misread the bond she felt with the bossy office manager. "Also, I was wondering if you'd be willing to stand by my side at the wedding. Can you tolerate the title matron of honor?"

Penni blinked at the tears seeping in the corners of her eyes. Her voice was strangled with emotion, "I'd be so honored you can't imagine." The tears won and streamed from her eyes as she forgot Dana's wound and hugged her tight.

Just when the pain was getting the better of Dana, Penni

let go of her, "Oh dear! Your shoulder. Did I hurt you?"

Dana choked back tears, "No. I'm okay. When you hugged me it felt just like when my mom used to hug me— thank you."

Penni wiped the tears from Dana's cheeks, "I'm going to leave before I use up all my tears today and have none left for tomorrow."

***

Simon dished up a serving of sloppy lasagna, large enough to feed two men. He placed the plate in front of Dana. She watched him as he helped himself to less than half the amount he gave her.

His eyes darted from the plate, to the kitchen, to the view from the patio door of the backyard in sore need of attention, before finally resting on her. He failed to mask the sadness in his eyes.

She switched plates with him and took his hand, "Tell me."

He returned her grip, "I was just thinking how perfect this is—how right it feels. I'm so sorry I didn't recognize my feelings for you sooner. I hate how much time we've wasted that we could have been together."

She studied his face, "The past is done. We're together now, that's what counts. But I get the feeling that's not everything that's bothering you. Tell me."

He looked into her eyes and took a deep breath, exhaling slowly, "The governor asked me to organize a militia from Whitley County to deal with the invasion threat. All the counties are organizing. It started by word of mouth but has grown much quicker than I anticipated. I'm afraid we might not get too many nights like this, especially if it comes to an armed conflict." He fell silent and rubbed his thumb over her knuckles. "We won't get much of a honeymoon either. I'll have to meet with the county leaders on Monday afternoon."

She tried to sound light and not betray the ominous dread creeping into her heart. "Then we should enjoy this meal, especially since I don't cook any better than you do, so we're not likely to have too many meals this good." She let go of his hand and picked up her fork, "Eat up while it's hot and tell me what's going on. I've been off the meds long enough that I might even remember what you say."

He relaxed, grateful for her companionship. He'd been looking forward to discussing his concerns with her, "The hard part is we don't dare do background checks, that would flag everyone joining and, heaven forbid if we lose, everyone joining could become targets for retribution. That means we might be fighting alongside someone who will turn their guns on us instead."

Dana's stomach twisted in knots. Suddenly not hungry, she pushed a piece of pasta around her plate. "What about our department? Do you think someone is a plant?"

Simon mulled her question over, "I hate to think it, but of course it's possible." He shook his head, "We have four employees who've been in the department less than ten years: you, Collins, Jackman and Murphy."

She choked on a bite of lasagna and said, "I hope you know it's not me."

He leaned over and kissed her, "Of course I know it's not you. But I need your help to figure out if one of them is in Hamron's pocket."

Dana mulled his words, "Not Murphy, I trust her with my life. I don't know Jackman too well. He's a big flirt with almost everyone. But I think he's harmless. At the core, I trust him."

Simon frowned, "He's a flirt? He didn't flirt with you

did he?"

She grinned at the jealous edge to his voice. "Sure. He even flirts with Penni. The only woman I've never seen him flirt with is Stephanie Murphy."

Simon's expression floated from relief to confusion, "Why not Murphy? She's a pretty girl. Good cop."

"I think he's carrying a torch for her." It was Dana's turn to feel a twinge of jealousy. "You noticed she's pretty?"

Simon winked at her, "She's pretty, but she doesn't hold a candle to you."

Dana's face flushed. How had she turned so possessive so quickly? She changed the subject, "So what about Collins? I don't know much about him. Where's he from?"

Simon pushed his plate out of the way and stretched his long arms to pick up some folders sitting on the kitchen counter. "I had Penni bring the files so we could look them over. I thought maybe a fresh pair of eyes might help."

Fatigue sapped what little energy she had left. Through drooping lids she glanced at Collins and Jackman's files. "Did you check all the references when you hired them?"

Simon said, "Yes, Penni called every reference and previous employer."

Dana yawned, "The first step is to do a reverse phone number look up and make sure you're calling who you think you are. Maybe see if there is an alternate phone number from the one on their application, then call and pretend you're doing a credit check for a car loan. My phone has the caller ID blocked so you can use it." She wrinkled her brow, "Where is my phone?"

Simon pulled a new phone from his pocket. "I had to take your phone as evidence but had all your messages and contacts transferred to this new one. It probably needs charged though."

She took the phone to the bedroom to plug it in. and stopped short in the doorway. Her twin-sized mattress on a frame was replaced by a king-sized wooden frame bed with matching dresser and two bedside tables. A white down comforter covered the bed, complete with pillows and pillow shams edged in Battenberg lace.

Simon followed her into the bedroom. He wrapped his arms around her waist and whispered in her ear. "Do you like it?"

Dana fumbled for words, "Where did this come from? I mean was it your bed?"

Simon bent to kiss her cheek, "No. I couldn't do that and I didn't think you could either. Matt Harris sold me the furniture and took my old furniture in trade. He, Tom and Max helped me move things in yesterday. That's why I was so late. Am I forgiven?"

"You already were forgiven. I'm sorry I snapped at you last night." She turned to face him and lifted her arms to wrap them around his shoulders but she only got her right arm elbow high before she gasped in pain. She bit her lip and moaned, "How did I forget that?" she breathed slow ragged breaths until the pain subsided.

Simon held her until her tension eased and she molded into his embrace. "You need to rest. We have a big day tomorrow. I'll work on the phone numbers for a while before I come to bed."

Dana kissed him tenderly. But when she broke from his arms to plug in her phone, she couldn't bring herself to meet his eyes. As she sat on the edge of the bed waiting for the phone to come to life, she tried to think of how to express what she wanted without hurting his feelings. "I know we can't have the usual wedding traditions, but I'd like to keep one." She forced her eyes to lock onto his, "They say it's bad luck to for the bride and groom to see each other before the wedding."

Simon wrapped his arm around her waist, "I don't think I'm going to like where this is heading."

She rested her head on his shoulder and pulled up her text messages. A grin spread across her face. "As much as I want to sleep in your arms, I want to keep that tradition. Max and Lucy are going to pick me up and we're meeting Lista, Tharon and Maisy at the church. They're going to help me get ready. Besides, I have a secret favor to ask of you that is going to knock everyone's socks off."

Simon kissed her tenderly, "If that's the way you want it, then that's what we'll do. What's the favor?"

She showed him the message. He grinned from ear to ear.

CHAPTER 36

November 18, 2056

Saturday morning found Dana so filled with excitement even her throbbing shoulder couldn't dampen. As if the heavens were smiling on their union, the clouds disappeared, leaving behind a clear, bright sky. Even the temperatures continued their moderate trend with highs in the mid forties.

Max arrived before ten to take her to the church. His suit hung loosely from his shoulders, his white shirt cuffs dangled from the sleeves and the hem of his trousers dragged the floor.

Every time Dana saw him he looked thinner. "Max, you're wasting away. Are you ill? Have you been to the doctor?"

Max straightened his tie and smoothed his suit coat, "I am kind of rumpled. Haven't been to church for a while and didn't realize how bad this fit. I'm healthy as an ox, though. Lucy hasn't felt well enough to cook so I've been the chef. I guess neither of us has an appetite for my cooking. I'm sorry to look so sloppy for your wedding."

Dana smiled, "Oh, I don't care about that. I just noticed you've been losing weight. Thanks for picking me up. I had a job for Simon to do today."

Max chuckled, "You're already starting the honey-do list?"

She smiled, "You'll understand when you see it." She looked at the empty truck, "Is Lucy feeling up to coming to the wedding? You can't imagine how grateful I am to her for loaning me her wedding dress. I want to thank her in person."

Max smiled, "She's happy to do it. Her friend Maisy is taking her to the church. That way she got to sleep for an extra half hour. She gets tired pretty quickly these days but you couldn't keep her away. It's like you're the daughter we never had."

Dana glanced at him and said, "I'm glad you feel like that because I have one more favor to ask. Would you be willing to walk me down the aisle and give me away?"

Max blinked rapidly and cleared his throat several times before he could answer. His face flushed all the way to his balding forehead. "It'd be my honor."

***

Dana's heart fluttered as Max pulled his pickup truck into the church parking lot. A mere week ago she never thought this day would come. The dizzying whirlwind transition from employee, to fiancé, to wife, was surreal and she often had moments when she wondered if it was all a dream. She walked up the cracked sidewalk to the stone church and accepted that it was indeed a dream—a dream come true. She was about to become Mrs. Simon

Ellis.

A pang of momentary loss touched her heart. How would being married change her? What of Dana Donovan? She thought of her solitary life and figured it was a sacrifice worth making.

Tharon waited for her at the side entrance with a wide welcoming smile. Her chin length hair was gathered back and adorned with a small spray of baby's breath and a delicate blue bow. Soft brown ringlets framed her heart shaped face. She wore a pink satin dress with a blue band at her waist that matched the bow in her hair. Dana noted for the first time the striking likeness between Tharon and her mother. Perhaps it was the difference in their hair color that kept Dana from noticing the remarkable resemblance earlier.

Tharon immediately grabbed her hand to guide her to the 'bride's room': a secretary's office with a full length, three-sided mirror. "Mom, Maisy and Lucy are waiting for us along with your friend Penni. The men have to come in the back door so you don't see them. Did you know it's bad luck to see the groom before the wedding?"

"Yes, I've heard that." Dana smiled as she hurried to keep up with the exuberant twelve-year-old. As they entered the bride's room her mouth dropped open in awe and disbelief. Hanging from the coat rack was the most stunning wedding gown she'd ever seen. "Oh, Lucy, how will I ever thank you?"

Lucy sat in a mauve wingback chair in front of the desk. Her pale face beamed with joy. "You can thank me by being as happy with Simon as I've been with Max."

Dana hugged the frail lady with her left arm; tears spilled down the cheeks of both women. Dana felt Lucy's hug weaken and eased her back into the chair. She exchanged a concerned look with Penni who snapped a handful of tissues from the box on the desk and distributed them among the women.

Tharon shook her head, "Why is everyone crying? I thought weddings were supposed to be happy."

Dana dabbed at her eyes and said, "Sometimes when you're very happy, the happiness spills out in tears of joy."

Lista hugged Tharon, "And you should never be embarrassed by any tears, especially tears of joy."

Penni and Maisy helped Dana into the dress as Lucy supervised which buttons to fasten in what order. The dress fit like a glove. Its scooped neckline dipped in the back as well as the front and Dana was grateful the cut of the dress covered her bandages. The bodice fit snug to her hips, then flared out into a princess skirt with a ten foot train that trailed behind. Beading and lace on the bodice accentuated her bust and waist and the satin covered buttons formed a perfect line from the back scoop to the top of the train.

Maisy stepped back and surveyed Dana from every angle. "I don't see anything that needs altered. It looks like I've brought my sewing machine for nothing."

Lista styled Dana's chestnut colored hair and secured the veil to the top of her loosely gathered curls.

The ladies refused to let Dana see how she looked until Penni applied her makeup.

Dana had never worn so much makeup in her life and worried it would be too much—but when Penni stepped back and Dana stood in front of the mirror, all Dana could say was, "That's me? I look..."

Lucy struggled to stand and put her arm around Dana's waist. "You look beautiful, my dear. The loveliest bride I've ever seen."

Penni dabbed at her eyes, "She's right. You're absolutely lovely."

Dana turned from side to side, then faced herself eye to eye and smiled wide, "I'm getting married." She knew her sparse circle of friends would only fill a small corner of the chapel, but she felt rich with their friendship. "I want to thank all of you for helping make my wedding special. You don't know how much this means to me."

She thought of her family and wondered if they were happy for her—wherever they were.

Penni took Dana's hand, "I'm sure they're here and they're happy for you."

Dana was certain she hadn't voiced her thoughts, "Who?"

Penni said, "Your family. I feel like this room is crowded with more than just us. Don't you feel it?"

Dana closed her eyes and reached out with her heart. The familiar presence touched her with peace and comfort. "Yes. I believe you're right."

A knock rapped on the door and when Tharon opened it, Max filled the frame. "Everything is ready but Simon called and said he'll be here in half an hour."

Lucy grinned mischievously at her husband, "Maisy and Lista, is there enough time to put a few tucks in Max's suit coat?"

Lista's smile brightened, "Absolutely." She opened her sewing box on the desk and strapped a pincushion to her wrist. "Max, let me have a look at you."

Maisy set up the sewing machine on the desk and handed Dana a bouquet of white roses and blue carnations. "Alterations are Lista's forte and I need to check on a few things in the fellowship hall. I'll see you all in the chapel." She bustled out of the door on the opposite side of the office without looking back.

Twenty five minutes later Lista helped Max back on with the jacket. He buttoned the top two buttons and said,

"This is amazing." He stepped into the office to check the fit in the mirror and turned to Lucy. "Now maybe you won't be ashamed to be seen with me in public."

Lucy grabbed his tie and pulled him down to eye level with her, "You old goat. You know I've never been ashamed to be seen with you." She gave him a playful smack on the cheek, "But now I'll accept no excuses that keep you from taking me to church tomorrow."

Max took in a breath to complain but when he saw the hopeful look in his frail wife's eyes he planted a light kiss on her lips and said, "It will be my honor."

An uncomfortable silence filled the room. Dana looked at the clock and said, "Max, why don't you take the ladies to their seats and give Tharon and me a few moments to ourselves?"

Penni noticed Lista's fatigue and helped her stand. She eyed Max with suspicion, "I'll go along, just to make certain everything really is ready."

Once they were alone, Dana said, "I want to thank you for being in my wedding. You look very pretty."

"I do?" Tharon fidgeted with her hands and shifted her weight from one foot to the other and back again. "I'm not sure what I'm supposed to do."

Dana bent towards her, "You know, I'm not sure either. I think you're supposed to walk down the aisle in front of me and keep pace with the music. But if you get the urge to run down the aisle, that's all right with me."

Dana hadn't had a chance to talk to Tharon alone before. "When we were in the woods, Officer Brandt wanted to take you with him. Do you have any idea why he wanted you?"

Tharon trembled and folded her arms tight across her chest She shook her head. "I've tried to figure out why anyone would want me and I can't think of anything. I asked my Dad but he just tried to make a joke that it was because I'm so cute. Only..."

Dana tilted her head, "Only what?"

Tharon searched Dana's eyes as if deciding if she should confide in her. "Only he won't let me go anywhere alone. Even today, he only let me watch for you because he was down the hall watching me. Do you think I'm still in danger?"

Dana felt bad that she'd brought a level of fear back into Tharon's eyes. "I think as long as you do as your father says, you won't have anything to worry about. He loves you very much and he is tremendously proud of you. Nothing is more important to him than keeping you safe."

Tharon lowered her lashes, "I guess so, but I think my tree climbing days are over."

"Well, perhaps he will go with you." Dana wanted to change the subject, "You seem to be walking well. How are your feet healing?"

Tharon smiled, "Oh, they're healed. They hurt a little in these shoes but that's just because the shoes are new. My mom said if they hurt too much I can wear slippers at the reception."

Dana raised her eyebrows, "We're having a reception?" she had no idea what plans had been made.

Tharon beamed, "Of course. The best part of the wedding is the cake! I helped Maisy bake it."

Dana grinned. That wasn't the part she was looking forward to, but she thrilled to see the sparkle of anticipation in Tharon's eyes. "Thank you for helping. I'm sure it will be wonderful."

They turned when Max filled the doorway again, "Are you ladies ready?"

***

Standing in the church foyer, Dana took Max's offered arm while Tharon and Penni helped arrange the train behind her as she stood before the closed doors of the sanctuary.

Matt Harris and Tom Trace opened the doors to the chapel and walked down the aisle to join their wives in the pews. Everyone in the chapel rose to their feet as the wedding march began. Dana gasped to see the sanctuary full to overflowing.

Penni held a nosegay of flowers and step-paused in time with the music until she stood at the front of the chapel.

Tharon took her place in front of Dana. Helm and Kaid flanked her, each offering her an arm. Tharon looked back questioningly at Dana.

Dana nodded that it was okay to take the boys' arms. She smiled at Tharon and the boys as they shuffle stepped a few times, adapting their pace to Helm's limp, and moved down the aisle in semi-unison—step, together, step, together— somewhat in pace to the music.

Dana wondered if someday Tharon would walk down this same aisle on Tom's arm to bind herself to one of those boys. The puzzling concern that someone wanted to abduct Tharon and not the boys resurfaced, but she pressed it to the back of her mind, determined that for the rest of this one day she would be a woman and not a cop.

When she saw Lista and Lucy sitting on the front row of the bride's side of the chapel, warmth stirred in Dana's heart. Next to them sat the strawberry blond nurse, Gretchen, with her now familiar crooked grin wider than usual. The hard loneliness deserted Dana's heart, crowded out by a full and open feeling of love and friendship.

Maisy dabbed at her eyes from the back of the chapel and Dana wondered briefly why she didn't sit with her friends.

Max took a step forward but Dana held him back, "Not yet," she whispered, "wait for Simon."

Simon entered from the side door at the front of the chapel. Most of the people were watching Dana so it took a moment before recognition swept through the congregation. Tom turned first and touched Lista's arm. Her hand flew to her mouth and tears sprang from her eyes.

Tharon and the boys were half way down the aisle when Shep stepped around the pews and limped towards her. "Shep!" her strangled cry sliced through the music; the organist hit the wrong cord and stopped playing.

Tharon and the boys ran to the dog and dropped down in the middle of the aisle, smothering him with love and affection. Tears streamed down Tharon's face as she hugged and stroked her dog's neck.

Shep whimpered, whined and yowled with love, and happiness—and maybe a little scolding at Tharon for not being there when he needed her. She threw her arms around his neck, taking care to not squeeze him too tightly where he was bandaged. For the first time in her life she wept tears of pure joy.

Dana wondered if her make-up was streaming down her cheeks but she didn't care, her heart was full. She looked around the chapel and nearly everyone wiped tears from their faces.

Max pulled out a handkerchief and mopped his face too. "You couldn't give a guy a heads up about something like this?"

Dana squeezed his arm, "Max, you're an old softie after all."

Grinning happily, Dana watched as Tharon led Shep to the front of the chapel and sat down on the step with him on the bride's side. Helm and Kaid sat on either side of her beaming with happiness.

The music started again and Dana locked eyes with Simon. Her heart pounded in her chest. When she'd resolved a few short days ago to get a life, she'd never dreamed it could hold this much joy.

She tugged on Max's arm, "Let's hurry, before he changes his mind."

CHAPTER 37

Tharon sat at the main table with the bride and groom. Shep lay on the floor at her feet. She slipped her dress shoes off and searched out Shep every few minutes to scratch behind his ears with her toes. Helm and Kaid sat on either side of her. Her cheeks ached from her near constant grin.

Dana and Simon got up to dance and Dana paused to whisper in Tharon's ear. "I'm sorry about keeping it a secret that Shep was alive. I didn't want to tell anyone until I was sure he was going to survive."

Tharon swallowed the bite of cake in her mouth. Her brown eyes sparkled with happiness, "That's okay. It was the best surprise I ever got. Thank you for taking him to get better."

Tharon looked around the fellowship hall and smiled at the decorations Maisy had put together so quickly. Small pine wreaths circled white candles on each table. She let Tharon sprinkle translucent glitter and blue ribbon curls around the pine needles and cones with some sprinkled on the white table cloths. Maisy told her, "It will be the dickens to get the glitter out of the cloth but you just wait, it will look wonderful."

Maisy had been right. With the glow of the afternoon sun streaming through the high windows, and the flickering, battery operated, faux candles; it looked like sparkling diamonds shimmered at each table.

At the youth table in the back of the room, Cody Miller, Veronica and Tracy sat with the Edwards twins and Sarah Felger. Cody had his back to her and when he got up, he turned and winked at her.

She grinned at him.

Everett pointed at her and said something which made everyone at the table, except Eddie, Sarah and Cody, laugh.

Tharon looked down at her plate. She didn't want to let them make her feel so worthless. Why did she still care what they thought of her? Her fingers absently touched her short hair and she wondered if she looked grotesque. The adults told her she was pretty but she wondered if they were just saying that because that's what grownups do.

Helm reached over and held her hand under the table. "What's wrong now?"

She smiled at him. "I was remembering how all this started. I just don't understand why I can't be friends with you and Kaid and with Tracy and Veronica."

Helm and Kaid both looked at Veronica across the room. She brightened and grinned at Kaid, who said, "I don't get why you want to be friends with them at all."

Tharon shrugged and picked up her fork to push a crumb around her plate, "I sure don't want to be enemies with them. Besides I never wanted to hurt anyone's feelings. I just don't see a way back to friends. I'd settle for them ignoring me. I don't do well in conflicts."

Kaid stabbed a piece of cake with his fork and said, "I think you do pretty good in a conflict. I'm sure Marty and Officer Brandt would agree." When his comment failed to produce a smile, he said, "We could make the first move and go talk with them."

Tharon wrestled with what she wanted to suggest. Even though it twisted her into knots she knew it was the right thing to do. "Maybe if you two asked them to dance, it might ease the tension between us."

Helm frowned, "I don't want to dance with Tracy."

Kaid screwed up his face, "Well I don't want to dance with her either. Yuck."

Cody walked up behind Tharon and tapped her shoulder, "Hey, Dork, would you like to dance?"

She slipped her dress shoes back on and smiled, "I'd love to, Nerd, but I'm warning you, I've never danced before."

Cody offered her his arm, "No problem, I'm wearing steel-toed dress shoes."

She looked at him with a raised eyebrow and laughed when she realized he was teasing her. She took his arm and followed him to the dance floor.

He held her right hand and wrapped his other arm around her waist. They circled and twirled around the floor.

Shep tagged along until he heard Tom whistle softly for him; he limped over to his master and lay down at his feet.

Tharon watched Cody's feet but kept stepping on his toes. "You might need steel-toed shoes with me."

He tipped her chin up to look at him. "Stop thinking about it. Don't watch your feet, just keep looking at my ugly mug and follow my lead."

Tharon did as he said and soon their movements became more fluid. Her face broke into a wide smile. "You don't have an ugly mug." She tilted her head and looked up at his face. His square jaw and strong chin were like his father's, but he had his mother's full lips and wide smile. She noticed his smug grin and added, "For a nerd."

He pulled her tight and spun her quickly around the floor until she was dizzy. "Are you ever going to stop calling me a nerd?"

She laughed, "As soon as you stop calling me a dork."

He slowed their circular motion. "Fair enough, *Tharon*. How come you got your hair cut?"

Her face warmed, "We were hiding in the woods and Helm was in bad shape. We needed to start a fire and there wasn't any dry kindling so I cut off my braids and Kaid used them to start the fire."

He frowned at Kaid, "I can't believe he asked you to do that."

She shook her head. "No one asked me. I just did it. I don't think Helm would have lived if we didn't get a fire going." She touched the back of her hair, "Does it look that bad?"

Cody tilted her head up and said, "No, it doesn't look bad. You look pretty. It's just a different look for you."

She winced, "Pretty is a different look for me? Thanks." Kaid and Helm walked to the youth table and she tried to focus on Cody's face which turned bright red.

"That's not what I meant. I always thought you looked cute."

It was her turn to blush. "Let's change the subject. That was nice of you and your dad to take care of our animals while we were...gone."

He squeezed her closer and his voice thickened, "I was worried about you. We all were."

Tharon hesitated, "Even your sister?"

Cody shrugged, "In her way, she was."

Kaid asked Sarah to dance. Helm danced with Veronica. Eddie stood and held a hand out to Tracy, leaving Everett to sit and scowl at Tharon. She didn't think Everett would ever stop hating her.

Cody was still talking, "You know with our dads in the militia, if you and your mom ever need anything, you can call me. I want to help you if you need me."

She smiled up at him. "Do you think we might have to put in the spring crops by ourselves?"

He shrugged, "Who knows? If we do, we'll help each other. Right?"

She locked eyes with Helm and tried to ignore the tug at her heart, "Right," she said absently.

Cody followed her line of sight and shook his head. "Come on, I'm going to show you just what a good friend I am." He twirled her across the floor and tapped Helm's shoulder. "How about letting me switch partners. Come on, Roni, let's show them what a waltz looks like."

In a smooth motion Cody deftly switched partners leaving Tharon in Helm's arms. As he waltzed his sister away Veronica snapped at him, "How many times do I have to tell you not to call me Roni."

Helm rested his hands on Tharon's waist and she held onto his shoulders as they managed a circling side-step. She was clumsier than when she danced with Cody, but she felt more comfortable with Helm.

Helm cleared his throat, "Did Veronica tell you why I said I didn't want to be Tracy's boyfriend?"

Tharon had almost forgotten the boyfriend fiasco. Almost. She shrugged her shoulders, "She said you think of Tracy as a sister."

He dipped his head to look into her eyes. "Did she say anything else?"

She lowered her eyelashes, "Just that you liked someone else and you wouldn't tell her who."

Helm inhaled nervously, "Ever since I saw you climb your dad's apple trees when you were seven years old, and then when I saw you in my dad's store shopping for the

Felger fam—"

She touched her finger to his lips, "Please don't say anything more. No one is supposed to know about that."

She searched for the right thing to say. She felt the bond between them but the whole boyfriend scheme still left a sour taste in her mouth. Besides, she just got them both back. What he wanted to say might cause a rift in her friendship with Kaid. And what if being more than friends didn't work out? Maisy used to tell her you can go from a friend to something more but it was hard to go from something more back to a friend.

She looked deep into his hazel eyes, "You and Kaid are both my friends and I don't want things to be weird between us. After everything that happened last week, I couldn't bear losing either of you as friends. Besides, I'm only twelve and my dad won't let me date until I'm sixteen."

He grinned and twirled her around as best he could with the walking cast, "Fair enough. But in four years we're going to finish this conversation."

Tharon laughed and hung onto his shoulders, "You'll be sick of me by then."

He kissed her forehead, "That'll never happen. I'll always be your friend."

She smiled up at him, "I'll always be your friend too."

Tharon smiled at Sarah dancing with Kaid. When they circled close enough, Sarah said, "I'm so glad you weren't hurt. I was praying for all of you. I'm happy you are all safe at home."

Tharon returned her warm smile, "Thanks, it's good to be home."

But always at the edge of her mind was the knowledge that Marty was still out there and she had no doubt he intended to make good his promise to kill her. She also worried that someone wanted to abduct her. She still couldn't figure out who wanted *her* and why?

CHAPTER 38

The hotel was much nicer than Simon had expected, but the wedding, the reception and the two hour drive to Indianapolis wore Dana out. She slipped into slumber soon after taking her pain meds.

He watched her even breathing and peaceful face and wondered if he'd made a mistake, insisting they get married right away. Was he being selfish marrying her, with the threat of secession and the increase of government troop activities on the state border mounting each day? Just like him, she had lost her entire family—parents, grandparents and siblings—to the influenza pandemic.

He'd waded through his grief, often working until exhaustion to keep from thinking about his lost wife and daughters. Out of concern for him, the county hired Dana as his driver and partner, tasked unofficially with easing his burdens and helping him accomplish his duties.

At first he resented being assigned a babysitter, but as they worked side by side, he found comfort in Dana's quiet strength. Their common loss forged a bond between them.

He remembered the time they were on the way to meet with the Health and Safety Commission on the dangers of abandoned houses and the threats posed by looters.

As they waited at a red light, a young family with two daughters crossed the street in front of them. Something about the older daughter reminded him of his daughter, Cathy. He pulled out his phone and looked at the date. A wave of palpable grief swept over him.

Dana must have noticed. She never said a word to him. She picked up her phone, "Penni, please call the commission and let them know the Sheriff is running about an hour late. Find out if they want to wait or reschedule and call *me* with what they want to do."

After that she drove him out to the country to the top of a hill where you could see for miles in all directions. They got out of the car and waded a half dozen yards into a wheat field. A warm summer breeze blew over the field, rippling the heavy laden stalks in waves. Dana inhaled deeply, her face bathed in the amber setting sun. "I love it here. It's so open and free. It helps me remember, there *is* still beauty in the world."

That was the moment he started to fall in love with her. Everyone else he knew looked at him with pity. Dana treated him with understanding and compassion. She never asked him about his family, but when he was ready to talk, she quietly listened. She helped him work through his grief without ever seeming to do anything but be there for him.

As she stood in the sunlight that evening he had asked, "So how long have you and Penni had a signal worked out to let her know when I need to be 'running late'?"

Dana chewed on her lower lip and looked down at her boots. "Too obvious?"

"Not too much. So how long?"

She sighed, "Since day one. Penni worked it out. I've never used it before, honest. You just looked like you needed this."

Simon breathed deeply and soaked up the warm breeze and fading sunlight. He drank in the scent of grain; the gentle murmur of the rustling wheat. "I did need this. Thanks. I just got caught off guard when I realized today would have been Cathy's ninth birthday. She's been gone two years now."

Dana's voice was soft when she spoke, "I thought it might be something like that."

Simon tilted his head as he looked at her. "How is it you got hired? I just realized, I don't recall interviewing you."

Dana said, "I wondered about that when I got hired. I think Penni pushed all the paper work through. She's the only one I spoke to. You may be the Sheriff, but I think she's the one who runs the department."

Simon smiled at the memory as he watched his sleeping bride. He thought he might just have to give Penni another raise, if she hadn't already given herself one.

He kept telling himself their marriage meant Dana wouldn't be left alone during her recovery, but that excuse rang hollow, even to his ears. They could have hired a nurse. They could have set her up with someone to stay with her, but something snapped in him when he saw Brandt leering at her—he was jealous.

When he found out Brandt tried to kill her, he nearly dispatched him to the great beyond on the spot. Had it not been for Max, Tom Trace and Matt Harris, he might have. He shuddered with shame at the rage that had filled him and almost driven him to something that went against everything he stood for and believed in.

Dana stirred and started to stretch.

Simon caught her arm before she pulled her stitches out and sat next to her on the edge of the bed. He kissed the palm of her hand. "How are you feeling?"

She purred, "Oh, I'm feeling gooood."

He raised an eyebrow, "Are you sure the pain meds don't have you too out of it? I don't want to take advantage of you."

Her deep throaty chuckle stirred his desire as she said, "I believe I consented today to giving you all the advantages you want."

He laughed at her, "I've never seen you act like this. When we make love the first time, I want you to be able to remember it."

She sat up and plunged her fingers into his thinning blond hair. She pulled his face close to hers, "You've never seen me like this because you've seldom seen me happy." She kissed him, softly at first, then deeper. When their lips parted she said, "This is my first time to make love. Ever. So I promise you, I'll remember it."

He cradled her face in his hands. "I didn't know you were a virgin."

Her face blushed crimson. "It's not something you bring up in casual conversation with your boss."

A war of emotions stormed through Simon. He closed his eyes and shook his head, "I *have* been selfish, pushing you to marry me so quickly. Do you want to slow things down and, I don't know, go on some dates first?"

She sat back and looked him in the eyes. "Simon Ellis, are you in love with me?"

His features softened. "Yes, deeply," he cradled her face and kissed her softly.

"I have loved you almost from the first day I met you. I have longed for this night. You can't know how much it means to me to be your wife; to be able to share our lives—" her voice caught with emotion. She took a deep breath, "—to not be alone anymore. We can date if you want. That might be fun. But right now, all I want is to show you how completely I love you."

She searched his eyes, willing him to understand the depth of her love, "I promise you, I'm not a naive child. I decided when I was a child that I wanted to wait until marriage. I have saved myself for you, for this night."

Dana touched the side of his face with her palm, "I will make you happy. I love you, Simon."

Simon eased her gently back on the pillows. He kissed her just below her ear. His kisses cascaded down to the nape of her neck.

His phone rang on the bedside table next to their heads. They both jumped with a start and Simon answered it out of habit. He barked into the phone, "Ellis."

Max's voice was solemn. "Sheriff, I hate to bother you, but Officer Brandt was killed today in his room at St. Joe hospital."

Simon rolled to Dana's side and laid on his back next to her as he talked into the phone. "How could that happen?"

Dana exhaled loudly, folded her arms over her chest and crossed her ankles.

Simon shifted the phone and took her hand in his, intertwining his fingers with hers.

She smiled and closed her eyes.

Simon heard the strain in Max's voice. "The guard was called to help with a security breach at the end of the hall. He was gone three minutes tops; just long enough for someone to inject an air bubble into Brandt's IV."

Dana snored softly.

Simon frowned, "Did you get a chance to interrogate him?"

"I got a call after the reception that he was out of the burn unit and able to talk. I was on my way over to question him but he was killed before I got there."

"Who knew you were going to talk to him?"

"On our end? Nobody. In Fort Wayne, it's hard to say." Max paused, "The nursing staff knew. They were to call me when he was able to talk. I'm not sure who they called in Fort Wayne."

Simon rubbed his head. "See if you can find out. Find out what you can about that security breach too. Whoever killed Brandt has just became our best lead to finding out who ordered Brandt to take Tharon. I've got a meeting tomorrow morning to fill in the gaps on Wil Silar. Any luck on finding Marty Phillips?"

Max hesitated, "I think I found out where he got his face sewn up. There was a fire at an after-hours clinic in Auburn last weekend. The doctor and nurse died in the fire. Yesterday they ruled it a homicide. It turns out both of them had their throats cut before they burned."

Simon sighed, "We're running out of leads and evidence. Double up your efforts on finding Marty. He's our best shot at finding whoever is behind all of this. Without a solid witness, we have no way to prove what the government is up to."

"Right," Max hesitated. "Sheriff, I just wanted to tell you how happy Lucy and I are for you and Dana."

Simon smiled at Dana's gentle snoring. "Thanks, but next time you need something, text me unless it's urgent."

Simon disconnected. He reached across Dana to turn out the light. She snuggled into his side and he wrapped his arms around her. He sighed with a blend of frustration and contentment, pulled the blanket up over them both, and settled down to sleep. Within moments he joined his bride in gentle snores.

CHAPTER 39

"Just call that number," the First Lady cooed as she perched on the edge of Vice President Larkin's desk, her thigh nudging his arm. She covered his hand and fingered the inside of his wrist with a delicate touch.

Larkin's eyes smoldered, his pulse quickened.

"Martin should have been in charge of the Fort Wayne contingent to begin with. I've found his dedication and discretion valuable in the past."

Larkin flinched at the flash of fire in her eyes, "Burt Payne came highly recommended by my strongest political ally in my congressional district. I had no idea he and his brother could bungle things so badly."

She hopped down and cupped her hand on the side of his face before trailing her fingertips along his jaw and down to his chin. The nail of her index finger lingered in the cleft of his chin. "Perhaps you can learn from this and not counter my wishes in the future."

Warmth flooded his face as he marveled at how he could be equally frightened and excited at the same time by this woman who belonged to someone else. Their shared hunger for power fueled his passion for her. "It will never happen again."

"I want the girl and her mother alive and unharmed. Be clear that the strike team knows that," she lifted her finger from his chin to her lips and pressed a kiss to it before transferring a smudge of dusky lipstick to the corner of Larkin's mouth. "Tell Martin to forget the hostage ruse. We will invade from two fronts. That will draw their pathetic militia away and the women will be unprotected at the house."

Larkin licked his lips and his hungry eyes followed her swaying hips to the door, the dusky lavender silk of her full skirt flowed with her movement, sending ripples of desire through him.

She stopped with her hand on the doorknob and turned to flash him a seductive smile, "Oh, and tell Martin not to leave any witnesses alive this time." She gave him a playful wave.

His face flushed with the heat of his desire for her. He could taste the power pulsing through his veins. Soon he'd have the Presidency and if he played his cards right she'd continue on as his own First Lady.

With his eyes closed he fingered the edge of the piece of paper she'd given him. Images played in his mind of her on his arm welcoming heads of state to White House—his White House. The razor sharp edge of the paper sliced into the soft flesh of his finger and brought him back to reality.

A drop of blood dripped onto the name of Martin Philips and began to soak into the paper, spreading to the phone number. Larkin gasped and snatched the silk handkerchief from his suit coat pocket to blot up the blood. Beads of sweat broke out on his upper lip as he struggled to read the ink before it blurred. He wrote down the number on another piece of paper and underlined the number he was uncertain of. He dared not let Mrs. Hamron know he might have lost the number.

He pulled out his cell phone and started calling different number combinations. After four wrong numbers, a surly voice answered, "Who is this?"

"I'm trying to reach Martin," Larkin sputtered. "Is that you?"

Marty hedged, "That depends on who's asking and what you want."

The Vice President swiped his hand over his brow, not realizing he left a smudge of blood in the center of his forehead. "A lovely and powerful friend gave me your number. She has a high regard for you to provide the desired results."

With a chuckle, Marty said, "I can think of several lovely ladies of that opinion but I don't imagine you want the same results they did."

Larkin reached his exasperation limit. "Confound it man! Are you Martin Philips or not? I am the Vice President of the United States and I have no time for dithering."

Marty paused before saying, "I'm your man. What do you need?"

"There has been a change of plans. No hostages will be taken. Two incursions will be made into the state on Thanksgiving Day. Our sources indicate the home of the girl will be unprotected. You are to secure the girl and her mother, alive and unharmed. You are to leave no witnesses."

"Am I to have any help?"

"A tactical strike team will rendezvous with you that morning with an air cruiser. You will be in charge of the operation and the responsibility of success or failure will reside with you and the entire team. We expect you to succeed or die trying. "

Marty's voice held no humor, "I understand."

CHAPTER 40

November 20, 2056

Fatigue plagued Lista Trace Monday morning. She was still tired from the Saturday wedding of Dana Donovan to Sheriff Simon Ellis. As much as the wedding contrasted the stress of her daughter's abduction and the loss of her baby the previous week, she had to admit, it took a lot out of her. She managed to go to church on Sunday—how could she not express gratitude for her daughter's safe return—but by the evening she was pretty well spent.

When Angela Harris spoke to her at church about Helm spending the next few days with Tharon, she was grateful for the opportunity to do something for the young boy who had calmed Tharon and helped her through the worst moments of their ordeal.

Lista's feelings of guilt weighed on her for trying to keep Tharon and the boys apart. If she hadn't interfered, Tharon and the boys wouldn't have been in the woods and witnessed the murder. They wouldn't have been abducted. She still had her concerns about the bond between Tharon,

Helm Harris and Kaid Walker. Perhaps it wasn't much of an issue yet. Tharon was only twelve, but as they matured, their interest in Tharon was bound to mature as well. If that happened, her husband Tom would have to deal with it. Lista's meddling days were over.

She smiled at Tharon's excitement to spend the day with Helm. She'd spent the night before picking out books to read and games to play. She'd organized the window seat at the front of the living room with extra pillows and even a couple of throws in case they got cold.

The window seat wasn't a bay window, since it didn't jut out onto the porch. Massive white book cases framed the front window with a storage bench between them beneath the window. The bench was covered with a thick cushion and several pillows. It was Tharon's favorite place to play and read.

The plaid cushion that covered the bench, coordinated perfectly with the red and yellow floral colors of the sofa and accent chair. She was sitting on the window seat watching for an hour before Helm arrived with his parents, Matt and Angela. "He's here!"

Tom tromped in through the back door stomping his feet to shake off the morning frost and any other debris from the farmyard. He risked Lista's wrath by keeping his shoes on as he strode to the front room to talk to Matt Harris before he left.

Tom ignored Lista's frown at his feet and slipped his left arm around her shoulder as he thrust out his right hand and shook Matt's hand firmly. "Did Simon give you a call last night?"

Matt's face was grave. "Yes. Do you think something is imminent or are these just precautionary measures?"

"I was under the impression things might progress

quicker than we thought. He asked me to be one of his lieutenants, what about you?"

Matt nodded, "Yeah, me too. It sounded like his wife recommended us."

"Do you want to ride with me to the meeting this evening?" Tom asked.

Matt looked to Lista who clung to Tom while Angela held onto Matt. "Lista, I know this is a lot to ask, but can Helm spend the rest of the day here? Angela will pick him up after she closes the store."

Lista said quietly, "Of course. He's always welcome here."

Tom smiled at her change of heart and covered her hand with his. He turned to Matt, "I'll pick you up so Angela will have your car. I'll see if Chuck and Doc want to come with us. Can you think of anyone else we should ask?"

"Well, there's Royce Edwards, I doubt he'll come, but he'd probably be offended if he isn't asked."

"Daddy?" Tom looked down at the Tharon who stood listening with rapt attention as she gripped Helm's hand. "Is war starting?"

Tom touched her face. "I don't want you two to worry about it. I think fighting will come sooner than we expected, but we're going to make sure all of you are safe."

Tharon's face was filled with worry, "But who will make sure you're safe?"

He patted her head, "Helm's dad and I are going to watch out for each other to make sure we both make it home, just like you, Helm and Kaid watched out for each other."

The school bus pulled into the semicircle drive and stopped behind the Harris's car. Chuck Miller hopped off the bottom step of the bus and turned to hold his wife Ginger's hand as she tenuously felt her way down the steps in her white stiletto boots, tight white slacks, and puffy white jacket with speckled fur trim.

Tom smiled as he watched their petite, bubbly, forty-something neightbor work her way up the steps. He held the door open for them as they made their way up the front porch steps.

Ginger wobbled on each step in her six inch heels, clinging to the rail with one hand and Chuck's arm with the other.

She clicked her heels across the porch and burst into the foyer, lighting it up with her radiant smile, "We thought we'd see if you want Helm and Tharon to go to school. Chuck and I are running the route together and he's packin' heat," she lifted Chuck's jacket hem to reveal a holster and gun strapped to his belt. Her throaty chuckle boomed in the quiet house. "And I'm packing my own surprise," she brushed her blond hair back over her shoulder as she opened her purse and proudly displayed a large red brick.

Chuck swung a loving arm around his bubbly blond wife, "We got a call from the state Commissioner of Education that there's been a terror threat targeting school buses and schools. With all you folks went through recently, we just wanted you to be reassured about the children's safety. We will protect them." His eyes twinkled when he grinned at Tharon and Helm. "We're glad you two and Kaid got home safe."

Lista and Angela exchanged the same panicked look. Lista said, "I'm sure they would be safe with you both, but we still want to keep them close this week. I'm sure you understand after everything that happened we want to anchor them to our apron strings just a bit longer."

Ginger's throaty chuckle warmed the foyer, "Oh, honey, of course I understand. I only thought with you being pregnant we might help you get a little rest. But that's fine if you want the children close by, I understand."

Lista's countenance fell. She sank into Tom's side.

Tharon voice was filled with sadness when she said, "Mommy's baby died."

Ginger's smile froze. She stared at Tharon as her words sunk in. Her lips quivered and tears dripped down from her rapidly blinking eyes. As her tears streamed down her cheeks they melted her mascara and her smile. "Oh, Lista, I am so sorry."

Lista found herself comforting her distraught neighbor. She drew Ginger into her arms and patted her back. "It's all right, Ginger. I'm going to be fine. But you can see why I want the children around me today."

Sobbing, now, Ginger nodded her head, unable to form coherent speech. She broke from Lista's arms and foraged inside her massive purse until she extracted a tissue from the inner folds of the bag. She blotted up her running mascara. Between sobs she repeated, "I'm—so—sorry!"

"Thank you," Lista said as she gave Tom an imploring look.

Tom turned his attention to Chuck, "We've got a meeting for the militia tonight. Would you like to go with Matt and me?"

Chuck raised an eyebrow, "Absolutely. What time?"

"I plan to leave at five."

Chuck shook his hand again, "I'll be here. Thanks for letting me know."

After exchanging goodbyes, Chuck had to practically carry Ginger down the steps. Angela and Matt hurried to pull their car around the semi circle drive and get out of the way of the bus, leaving Tom with his arm around Lista, and Tharon holding Helm's hand.

Tom led Lista to her chair and covered her knees with a knitted afghan, "You rest and relax while I enlist those two hooky players to help me make pancakes." He kissed the top of her head.

Lista eased back and sighed, "That would be lovely."

CHAPTER 41

Max thumbed through reports stacked on Simon's desk. Penni dropped another one on top eliciting a grumble, "What is going on? Most of these deal with trespassers and break-ins. Is there usually this much activity on the weekend?"

"No. I talked to the Sheriff's departments in the northern counties and they say there's been a significant increase in traffic and incidents along I-80. Most of it clustered around I-65 and I-69. And get this; almost every county has reported dogs have been killed in rural areas."

Max furrowed his brow, "Why kill the dogs? This doesn't make any sense."

Simon entered his office, his arm looped around Dana's waist. "It makes sense if reconnaissance is eliminating nature's security alarms."

Penni frowned, "You two are supposed to be on your honeymoon. We can handle this. Now scoot. Go bask in your wedded bliss."

"I promise you, Penni, there's nothing I'd like more," he shut the door behind him. "I met with the governor early yesterday morning. It looks like Indiana will secede from the Union along with at least twenty-three other states. We're still not sure which way Ohio is going to go. And there may be cities that stay with Hamron while the rest of the state goes with us."

Max's mouth dropped open. "I'd heard talk of it but had no idea we were this close yet."

Simon still draped his arm around Dana's waist. "I'm going to need help from all of you. Penni, please get me a list of the names and numbers of all the mayors, police chiefs, township commissioners and school principals for Whitley County."

He turned his attention back to Max, "I've been tasked with leading the militia regiment from Whitley County, so I hope you feel comfortable in that chair, Max; because I'm going to need an interim Sheriff if fighting breaks out."

Max shook his head and pointed at Dana, "You've got your arm around your interim Sheriff. If fighting breaks out, I'll be there with you."

Simon locked eyes with Dana and seemed to be considering the merit of Max's suggestion. He raised an eyebrow to his bride, "That's not a bad idea. But Max, I still want you here to help her."

Dana shook her head and pressed her palm against her husband's chest, "I'll be going with you, too."

"No, Sweetheart," Simon touched her face, "I don't know about the other counties, but we won't be taking any women of child bearing age. You ladies are too important to rebuilding the population. Besides, if you were there, I'd be too distracted and worried about you to do my job." His gentle kiss stilled any more protests on her part.

"What can I do now to help you?" She rested her hands on her hips to let him know she meant business.

Simon shook his head, "Since you refuse to follow doctor's orders and rest, it would help if you mark on a map all the complaints of trespassers and killed dogs." He rummaged in the file cabinet and pulled out a map. "I think for now, we'll go old school and use a map with pins in it. I question how secure our computers are."

She started to leave the room but Simon grabbed her hand and pulled her back into his arms. He ignored Max and Penni as he told Dana, "This is just to remind you that even though we're back to work, the honeymoon is far from over." He kissed her with a gentle passion that made her lift one foot off the floor.

Max and Penni grinned at each other.

After Penni and Dana left the room, Max got up to turn the Sheriff reins back over to Simon. Max said, "So, what was the lead you followed up in Indy?"

Simon settled back behind his desk. "Wil Silar was an undercover cop. He'd been given a fake criminal record so he could infiltrate the cell run by Burt Payne. I guess cell is about the best description for it. Did you hear what Burt said at the hospital? The plan was in motion for ten years. That was before Hamron even hinted an interest in politics. Is he behind all of this or is there a bigger machine pulling the strings? Who knows how many more groups there are out there hidden in plain sight? For all we know, if it comes to street fighting, we might have some of our own turn their guns on us."

The thought of such betrayal sickened Max. "So why did they kill Silar?"

"There have been credible reports of plans for the government to invade Indiana. Silar was the source of those reports. Apparently the Payne Brothers were to signal other groups to initiate a widespread incident. They planned to claim the secession movement was behind the incident. That would open the door for the government to justify invading the state and establishing marshal law. Silar was trying to find out what that plan was but he was discovered and murdered before he could report it."

Simon frowned, "Of course, now we know they'd planned a mass abduction of school children. Brandt was part of the network too. Now our only leads to uncovering the rest of the network are to find either Marty Philips or whoever killed Brandt."

Max let out a low whistle. "There's one other way, but it's the worst option. We wait for them to strike."

"Regardless of what else we're doing, we've got to place top priority on assembling our militia and making sure our schools are secure and their bus drivers are trained and ready."

***

Penni gave Simon the list of phone numbers he requested and then she split the northern counties up with Dana and together they contacted the other sheriff departments and pegged each incident on a regional map and a large corkboard which she found in storage. They used blue pins for the trespassers, yellow for the break-ins and red for the killed dogs.

When they finished the two women stepped back and stared at the map with their mouths open. The blue and yellow pins were scattered in a haphazard fashion all over the region. They tended to cluster around the more affluent areas. The red pins formed two lines that followed rural roads. One stretched from near Gary to Indianapolis. The other skirted the back roads from south central Michigan to Indianapolis—it snaked through the center of Whitley County. Penni let out a low whistle and said, "I think you'd better go get your husband."

CHAPTER 42

Every mayor and township commissioner responded to Simon's call and assembled in the Columbia City town hall. Dana stood in the back of the room observing the commotion.

Mayor Shanna Brice from Columbia City was the most vocal. "What do you mean? How can we declare war on our own country? This is ludicrous. Governor Talbot can't get away with this. This is outrageous." Her face grew redder with each word until it was almost the same shade as her bright red blazer, which gave her quite the patriotic appearance with her white hair and blue slacks.

Dana wondered what word ending in 'ous' she'd inject into her rhetoric next.

Dana's eyes wandered to her husband, who stood at the podium, somber and calm. Her heart fluttered when their eyes met and a happy smile curled on her lips. Her shoulder still throbbed from her gunshot wound, but she wasn't about to dull her senses with pain killers.

Simon's eyes warmed as he looked at her, but he fought to maintain his stony expression while Mayor Brice continued, "How on earth does Talbot think we can survive surrounded by states loyal to the administration? It would set us up for a blockade or siege. It is audacious!"

The room erupted in another chorus of murmurs.

Simon pressed his palms to the air in front of him calling for quiet, "I appreciate your concerns Mayor Brice. First of all, Governor Talbot alone cannot call for secession. Both houses of the state legislature would have to vote for such action. Second, secession does not mean we'd be declaring war on the United States. The governor has requested that the counties ready a militia for our defense should the government attack us. And third, I've been told that at least twenty-three other states are considering similar actions."

Mayor Brice bristled and took a step back. Her shrill voice made Simon clench his jaw, "Which other states?"

Simon ignored her question. His steady tone calmed the room. "I want to emphasize that no vote has been taken in any state. The formation of the militia is a contingency only. What we are asking all of you to do is inquire of your constituents for a list of those willing to join the militia. Can I see a show of hands of those willing to assist in this effort?"

Dana was relieved to see most of the hands in the room raised to the affirmative.

The tension eased from Simon's face, "And those unwilling to assist?"

A smattering of hands timidly rose, except for Mayor Brice who shot her hand defiantly into the air.

Simon jotted down the names of those unwilling to help.

Mayor Brice's voice shrieked above the din of the room, "Why are you writing down our names? Are we going to be targeted by some secret government agency? I demand to know why you are recording our names?"

Simon sighed, "Madam Mayor, I am merely recording the townships and cities where the Sheriff's department will need to recruit because you have elected not to help. The constitution affords us the right to form a militia and a regiment will be formed from Whitely County, with or without your help. This does not mean we are going into battle. It means we are organizing a force to defend ourselves should the need arise."

Mayor Brice stumbled over her words, an experience obviously foreign to her. When she gathered her composure, her resolve was clear, "I misunderstood. I thought the decision had been made. In that light I will be delighted to talk to my constituents to help organize a state militia," her voice grew stronger and took on a campaign rally edge, "Those with me? Say aye."

The room erupted in a thunderous "Aye."

Brice continued, "Any opposed say nay." The room fell silent. Mayor Brice turned to Simon, "Sheriff, you shall have a regiment of the finest militia in the state if not the nation!"

Simon smiled at Mayor Brice, "Thank you, Madam Mayor. I'm sure that will be true, and your assistance will be invaluable."

Mayor Brice tugged her jacket smooth, squared her shoulders and nodded to Simon. "Sheriff, I have just one more question. How will we be protected here at home if you do get called upon to fight?"

Simon held out his hand towards Dana and flicked his fingers summoning her to him, "I'm glad you asked that, Mayor. Most of you know Deputy Donovan, who rode with me for three years and has been integral in the solution of many of the problems we have faced since the pandemic. She has been primed as no other to step in and serve as interim Sheriff in my absence. As an added credit to her character, last weekend she took on the supreme challenge of becoming my wife."

As Dana made her way to Simon's side, the room erupted in the applause of a standing ovation. Simon motioned to the microphone for Dana to say a few words. She gripped the podium so hard her knuckles turned white, "Ladies and gentlemen, I want to assure you that I have no desire to assume the duties of the Sheriff. I want my husband to stay right here with me. But I also want to assure you that should the state require the defense of the militia, the leadership of our regiment would be in the best possible hands."

She waited for another round of applause to die down. "And I further want to assure you that the quality of service from the Sheriff's department will continue with the same level of excellence you've come to expect from Sheriff Ellis."

Dana stepped back from the podium as applause thundered in the room. Simon took her left hand and raised it high, showing the county leaders their bond of unity.

CHAPTER 43

Maisy rolled out a ball of pie dough the size of a baseball. She fussed at Lista who stood watching her, "You can help by keeping an eye on those two kids. Read a book to them; get them busy drawing pictures or doing their homework. I have a system. It might not be as nice a celebration as you can prepare, but there will be plenty of food and I wager there won't be too many complaints about the flavor either."

"I know it will be wonderful. It's just so hard for me to sit still knowing how hard you're working out here." Lista tried to stifle a yawn.

Maisy waved her rolling pin at her as she spoke, "That's exactly what I'm talking about. You're exhausted. Go to the living room and relax or go lie down and take a nap. Those are your choices, young lady."

Lista nodded as she yawned again and reluctantly agreed. She padded back down the hallway, passed the dining room and turned the corner into the living room. She paused at the edge of the sofa to watch Tharon and Helm sitting next to each other on the window seat. Helm read to her as she drew on a spiral bound sketchpad.

Helm paused mid-sentence and craned his neck to see the image Tharon drew, "What are you drawing?"

A mischievous grin lit her face as she scooted to the other side of the window seat and sat facing Helm, hiding the drawing from him. "It's a picture of you."

He raised his eyebrows, "Let me see."

Tharon giggled, "No. Keep reading. The story is getting good."

"Where was I?" he grinned and reopened the book.

"The witch raised her wand," she said without looking up from her tablet.

Helm feigned a straight face, "Right. *The witch raised her wand and waved it over her head. When she pointed it at the handsome prince she said, hit the road, now you're a toad—*"

"It does not say that!" Tharon giggled even harder.

"Sure it does, right here," he pointed at the page but held the book so she couldn't see it.

"No it doesn't, let me see it," she wiped a tear from her eye from laughing so hard.

He grinned at her, "You show me the picture first and then I'll show you the book."

She looked down at the drawing and the smile left her face, "It's not a picture of you," she turned the notebook so he could see it.

The smile left Helm's face too. "That's Marty. I didn't know you could draw so good. It looks just like him. Is that mark where you cut him?"

Tharon nodded and handed the notebook to Helm. She drew her knees up and wrapped her arms around them. "Yeah. Even though I didn't mean to, he's going to come after me someday." She shuddered, "He's going to kill me."

Helm laid the notebook on the bench and scooted close to her side. He put his arm around her shoulders, "I won't ever let him hurt you, I promise."

Lista walked to the window seat and picked up the drawing. She studied it and felt the skin at her temples tighten as she recognized the face her daughter had drawn. "Helm's right, Sweetheart, we won't let him hurt you. I promise, too."

She tore the picture from the notepad, folded it and stuffed it into the pocket of her bulky sweater, "I think I want you two to play either on the floor or over on the sofa. I'd rather you stay away from the windows."

Lista moved mechanically to her chair by the fireplace. On the stand next to her chair, she saw the card Max had given her the day the children were taken. She picked it up and tapped the edge of it thoughtfully before stuffing it into her pocket as well. She wondered if she dared to tell Max or Dana or anyone who Marty was and ultimately decided that she needed to discuss it with Tom before she did anything. But Tom had so much going on now. Should she burden him with it when he needed to focus on the militia?

He was hunting turkey for their Thanksgiving dinner. She decided if he got home early enough, she'd talk with him before he left for the militia meeting. If not, it was up to her to keep them safe until he returned.

She locked the front door and checked all the windows in the front of the house to make sure they were secure. In the kitchen she locked the back door and the windows and paused long enough to search outside for trespassers.

Maisy watched her with a puzzled look, "What on earth are you up to girl?"

Lista pulled the drawing out of her pocket and showed it to Maisy, "This is the man who attacked Tharon. He swore to kill Tharon someday. Do you realize who that is?"

As Maisy studied the picture, Lista retrieved a key from the spice cupboard.

Maisy's mouth went dry, in a hoarse voice she said, "I thought he took off for South America. I thought..."

Lista's voice was hard and resigned. "We all thought we were safe. We were wrong." She unlocked the closet under the stairs where Tom kept his weapons. For the first time in their marriage she was glad he was such an avid collector of guns, knives, arrows and bows. She was also grateful he'd insisted she and Maisy learned how to shoot.

She selected two revolvers, loaded them, and stuffed one into her sweater which bulged and hung significantly lower on that side. She presented the other one to Maisy.

Maisy quickly wiped her hands on her apron, checked to make certain the safety was on and hid it behind the flour canister. Tears glistened in her eyes as she looked at Lista. "I honestly thought we'd be safe here."

Lista hugged Maisy, "It's been a fabulous home. I'm grateful that you shared it with us. I've grown to love the land and the people here. If we have to leave, I'll be heartbroken."

Tharon and Helm listened from the hallway. He took Tharon's hand and led her back to the living room. "I hope you don't move away."

She looked up at his face and her bottom lip quivered; tears welled up in her eyes, spilling down her face. The lump in her throat kept her from speaking. The thought of leaving her home, of leaving Kaid, of leaving Helm—was more than she could bear and worse than anything they went through a little over a week ago.

Helm wiped the tears from her cheeks and kissed her lightly on the forehead. "Don't worry. I'm sure you won't have to move. Everything will be okay." He held her hand as they sat down next to each other on the sofa.

After a few quiet moments he tried to lighten her mood, "So what's the plan for Operation Secret Santa this year?"

Helm kept her talking in hushed tones about the elderly Culpepper Sisters. She'd overheard them lament about not being able to purchase materials to make gifts like they have in the past. Gifting to them seemed a perfect way to help many people indirectly. She chatted until fatigue overcame her.

Helm put his arm around Tharon's shoulder and pulled her close. She pressed her ear to his chest and listened to the steady drumming of his heart and once more felt safe in his steady strength.

She was only twelve years old but in just a little over a week, her whole world seemed to be turning upside down. The only thing she knew for certain was she couldn't lose the friendships she'd found again with Helm and Kaid.

She and Helm curled up on the sofa together and fell asleep in each other's arms as the early afternoon rays warmed them from the windows next to the fireplace.

Lista returned to the living room and when she saw her daughter asleep in Helm's arms, she realized running was not an option. Even if they ran, the Hamrons no doubt had operatives throughout every state. She couldn't uproot Tharon. She couldn't take her from the friends she'd made. She couldn't let her become a victim of fear. Her courage and kind heart deserved at least some semblance of a normal life for as long as they could give it to her.

No more running. It was time to stand and fight.

CHAPTER 44

Tom bagged two hen turkeys, field dressed them, but brought them to Maisy to pluck and finish cleaning. "I'm sorry I don't have time to properly clean them for you. I was beginning to fear we'd be having a vegan Thanksgiving."

Maisy gave him a bleak smile, "That's fine. I'm glad you got them."

She seemed distant, not her usual self. The sparkle and fire of her eyes dimmed, replaced with an edge of sadness.

Tom waited until she looked into his eyes, "Are Lista and Tharon all right? Is something wrong?"

She waved her hands in a weak attempt to display her usual bluster. "No, no. Everything's fine. You go get ready. I'll fix a couple sandwiches for you to eat on the way."

She was right, he had barely enough time to shower, pick up Matt and get to the meeting on time. Still he hesitated. He'd known her all his life and there were few occasions when he'd seen her like this. In a gentle but firm voice he said, "Maisy, what's wrong?"

When her eyes met his, her fear gave way to tenderness,

"Go get cleaned up. Lista can tell you while you change."

He ducked his head into the living room. Tharon, Helm and Kaid sat on the floor around the ottoman playing Chinese checkers. "Who's winning?"

Kaid spoke without taking his eyes off the board, "Tharon's won three out of four games, but I think this one is mine."

Lista got up from her chair where she'd been watching them play. "I'll keep you company while you change."

When she stood, Tom noticed the bulge in her low hanging sweater pocket. He also saw the set of her jaw and knew she intended to keep something from him.

He took her hand and led her into the bedroom. When the door was closed, he pulled her into his arms and kissed her lips gently at first, and then with fervor as he let loose of the pent up emotions of the day, if not the week.

He pulled the pins from her hair and let her tresses fall about her shoulders. Easing her onto the bed, he kissed her cheek, nuzzled her ear, tickling her with his whiskers, and ran his thumb along her jaw line. He gazed into her deep brown eyes smoldering with desire and asked, "Honey, is that a gun in your pocket or are you happy to see me?"

She laughed louder than she intended and covered her mouth to stifle her amusement. "Both."

The tension she'd felt all afternoon shook loose with her laughter and eased from her shoulders.

He kissed her again with tenderness. When their lips parted he smoothed a lock of hair from her cheek, "All right, beautiful, tell me what has you and Maisy so spooked."

"I shouldn't tell you. You already have so much to do and worry about." She started to sit up.

He pinned her shoulders down and gave her a playful

warning look. "Do you want me to start kissing you again?"

She tilted her head to the side, thinking that would be a welcomed punishment. "Absolutely."

He hovered over her mouth without touching her but so close she felt his warm breath on her face, "Then spill it, or there'll be no more kisses for you, woman."

She narrowed her eyes at him, "You fight dirty."

He nuzzled the tender spot below her ear, "Come on, what's got you so spooked?"

She sighed and pulled the picture from her pocket. "Tharon drew this today. It's the man who's still loose—the one who threatened to come after her. That's Martin Cutler."

Tom sat up on the edge of the bed and stroked his beard. His shoulders sagged. "That's one face I never thought I'd see again. If we're going to stay here—," he looked at her to make sure they were in agreement.

"Yes. I thought about running, but then I saw Tharon asleep on the sofa with Helm and I couldn't imagine taking her from Kaid and Helm again. The bond they've formed is so strong. Whatever is coming, we need to stand and face it here."

Tom nodded, "We might need to tell someone the danger we are in and why. I'm thinking Simon can be trusted."

Lista grazed her fingertips across her husband's back, "Okay. Should we tell Dana too? I don't know what it is about her, but I trust her."

Tom hunched his shoulders to redirect her fingertips lower. "I trust her too. When we were tracking the kids, she had a determination that she'd bring them home safe or die trying. Who cares that much for someone else's children?"

Lista sat up next to him and ran her fingers through his long brown hair. "You do. It's just one of the many reasons I love you." She touched his face and kissed him with all the intensity of her passion and love for him.

He groaned and pulled away from her, "Now my shower is going to have to be a cold one." He got up and headed for the bathroom, leaving a trail of clothes as he went.

She lay on her side watching him, "Serves you right for trying to start something that you know I won't be able to finish for several weeks."

He flashed a brilliant smile, performed a series of muscle man poses for her in the buff, winked and said, "Until then, my darling!" He turned on the water and stepped into the shower. "Brrrrrr!"

She shook her head and smiled. Her eyelids drooped closed as she listened to the water thrumming against the shower curtain.

When the water stopped Tom wrapped a towel about his waist and walked to the dresser, picking up his dirty clothes on his way. He tossed them into the hamper in the corner.

Lista stood and walked over to him as he rummaged for clean briefs and socks. She wrapped her arms around his waist and hugged him tight. "Thank you."

He twisted in her arms until he was facing her. "Now what did I do?"

She caressed his solid chest with her palms, moving them downwards to rest on the miniscule love handles at his sides and went up on her tiptoes to kiss him, "You made me forget to be sad. You made me smile and laugh. Thank you."

He tossed his underwear onto the bed and framed her face with his hands, "We'll get pregnant again, and we'll have healthy babies—a whole house full of them. I promise. And I won't let Martin Cutler or anyone else hurt us or drive us from our home." He kissed her again.

The front doorbell rang. Tom reluctantly parted his lips from her supple mouth, "That'll be Chuck. Much as I hate to, I've got to go. Will you tell him I'll be right out?" He kissed her forehead.

With an impish grin, she said, "I'd be happy to." She loosened his towel as she broke from his embrace.

He caught the towel before it hit the floor and snapped the air behind her with it.

She turned and blew him a kiss before she ducked out the door.

The smile left Tom's face as soon as the door closed. He dressed quickly and reopened his top drawer. He reached up under the bottom of the drawer and pulled out a digital bridge which had been taped to the underside of the drawer. He slipped it into his wallet with a determination to do whatever it took to protect his family.

CHAPTER 45

Thursday, November 23, 2056: Thanksgiving Day

Lista tried to hide her frustration at not being permitted to help cook Thanksgiving dinner. Every time she wandered into the kitchen, Maisy shooed her out to go rest. If she got any more rest she feared she'd explode. Instead of focusing on what she couldn't do, she occupied herself with creating works of art with the dinner napkins.

Tharon set each place setting, standing back to make sure everything was even. Lista said, "Do I step back and look at each place setting like that?"

Tharon tilted her head from side to side, "Uh huh. I guess that's why the table always looks so pretty." She looked at the napkin in her mother's hands, "What are you making?"

Lista shook out the napkin she'd been working on. "I'm trying to make a turkey but they just don't look right. I think I might just make a swan or a bird of paradise and be done with it. What do you think?" She quickly folded one napkin into a swan and another into a bird of paradise.

Tharon shrugged her shoulders. "I guess if you can't do a turkey, either one is okay." She bounced on the balls of her feet, "How much longer until everyone gets here?"

Lista smiled and pulled Tharon into her arms. "I don't think I've ever seen you this excited for Thanksgiving. What makes this holiday so special?"

Tharon melted into her mother's side. "Well, you know, we've never had Thanksgiving with anyone but the Walkers before. And this year Helm's family is coming and the Sheriff and Dana. And Shep is home and well, it just seems like there's a lot more to be thankful for this year."

Lista's eyes glistened. "There is a lot to be thankful for."

"Mom, don't get all mushy and weepy. You still have a lot of napkins to fold." She wriggled out of her mother's grip and then planted a sloppy kiss on her cheek.

Lista playfully smacked Tharon's bottom as she skipped away to finish setting the children's table.

Lista thought about all the bad that had happened and weighed it against the good and decided Tharon was right, they had a lot to be thankful for. She frowned at the floppy turkey shape in her hands and decided bird of paradise would be just fine for this year.

As she focused on the napkins she started humming and then when the tune in her heart turned into a familiar song she softly whistled a happy melody. A movement caught her attention and she turned to find Tom leaning on the pillar by the dining room with his arms folded. She stopped whistling and focused on her napkin folding, "How long have you been standing there watching me?"

He chuckled, "Not nearly long enough." He moved to her side and lifted her chin so she was looking at him. "It's good to see you happy. Whistle that tune again for me?"

She puckered her lips to whistle and he bent down and smothered the tune with a kiss. When their lips parted he said, "I know I don't say it enough, but I love you, Mrs. Trace."

She gently caressed the side of his face, "The feeling is quite mutual, Mr. Trace."

Their tender moment was interrupted by Tharon's squeal from the living room. "They're here!"

Roused from his bed by the fireplace, Shep barked as he wedged himself between Tharon and each visitor. His wet nose sniffed each dish carried in as if he were a trained bomb sniffing dog.

The Walkers arrived first, each person carrying a contribution to the meal. By the time Matt and Angela carried in their a sweet potato casserole, Shep had deemed anyone carrying food a welcome visitor so he barely acknowledged Simon and Dana and pranced eagerly around the fragrance of the chocolate cake in Simon's hands.

Angela and Marilyn joined Maisy in the kitchen where they prepared the final trimmings of the meal, while the men stood in the living room, discussing the militia in hushed tones.

Dana and Lista shared a companionable silence as they listened intently to the men's conversation. Simon expressed his concerns about troop movements in Michigan and northeastern Illinois. They had spotters positioned along the suspected lines of attack and if there were any movements, he was to call up the militia for a defensive maneuver.

Lista frowned, "Do you think they might have to fight tonight?"

Dana met her gaze. "I hope not, but I wouldn't be at all surprised."

Lista folded her arms and tried to suppress a shudder. "I'm glad we decided to have an early meal."

Maisy bustled out of the kitchen followed by Marilyn and Angela. "Dinner's ready."

After Tom herded his family and friends into the dining room he asked them to gather in a large circle. "We have a Thanksgiving tradition in our family. We join hands and after the prayer, we each take a turn to express our gratitude. Please don't feel pressured if you don't want to participate, but if you do you are most welcome."

Helm and Kaid each claimed one of Tharon's hands while Tracy quickly wedged in between Helm and Angela.

Tom waited for everyone to join hands and said the prayer expressing gratitude for the safe return of Tharon, Kaid and Helm; for friends and family; for the food. He asked blessings on the food and sought blessings of protection for their home and families, for the militia, for the state and for the nation. When he finished a round of *Amens* expressed perfect agreement with his prayer. After the prayer he said, "As head of this household, Lista has given me permission to go first."

Lista gave Tom a gentle elbow in the side as a chuckle went around the room.

Tom continued, "I would be remiss if I didn't express my profound gratitude to everyone who helped find the children. I'm especially grateful for Dana's determination, stamina and her good eyesight to find Tharon in the tree. I shudder to think what might have happened if she were even a minute later getting to them. And I'm grateful for Tharon, Kaid and Helm and for how well they took care of each other. There are always blessings that come through trials and we've cemented some great friendships after what we've all been through. Thank you," his throat tightened as he choked out the final two words.

Lista cleared her throat but when she spoke, her words were still choked with emotion, "I'm thankful for my husband whose skill in tracking and training helped find Tharon and the boys. I'm also grateful that he knows just what to do or say to make me smile. And I'm thankful for friends, old and new." She buried her face in Tom's sleeve and he wrapped his arm around her.

For all his political speeches during election years, Simon struggled for words, "I'm grateful for new friends and my new bride." He slipped his arm around Dana's waist.

Dana looked around the room; never had she dreamed her life could change so quickly. Her heart was overcome with gratitude for so many things that she feared if she named them all she'd blubber like a baby. "I'm grateful that Tharon likes to climb trees. And I'm grateful to not be alone anymore."

Maisy wiped her eyes on her apron. "I'm grateful for many things, but right now, I'd be grateful if we can stop talking and enjoy this meal while it's still warm."

Another chorus of *Amen* resounded throughout the room.

Maisy clapped her hands together, "Just grab a plate and file out into the kitchen, feel free to refill it as many times as you want. The fewer leftovers we have to deal with, the better."

Conversations centered on the food as everyone settled around the table.

Marilyn nibbled at her modest portions, "Lista, this is delicious but you did too much. You should have said something, I'd have been happy to help."

Lista smiled, "The turkey is perfect, isn't it? I wish I could claim credit for it but Tom and Maisy wouldn't let me near the kitchen all week. I'm afraid all I did this year was fold the dinner napkins."

Marilyn pushed the turkey to the far edge of her plate, "Oh, well, it is a tad dry."

Maisy's smile faded as she cast her eyes down at her plate, her fork frozen in her hand.

Tom shoveled a large bite of turkey into his mouth, "Dry my eye, it's perfect. Thank you, Maisy. Everything is superb." He winked at her and Maisy returned a warm and grateful smile.

Lista nudged Tom's foot under the table and when she got his attention, she took a spoonful of Marilyn's gelatin salad.

Tom spooned a heaping mound of the cranberry salad into his mouth. "Mmmm. Marilyn, you're cranberry salad is wonderful. It wouldn't be Thanksgiving without it."

Marilyn sat a little straighter, "I'm glad you like it, Tom."

Lista rubbed her toe gently on Tom's ankle. He leaned over and kissed her neck, his beard tickling her and sending a shiver down her spine.

Dana felt perfectly happy. She reached for Simon's hand under the table and held it as she wondered how long it would be before she and Simon were able to communicate without words.

Simon put down his fork, tipped her face towards him and kissed her gently. Conversation stopped in honor of their tender kiss. Simon said, "Sorry folks, technically, it's still our honeymoon."

Simon's phone rang. He answered it, "Ellis here...Right....We'll be there."

He ended the call, sent out a blanket text message to the militia. Tom, Matt and Doc's phones chirped when the text came in.

Simon stood, "Grab your guns, gentlemen, we're up."

While the wives each gathered their husband's coat, Tom opened the gun cabinet and armed himself with his rifle, complete with night scope, a Glock and a Bowie knife. He filled his pockets with as much ammunition as they would hold.

Matt took a .22 rifle and Doc picked up a shotgun and stuffed his pockets with slugs.

Marilyn helped Doc on with his coat. She buttoned his top button, "Graham, don't be a hero. Come home to us. Do you hear me?"

Doc kissed her forehead. "Don't worry," he started to turn away but then drew her into a fierce hug and kissed her soundly on the lips. When their lips parted he cupped her face in his hands and said, "I want you and the kids to stay here until we get back."

Marilyn blinked rapidly and nodded. She stepped back so Tracy and Kaid could hug their father.

Angela and Helm helped Matt on with his coat. Matt tousled Helm's hair. "You take care of your mom. Doc's right. I want you two to stay here as well."

Angela kissed Matt and held him as they walked out onto the front porch. "What about Black Friday?"

Matt shook his head, "No. I don't care if we go under. I want to know you two are safe. Stay here. Be safe."

Tom picked Tharon up and hugged her tight. "Listen to your mom and Maisy. Be a good girl. I'll be home before you know it."

Tharon hugged Tom and kissed his cheek. "I love you, Daddy."

Tom put her down and kissed Maisy on the cheek. "Will you stay here until I get back?"

Maisy wiped her palms on her apron, "You just remember everything Frank taught you and you'll be fine."

Tom nodded and then turned to Lista. He drew her into his arms and kissed her deeply. His hands caressed her sides until he felt the gun resting on her hip. He parted from her lips and smiled, "Still happy to see me?"

She smiled back, "Always."

His tone turned serious. "Lock up all the doors and windows. Keep that handy. I'll be back as soon as I can."

They moved out onto the porch. Simon and Dana were embracing at the bottom of the steps. Dana said, "Let me come with you. I can help. You know how good a shot I am."

Simon framed her face with his hands. "You're not completely healed. Besides, you're Sheriff Ellis now. I want you to stay here. I don't want you to be alone tonight. I'll let you know when we get done. Call Jackman and Murphy to let them know what's going on. Don't use the radio if you can avoid it; I'm sure those channels are being monitored."

Dana nodded and kissed her husband. "I love you, Simon. You be careful and come home to me."

Simon hugged her tight, being careful not to crush her still tender shoulder. "I love you too. We have to go."

Dana climbed back up the steps and stood with the other wives watching the men load up in their cars. Chuck Miller pulled in behind them and Doc got in and sat in the truck cab next to him.

Lista watched Tom settle his rifle in the trunk of Simon's cruiser. Panic seized her chest. "Tom!"

Tom grinned and treated her to a few muscle-man poses and then blew her a kiss.

She laughed and blew a kiss back to him.

Dana grinned, "What was that all about?"

The tension eased from Lista's shoulders, "We have a date scheduled in a few weeks," her fingers touched the smile playing on her lips, "That was his way of telling me he intends keep it."

ABOUT THE AUTHOR

Jan Hinds was born and raised in the Mid-West of the United States. She has a deep love for her family and her country. Growing up her parents planned family vacations that touched most of the lower forty-eight states. She grew to love the forests and mountains; the plains and the bluegrass; the varied beaches of the Atlantic, Gulf of Mexico and the Pacific; but her heartstrings remain tied firmly to the heartland.

She spent her childhood in the small town of Minerva, Ohio and met her husband while attending graduate school in Kentucky. They have five children and have lived in southern Indiana, southern Wisconsin, western Kentucky, northern Illinois, and Fort Wayne, Indiana where she resides with her husband, son and two dogs.

Sneaking Suspicions is the first book in the Tharon Trace series and will be followed in 2014 by Book 2.

In addition to Sneaking Suspicions, she is the author of the cookbook series, *Not So Secret Family Recipes*, which is an effort to preserve family recipes which have been handed down and collected for five generations.

Books in her cookbook series to date include:

Pies
Breakfast & Brunch
Cakes
Cookies
Candies & Holiday Treats
Just Desserts
Breads
Soups.

She loves to hear from her readers and can be contacted at janhindsauthor@gmail.com or on her facebook author page at https://www.faccbook.com/JanHindsAuthor.

Made in the USA
Charleston, SC
08 August 2014